Bound by Blood and Shadow

Book One: Tree of Offerings Trilogy

L. R. Bryant

L.R. Bryant

For You.
Reader.
Lover of fantasies.
Curious human.
Those who know me.
Those who don't.
You who picked this novel,
inspired by the cover...thanks Steve.
For Sadie – who dreampt with me long ago.
And for me.
Because some stories, some characters,
aren't content with staying silent.

Contents

	Copyright	V
1.	Chapter 1	1
2.	Chapter 2	8
3.	Chapter 3	17
4.	Chapter 4	28
5.	Chapter 5	43
6.	Chapter 6	55
7.	Chapter 7	64
8.	Chapter 8	74
9.	Chapter 9	85
10.	Chapter 10	97
11.	Chapter 11	106
12.	Chapter 12	117
13.	Chapter 13	129
14.	Chapter 14	142
15.	Chapter 15	153
16.	Chapter 16	160
17.	Chapter 17	167

18. Chapter 18	177
19. Chapter 19	187
20. Chapter 20	200
21. Chapter 21	213
22. Chapter 22	225
23. Chapter 23	233
24. Chapter 24	243
25. Chapter 25	253
26. Chapter 26	263
27. Chapter 27	274
28. Chapter 28	285
29. Chapter 29	299
CHAPTER ONE Veiled in Glass and Silence	307
Acknowledgments	314
About Author	317

Copyright © 2023 by L.R. Bryant

All rights reserved.

No portion of this book may be reproduced in any form without written permission from the publisher or author, except as permitted by U.S. copyright law.

Chapter 1

*"Being told you're insane is one thing.
Believing that insanity is another entirely."*

The whispered words came so audibly I thought it might be real this time, but Shadow and I were alone in these wooded hills. That is until two brown figures bounded from the tree line on my right, flying through the air and landing a few feet from Shadow's nose. In an instant my balance faltered, the animal beneath me snatching his face away before coming to a hard halt, now frozen more solid than stone. There was no amount of gentle urging that could engage a response from the fear-stricken creature.

A chuckle escaped my mouth, eyes following the surprise intruders.

"Just deer," I whispered, stroking his firm neck gently.

The horse didn't dare a breath, refusing to blink in fear they might see him.

Pivoting their necks in unison, the deer locked big brown eyes on mine before returning to their mission. Long legs brought the majestic creatures gracefully into the tall grass that no doubt held some small amount of water causing them to slow their movement. It was a strange yet beautiful grass they had found. Lovingly, I marveled once more at the long silver-white strands that seemed to feather and sparkle, refusing to match the brown or green foliage around it. In all my years I had never seen anything like it anywhere in my travels, except here.

Not far from where we stood the road would curve past our simple homestead nestled in the middle of a mighty forest, surrounded by protected family lands. It was all I ever wanted, complete with deafening silence and a stary sky that would put Van Gogh to shame.

Clicking to urge my horse forward, followed by more pressure to his side with my heels produced nothing. "Come on Shadow, clearly they don't want to eat you." Nope. He refused to budge, still frozen, facing in the direction of the does in that whimsical grass.

Resigning my fight with a huff, I followed his sight back to the two deer. Drifting on the breeze was the faintest tinkling of bells, like a melody of miniature wind chimes.

It wasn't odd for me to imagine strange things in the forest. Although I didn't believe in fairies, I knew it held old secrets the trees couldn't share. As the bells continued to tickle some unknown corner of my mind, I watched the deer wander farther into the silver grass, mesmerized with the serene beauty of it all. A glint of glass caught my eye mere inches from the first doe's nose, and with it they both vanished into oblivion.

Blinking to find relief for my dry eyes, I sat baffled. My ears were still ringing as the bells faded into the distance.

Shadow was staring in the direction of where the deer had been.

"That's simply not possible," I whispered, barely able to find words with no explanation for what I had seen.

The deer were there, I was sure of it. We had both watched them cross by us, had watched them moving through the grass. It was an open field. There had been no trees they could hide behind.

My curiosity perked as a ghost of my past self begged to investigate the area, scratching like a caged animal desperate to be heard.

The old me would have gone searching, adamant to learn some hidden secret or logical explanation. Nothing would have been able to stop the grand adventure once it had begun.

But I wasn't that girl anymore. I was different.

Somewhere inside my mind clanking sounded, banging against iron bars. I didn't know what resided there, but I had no desire to learn. The voice inside simply laughed while it cried before screaming, begging to be set loose, mocking my fear.

This time I thought I was truly going mad, so around we turned to head back home, both of us eager and relieved to be heading in the opposite direction of whatever had just happened there.

It only took a few minutes to shake off the discomfort, looking down at the sleek black neck under my hands. "He's not Raya," I gently reminded myself. Those forward ears and peppy step that I remember so well had my mind drifting into old memories. So many memories that spurred a desire to fight with that ornery mare just one more time.

No tears, yet.

Breathing a heavy sigh, I prepared to fight back the all too familiar wave of emotions that would take hold, pushing me to be angry once more with this animal I now rode that simply wasn't her. Instead, the birds sang and the clop of hooves against the hard Georgia clay rang loudly through my mind while the breeze rustled the leaves.

He looks just like her.

It's maddening how I can't tell them apart from up here. The curves around his head that went to his ears seemed to be the exact view I had studied for decades without difference.

Recalling when I first laid eyes on him, my heart had stopped.

That beautiful black horse with only one back hoof being white below a short sock. I'd initially thought it was her reincarnated, but we all know that Raya would never come back as a gelding. She'd think it beneath her.

That fire in her belly was the cause of our attraction; we were a pair for sure, and as I delt out my teenage angst, she demanded respect. Eventually I gave it. Each of us left our mark on the other. On more than one occasion blood was involved. Simply another reason I'm convinced she made a deal with someone to have the lightning from that storm end her life. It was dramatically fitting for her.

Shadow wasn't her though. He was missing that sharply dished face only Arabians had, replaced with a straight line from nose to ears. Morgan, or a combination of a million other breeds that were possible. He walked too willingly; Raya wanted to run everywhere, and most of the time I let her, truly craving the power she wielded underneath me to gallop like the reaper himself were behind us.

Moving further down the road, we headed home to conclude our first ride together. It wasn't easy to tell who was more tense, neither sure we could trust the other.

What I knew about him was vague because most of his past was unknown. He'd lived in this world for over ten years, but I only had knowledge of the last one. The previous owner had bought him from a horse trader, and he had little formal training. Tipping his nose to the right, I pushed my left heel back on his side. He did nothing. Opening the rein again, I asked him to move across the road. It was clear he was very green, unsure how to respond to my cues.

As for me, I wasn't the same rider or woman. The last five years had been a whirlwind of change, and I'd transformed so much in this past year I'm not sure Raya would even recognize me.

There was an anxious shadow that had been stalking me for a long time, but only recently did I acknowledge its presence.

Stopping at the gate, Shadow turned his neck around to face me. One more look into those deep eyes and I realized he recognized; he knew. This gelding had a story. We both did. A past full of anguish, but flickering in that moment was hope and willingness. Despite the fear, we wanted to try.

"Animals, always causing trouble." Cillian stood still, watching the two does enter the forest.

He'd have to report this. Hopefully, the human girl would believe her eyes had played a trick and turn around. Not that there was anything to worry about. She would never find the waning spot and even if she did, the Elder's magic wouldn't permit her to slip through, unlike lesser creatures.

Cillian's gaze began to follow the does as they wandered further into their new world, a sadness weighed heavy in him while they passed by unaware of where they had stumbled into.

"You won't survive the day. For that I am sorry," he whispered softly.

He had a deep love for all living things but truly pitied the ones from the human realm. Their fragility was no match for the wilds of a Starpathian forest and the beings that lived here.

Throwing his leg over the massive creature who silently crouched beside him, Cillian made way for the nearest town.

"Ready, Diadred?" he questioned, meeting those bright yellow eyes.

Diadred leapt into a run, eating the ground with his long stride while his golden claws threw the earth behind him.

The only one of his kind, Diadred was a fierce companion and loyal to a fault. His body resembled that of a panther, except he was covered in scales as black as ebony and stronger than steel. Seven tails like leather whips sliced behind him and his powerful chest bore a golden sigil only given to the guardians.

Faster they tore through the wood.

Cillian needed to reach Temani and the South Tower sooner rather than later to file a report from his scouting efforts.

The concern the Elders maintained seemed dramatic over such harmless things. The waning spots had been there for centuries and the wards had only ever allowed small animals to slip through on rare occasions. It was a big world to maintain, difficult to keep safely hidden, and there had always been spaces not fully sealed since The Closure.

All humans outside their realm were easy to scare off and usually did it to themselves without any intervention needed from him.

Strange lot.

They were too scared to believe in anything outside what they could see. Shame, really, how much of the magic they missed in their own world because of it.

Still, as much as Cillian believed the concerns with the breaches to be over-dramatized, he knew Master Olam had his reasons.

Ruler of All, the wisest of the Elders, Master Olam resided in the Ivory Palace. Quiet and kind, he approached you in a way that made even the most difficult people respect him without hesitation. Old, Olam was old. No one really knew just how long he had lived.

Off to the right water was purring from a stream, singing a melody. The pounding from Diadred's paws began to drown out while Cillian focused on the water, the rustle of the leaves, moaning of the great pines, an ancient song all their own.

Wings.

The flapping of them close by interrupted the song as he quickly shot a look over his shoulder, but all he could see was the blur of the woods. Diadred's muscles tensed, sensing the danger and pushing him faster.

There were more now. He felt the air move across his back while the trees stayed silent. Two, no three of them, unseen, but Cillian could hear each as they flanked them from behind.

Gangors.

Naked wings, sharp teeth, and bad attitudes.

If you ever saw one.

They moved with unnatural speed and agility that rivaled anything in the skies. There had not been a sighting this far south, ever, that Cillian could recall. Gangors kept to the Norwood, in the mountain caves serving the Fallen.

No, he was certain he had never even heard of them going this far from their mountains.

Pin pricks began snaking up his neck. He took a deep breath before shoving the creeping fear back down where it belonged.

Nothing good could come from this.

Chapter 2

Roosters crowing woke me earlier than the sun. Climbing out of bed, I began questioning my reservations of frying chicken.

Tea. I needed tea.

Humming from the microwave ensured a hot mug of water while I took time selecting some wonderful bags of chamomile accented with rose hips and licorice.

My favorite mug was handmade with red clay, cold in my palm. The potter had drawn tall pine trees all over it, a magnificent forest with mountains over the tops. Glazing of brown and white with flecks of orange or blue dripped down the peaks before fading behind the pines.

It was a superb work of art.

Not perfectly round, dents in places where a potter's fingers had molded the handle attaching it firmly to the side.

Herbal scents were soothing to my soul while I inhaled the wonderous harmony. Sipping the tea slowly, I tried to forget the events from yesterday gnawing in my head, demanding to be pondered.

Deer.

They had vanished.

No, it was some trick or I just needed sleep.

Sleep.

That had been far from me lately.

Pulling the blanket tighter around me, I welcomed the warm barrier between me and the leather love seat as I glanced at the RV kitchen to my right. This small and quiet space was comforting, surrounded by pieces of furniture I had refurbished myself.

Looking to the left I caught my reflection in the small vintage mirror on the wall. Long brunette hair that always fell straight matched my olive skin well. My sharp nose, that I hated, blended into a full set of lips and round face.

Turning away from myself I glanced back into that mug, remembering when it was full of coffee. It used to brew early every morning as I prepared for a busy day, but what once was a life blood became a nightmare. I had to give it up after the panic attacks got out of control.

Panic attacks were demons of their own.

Those dreaded things.

Everything triggered them lately.

Small spaces, loud noises, large groups, certain conversations.

There was a time they didn't exist, I argued.

Apparently, our bodies are intelligent.

According to the professionals, my body had been screaming at me for some time, but I didn't stop to listen. My life was too busy, and I didn't want to admit what I had been doing to myself to forget for so many years.

After I gave up those harmful ways, the caged voices became louder, reminding me they existed, and I could hear them now. Hyperventilation and hives had become common that first year before I kept counting how often the doctor repeated therapy.

"Who actually wants to dig up their skeletons," I had memorized as a response.

Rest, I was supposed to rest and clear up my schedule. For two years I had been unlearning unhealthy habits and trying to rewire my mind. Funnily enough, the less busy I became, the more I had time to get lost in my head, a treacherous place to be.

The clock ticking on the wall brought no comfort while I stared out the window, watching the chickens scatter about scratching for bugs. Horses' breath could be seen in the cool morning, gently sloping hills of green pasture with magnificent oaks spread into the forest where a small spring-fed pond could be found.

This view, meant to inspire joy, did nothing of the sort today.

Outrunning them was futile, and Diadred was better suited for fighting.

Diving off to his right, Cillian tucked and rolled as his shoulder contacted the damp ground, shooting pain up his neck.

Once Diadred no longer felt Cillian's weight, he pulled to a halt. No sooner had he stopped before spinning around with all seven tails raised up behind him, like serpents awaiting instruction to attack.

Cillian dug inside his mind and created a weapon.

From his left hand sprung a wooden bow with gold engravings. His right hand now held a quiver of arrows with barbed heads. Knocking an arrow, he swept from one side to the other.

Silence.

They weren't gone.

Gangors were used primarily to track, and with good reason. They were near perfect at it, and not keen on losing their targets.

Being in the forest provided cover, as it was full of tall trees wide enough to conceal most anything. Little help it offered their case though, since these dark creatures were blind. They didn't need eyes; they could smell their prey.

Diadred let out a roar that ripped through the trees as he leapt onto the first threat. His claws shredded the Gangor's leathery wing in one swipe, spraying black blood across the nearest pine. It released a shriek that drove tremors down Cillian's spine.

To his left emerged a second, slowly crawling down a tree trunk ten yards off. The wings were folded back and claws gripped the bark as it shuffled itself sideways.

In one leap it almost cleared the distance to where Cillian stood.

A second cry ripped through the air as the arrow he immediately released found its mark, directly centered on the forehead, causing the creature to drop with a crumpling sound.

Where was the third?

Looking to his right he found where Diadred was further mangling the first, ripping at its chest with his powerful jaws. Satisfied he had succeeded, he looked up, what was left of its body slumped over at the base of a tree.

Moving silently, Cillian crept further into the forest.

He knew these woods, better than they did.

Bits of bark fell from above and hit his head, stopping him hard.

"Olam have mercy..." he shuddered under his breath.

He knew what was there before he saw it.

With one slow look towards the sky, Cillian faced an image out of nightmares. Not a foot from his face was a sleek head twisted at an unnatural angle with black holes where eyes should be, slitted nostrils and forked tongue that flicked behind a circle of sharp teeth.

The stench hit him, flipping his stomach as blood began to drain from his face.

Was it smiling? Cillian thought.

He heard the distant thundering of Diadred's paws but knew he wouldn't make it in time.

Without warning the Gangor launched off the tree into the air, releasing another scream that would make anyone's blood run cold.

It was flying away.

Diadred reached Cillian moments later with a matching expression of confusion, sliding to a stop as he tossed forward debris from the ground.

"It could have, should have killed me." Cillian blankly stated.

His heart was racing, hands clammy, still clutching his bow tightly as he exchanged a look of dread with his fierce companion.

This was a far more concerning encounter than the deer breach.

"We're going forward." I fumed at Shadow while he backed up.

You are fine, we are fine, you can do this. I was trying to reassure myself and him.

He really didn't believe me or really didn't care.

We continued to fight, slowly making our way back down the clay road. Me fussing, kicking and begging him to just walk away from our land, Shadow continually trying to turn around, back us into a ditch or just stand in protest.

"You are stubborn, you know that? Maybe part donkey," I stewed, bouncing from the saddle to the ground to drag him forward on foot.

This is what our ride was unfolding into.

Raya never did this. I mean sure, we would disagree, but never to go explore. She was happy to move out swiftly with eagerness to the trail ahead. Often at a faster pace than I preferred, but she oozed confidence with every step. That assurance helped me feel safe even when she would spook at silly things.

"Oh, how I miss you. Why did you have to leave me?" My cheeks went damp as I barely pushed the words out from my heavy heart.

Ten more years. I was hoping for another decade with my heart horse.

That storm was so unfair. I needed that extra time with her, I wasn't ready to live alone. I guess no amount of time would have been enough, but the suddenness of her death left such an ache in me. She had been there through it all, twenty years from a child to an adult.

Nothing had been taken from my house of origin, except her; I had wanted to run away so often and tried quite a few times. Raya was my safe space, the place I could voice my feelings without fear or punishment. In mere moments we could be gone, running anywhere, just away. Away from the chaos, the hurt, the fear and anger.

Off to another world, one we would create that was all ours.

Worlds that no longer existed, adventures that had ceased to be.

Shadow finally gave up the fight, although I was still on the ground with him in hand, wanting to gain more distance before I attempted to remount.

Approaching the field I hesitated; I wished I didn't think about it so often. Shadow kept himself cautiously on guard too while we ventured closer to where the deer had vanished.

Madness, this was insanity.

Try as I may to forget, the past few days still had my mind swarming with thoughts of the deer. The way they moved slowly into the grass, the look the one in front had before she vanished. Even smells of the wildflowers and the eerie bells had invaded my dreams at night.

My goal was to ignore the fact we were so close to something so strange. Keeping my gaze forward while dragging my sluggish mount behind me was the best course of action I could come up with.

It didn't matter. Like the flipping of a switch, the bells returned. Softly the tinkling of windchimes sang in my head.

Such wonderous harmony, almost enchanted.

Turning to look at the beautiful silver-white grass swaying in the breeze, I heard someone sing a song so sweet and gentle, a language I didn't know. So serene, so perfect, it deserved an applause.

"We should ask them to dance." I said to Shadow, unaware now of where I was going.

There was no hesitation from either of us in those moments. It would seem the pied piper was playing his tune and I would follow him anywhere. Gently the grass brushed my thighs as I moved deeper into the field. At the crescendo of the harmony, my chest swelled, responding to every vibration I heard. Ears becoming attached to my very soul, describing an entirely new meaning to sound.

Bells, windchimes, the voice, grass rustling, Shadow's footsteps, my breathing, everything was heightened, getting louder and louder as I continued forward, deeper into the grass.

Then as quickly as they arrived, they faded into silence.

"Wait," I begged the harmony to keep playing. Reaching my arm out for something I could not see or hold, even understand.

Picking up my speed I forced Shadow into a trot and ran smack into a tree.

Shadow seemed as genuinely surprised as I was that it was there, like it had apparated out of nowhere, not in front of us seconds ago.

Pulling myself away from the stunned feeling, I sensed something was terribly wrong. Staring me in the face was a big, big tree. This trunk had to be wider than three of me, and it wasn't an oak. No, this was a pine, like something I had never seen in these woods before. Looking around, my eyes beheld more massive pines in a forest I didn't recognize. The clay road was gone, the field was gone, the mystical grass was gone. Even deeper than that, I felt a part of me was gone, like something had escaped, something important but something I couldn't quite recall to memory.

Confusion reeled, my mind tingling with panic.

Wait, no.

This is a dream.

Immediately I pinched myself, hoping for an awakening.

That's it, it's a dream.

I've been led into this weird corner of my subconscious.

But nothing changed.

Frantically I turned around, sprinting back in the direction we came from with Shadow in tow behind me.

We had gone too far, wandered onto someone's property and they had towering trees. This was the most logical explanation my mind could consume.

Heart racing, the space around me closing in, my chest grew tight and I began gasping for air. "No, no, no. Not here, not now," I begged to some celestial being.

Tears were welling in my eyes. Looking for an escape was all I could do, but there was none to be found, just vast forest in every direction.

My gut took an internal blow as I spun on my heels, it felt as though someone punched me before preparing to vomit.

Everything I knew was gone.

I was alone.

Grabbing Shadow's neck, hoping he would stand for it, I began forcing myself to smell, to feel, to see, to hear, anything to keep the overwhelming panic at bay.

As I looked up at him, hot tears ran down my face. He was drawing the same conclusion with the deep tension he held in every muscle while he returned his body to stone.

We didn't know where we were, but we both knew home was far, far away.

Chapter 3

Master Olam sat at the head of a lengthy wooden table wearing his spectacles while he ran a single hand over the manuscript. The animal hide had been worn down until it was very thin, the ink faded but still legible to those with patience. It was a beautiful piece of poetry set to music, one that was written by a man he would love to see again.

This was his finest work of art. There was such emotion, vulnerability, and honesty in his writing. Qualities that had long since become a rarity seen from his people.

Knock, knock.

"Master Olam," came a light voice from behind the large wooden door.

"Come in," the Master responded, eyes lifting from the page to meet those of a small-framed man with curly red hair.

"I beg your apologies, sir, but I have urgent news from Temani and Elder Feldrid of the South Tower. It would seem there has been a Gangor attack just north of our borders in the forest." The gentlemen bowed as he released his words.

"Who reported this?" Master Olam eyed him intently with a raised brow.

"Cillian, Master. He arrived just hours ago in the south. He'll be headed this way come first light. How would you have me assist you, sir?" The man took a step back as Olam rose to his feet.

He was unusually tall, Master Olam, medium build with long blonde hair. He did not look as old as he was, and his face was soft with gentle features. Only his heavy, crystal white eyes outlined in dark gray told a story that he had been around for a long, long time. "Send word to every region. It's only rogues, but have the Towers put on alert just to be safe. Let me know the moment Cillian arrives. I feel there's more to this encounter than what was divulged."

"Yes, Master, right away," the small man replied as he rushed back out the door.

Master Olam walked to the far end of his room to put the manuscript away. After he safely tucked it in a drawer by his bed, he pulled an old book from the top of the nightstand and rubbed the inscription longingly with his thumb. It read: Love is the Ultimate Law of Life.

He thought back to a different time, one that was cold and dark. A time before color and light had entered the world he loved. There was an evil who wished to see that time again, those who refused to accept what the light brought them. Instead of freedom, they wanted revenge for their pain. It was that sickness that kept the Fallen locked in darkness; dwelling in mountain caves of the Norwood.

The Gangors couldn't make a move without their knowledge or permission, which meant the Fallen were involved, but Olam wasn't ready to worry his people yet. The leader of the Fallen always had direct intention of chaos and destruction. Most threatening to Olam's people was the patience and cunning that leader possessed, dedicated to playing the long game that would claim lives to its cause in a slow and slippery way.

The Elders had kept the followers of this menace in check for some time, letting them brood in the farthest reach of the realm. Everyone knew, and most kept away from those borders. Tales of their trickery in the darkness was known far and wide. They flamed through generations to keep his people from falling prey to such dark influence.

Sadly, it was impossible to protect each one and by their unfortunate choice more had fallen; they were a free people after all.

He would give anything to keep them from such a fate.

Cillian drew in a deep breath; the smell of fresh bread filled the air. He had missed this place dearly, like a second home long without visit.

Temani was one of the most rural of the regions found in the deep south, filled with small communities of farmers that worked from dawn to dusk. These simple folk delighted in each other, tasty food and better beer. Rivaled only by the Norwood in lack of population, the bitter winters and dangers kept the area vacant.

Even more enjoyable was the fact that people of Temani didn't use magic often. They loved the everyday things they could do themselves. Cillian treasured that about them, just the genuine enjoyment of slow living with those they loved.

Stopping by Martha's for her famous pot roast was on his list of things to do before he left the next morning. As he walked in the door to her small inn, the meaty aroma hit his nose, filling his chest with hints of onions, carrots, potatoes and fresh herbs.

He strolled over to the bar to grab the last stool, taking in the scene before him.

There were five other men at the bar, plus another ten or so guests scattered about the dining room. They were mostly locals, tired from a day's work and dressed in denim work clothes or plain dress coats. Martha merrily scooted around the room from table to table, dropping bowls of hot roast in front of hungry mouths. To his left was a server's helper busily clearing a table. He couldn't have been more than twelve. Near the bar was a young woman checking in weary travelers happy to have a bed for the night.

Martha's Inn was the busiest spot in town, the only place you could eat, sleep and drink. She was a stout woman with blond hair pulled back from her round, red face. Her husband had died a few years back and only her daughter remained to help run the Inn, a mighty task.

"What can I get you, sugar?" Martha let out with a drawl.

"Just roast will do, Martha, thank you. How have things been around here since I last stopped through? I'd swear you were busier than my last visit," he observed, tipping his head to the bustling dining area.

"Well, it's been nonstop since Fall started changing them leaves. People flocking to get some warmer weather I suppose and use it as a reason to visit that ol' cousin of theirs twice removed," she winked as she turned to get a fresh bowl.

Returning with a slab of roast surrounded by the accompanying veggies, Cillian quickly thanked her before devouring the first hot meal he'd had in a week.

After thanking Martha again for her warm hospitality and swearing her food just kept getting better with her age, he headed back in the direction of the South Tower.

The tower was just that; a stone cylindrical tower with stables and other official outbuildings extending from the base. Each regional tower was different, depending on the needs of the area. Here in Temani they were simple and easily met. Surrounding the town was a small stone wall about five feet tall, extending to the outskirts with the tower in the center. Two large gates located on the west side would close at night to offer some protection to those that lived in town. It wasn't that the area needed much, but there was a time when darker things roamed these lands.

A time that might be trying to return. The thought paraded across his mind.

The outlying areas in Temani were mostly hilly, green with multiple streams and one large river that allowed for constant watering of crops or livestock, even in the dry months. A large pine forest ran around the southernmost border of their lands, enchanted with strange creatures to keep curious eyes from finding the waning spots along the Southern border.

Diadred had been confined to the stables, to his disgust. Cillian had offered to share his quarters, but once again the reigning Elder wouldn't hear of it. "No animal is sleeping anywhere but the stables, regardless of their known nobility," she had abruptly stated, wagging a finger.

Thankfully for her, Diadred was too tired to argue, although Cillian knew he was making things difficult for the stable boys.

Feldrid was petite with gray hair and dazzling green eyes. She was a stern woman, cranky even, but a wise Elder and good to her region. Being unwavering in her rules was a hallmark of her known personality.

Come to think of it, most older women in Temani were that way.

Cillian retired for the evening, putting his boots by the small chest in the corner of his room. There was a four-post wooden bed, a side table and a single chair in addition to the chest. Modest accommodations for a modest town. All the pieces were wood and hand carved by the local carpenter fifty years ago.

In a few days he would have a vastly different room. Anxious thoughts bit at memories he wished to forget.

He was going to meet Master Olam in the Shining City.

Located at the center of all four towers was a palace of ivory stone, polished to glisten in response to the surrounding light. The city was massive, spreading out around the palace to claim a piece of all four regions, making it a shared gem for all their people. A beautiful city on a hill, full of magic and wonder, but most importantly perfect peace.

It had been years since Cillian had gained favor to step inside those walls, yet he truly had never wished to visit again. That place was too beautiful for him to stay after what he had done.

Quickly he cut that memory off, pushing it back into the box and locking it there.

Tonight, he would sleep better without it.

Terror gripped me as tightly as I gripped Shadow's reins, the whites of my knuckles gleaming from the pressure.

I had decided it was safer up here in the saddle than on the ground.

Foolish comfort. I could just as easily be thrown, then have my horse run off, but I tried to ignore that thought.

The forest seemed to stretch on and on with every tree looking the same as the last. There was a light fog settling in some of the lower areas where I believed there to be thick mud. We had actively avoided those spots, journeying around them regardless how large.

"Last thing I need is you or I with a broken neck. On second thought, it could be a better outcome for us." I forced a laugh while Shadow pinned his ears in response to my bad joke.

Although we had started our ride mid-morning, the sun was already setting in these strange lands. The possibility of us still being lost in this forest in the dark made my head feel light as bile hit the back of my throat. "Come on, you can do this, you have to keep your head," I demanded with more confidence than I had.

Shadow had already watched me vomit, hyperventilate, sob and shake for longer than I'd like to admit. He had thankfully endured all my panic with little annoyance, or at least he hadn't shown much. Honestly, he was too concerned with looking around awaiting some demon to come for his hide.

We both were.

Silence was never encouraging when you were in the forest. Usually you heard the birds, squirrels or other small scuttling creatures that made the forest floor their home. Only when the little guys were quiet was there usually some predator they didn't want to alert to their presence. I tried to convince myself we were predators, but it was more likely we were being hunted.

Nothing had happened yet to make me honestly believe that, just the tingling on my neck from that hard wired fight/flight response. After the initial panic had subsided, the deep knowing that we were being watched just wouldn't go away.

No deer.

A forest like this should be teeming with deer, but I hadn't seen any trace of them.

To my right I heard the babbling of a stream, and I tipped Shadow's head in the direction of the calming, familiar sound. The rest of him followed as we made our way towards the water. He picked up his pace when he finally caught sight of the sparkling movement.

Down we went to the bank's edge where he greedily shoved his nose into the pulsing stream. I dismounted, noticing how clear the water was, and decided to risk drinking it myself.

My mouth welcomed the cool liquid as I rinsed the lingering taste of vomit away. Cupping my hands together I splashed it all over my face and down my arms. It was a refreshing sensation, and for a moment I thought about just dunking my entire head in, but I doubted it was deep enough.

Warm air still hugged my shoulders as the light started pulling further out of the forest. I had been thankful for only wearing a tank top and jeans earlier, but I began to wonder if there would be a chill once the light was gone.

More worrisome was the creeping in of darkness. I kept trying to pretend it wouldn't be pitch black here within the hour.

Shadow began pawing at the water which quickly turned to mud, ruining my drinking spot. Spinning to my right I shot him an annoyed look, about to make fuss when just past his shoulder my eyes caught movement.

Big movement.

Shadow felt my anxiety as his gaze followed mine and he froze, nostrils flaring.

Hurriedly, I scrambled into the saddle, refusing to take my eyes off the dark mass not twenty yards away.

A bear, the back of a huge bear.

Grizzly, I thought, but as it turned around to face us, I realized I was terribly mistaken.

Large ears pointed sharply up; his muzzle elongated more like a wolf than bear, with two large fangs coming down on either side. His shoulders were bigger than any grizzly as he stood on two hind legs that also resembled a wolf's, but that upper body screamed bear. He locked his gaze on us, and I noticed how gold his eyes were, matching the strange gold sigil on his chest.

We needed to move, but neither Shadow nor I dared the risk as the creature shot his head up, nose in the air to release a deafening howl straight to the sky.

Every hair on my body stood up. My mind was screaming *run*, and finally we did.

Digging my heels into Shadow's sides with everything I had, I leaned forward while pulling my left rein to snatch his head away from the animal. It was a direct order, not a question or suggestion, to move, now.

And boy, did he move.

Heaving forward with a jump, his hooves hit the ground and we were off into a full gallop. I had never asked him to do more than walk or trot, but he ran as if the devil himself were at our heels.

For a small horse, he moved impressively fast.

Refusing to look behind me, I focused ahead. Tearing past trees, we just kept straight, going who knew where. Although I wouldn't turn around, I could hear the creature gaining on us, his legs swallowing much more ground than Shadow's could.

We weaved ever so slightly when the trees forced us to, my arms forward as I centered my weight over his shoulders to ease the burden.

Shadow began to slow ever so slightly as his muscles screamed at him. Neither of us were in the best shape of our days.

We wouldn't, couldn't outrun this thing.

Dread crept in, slithering into all corners of my mind, heavily covering it.

We were going to die, here in a place I didn't know.

Scared, alone.

It would be a gruesome death, shredded and eaten alive. I had seen the claws on that thing. With one movement it could have Shadow and I too injured to move.

This was it, the end of my story.

There was this odd relief that began to find me. I wouldn't have to fight the darkness in the corner of my mind anymore. If I were gone, it would be gone too. No more attempts to keep the voices quiet. I had always feared death, but in the moments I didn't, I welcomed the peace it brought me. Sometimes I had even considered if it would just be better to have not existed at all.

Lurching forward Shadow suddenly picked up speed, giving everything he had, and I looked up to see a break in the trees. There was an opening, an end to the forest.

Tearing the dark blanket off my mind and urging Shadow forward, I screamed for him to move faster. Within seconds we burst through the tree line into an open field, catching the last bits of an orange double sun as it found rest with the horizon.

After we made it out, no longer did I hear the clamor of pursuit from that monster. I listened closely for another minute, and still nothing. Daring to look, the gold-eyed creature was gone, there was nothing except the line of an intimidating forest off in the distance.

"Whoa boy, easy, easy." Sitting back deeply in my seat, I gently put pressure on the reins.

Shadow reluctantly moved into a trot, slowing into a walk, then stopped as we topped a small hill, breathing heavily as my legs moved with his chest.

Surveying the area quickly, I noted a road in the distance, cutting in front and continuing to my right. It was dirt, but a road. To my right there were more fields stretching far beyond where my eyes could go.

Looking down, I scanned my horse for injuries. He appeared fine other than being drenched in foamy sweat. My hand found my face and wiped the itchy drip from my cheek to my chin. It had started burning only moments ago, and upon inspection of my wet hand I wasn't surprised to find streaks of blood. Moving through the forest I had taken a small branch to the face, not the first time that's happened.

Clicking to ask Shadow forward, we turned towards the road, hoping it would take us somewhere, and that whomever we met would be kinder than that beast in the forest.

Chapter 4

"What a perfect evening. Marvelous weather we're having, don't you think, darling?" came the sweet voice of Lilith as she looked out the window with her back against the black marble column. Her long-sleeved dark gray dress hugged each curve tightly with a slit halfway up her thigh revealing the ivory skin beneath. She had her black hair tied up loosely on top of her head with ice blue eyes sweeping across the mountainside watching the rain and sleet fall.

"Yes, I do believe it's perfect. Here you are, my pet," Abaddon whispered in her ear as he handed her one of the two silver mugs he was carrying.

She brought the mug under her nose, inhaling the sweet metallic scent.

"Cheers, to a new age," she offered up a nod and a mischievous smile.

"No, to the return of an old age long forgotten," he corrected as he held her gaze, his ebony eyes popping against his olive skin. His face boasted high cheek bones, full lips and a firm chin. This evening his black hair was combed to the side with a freshly trimmed goatee.

"Excuse me, my lord, how should we prepare the second doe?" came a voice from the other side of the room. A large man had emerged carrying a letter in his left hand. He bowed at the waist as he stopped and handed the letter over.

"Drain it. You're welcome to do as you wish with the leftovers. I'll have to thank my creatures of the night for retrieving such a delicious night cap." Abaddon answered.

The corner of Lilith's mouth lifted in a smirk as she waved her hand to dismiss the servant. Taking another sip from her mug, she relished the salty thickness of the blood before crossing the room to set it down on the long metal table.

"Oh dear, it would seem our Gangors have been spotted. That will reflect poorly on our management, don't you think?" Abaddon mocked with a smile while he tapped the letter he held in his hand. "I'll bet the old man is turning it over in his head right now, the thoughts driving him half mad. Pity I can't see his face as he questions 'why now'?"

Lilith rolled her eyes as she responded curtly, "I just don't understand why we play these games; they are tiresome after all these years. Why not just kill him? We could."

"You know I like to play with my food. Besides, hot-headed battles never last long. I want something eternal, and you'd be a fool to believe Olam could be so easily removed. Don't underestimate him." Abaddon sent a warning look her way as he finished the letter.

Lilith went to defend her position as the rage began piling up inside her, so hot her fists began to smolder.

Fool, he insinuated she was a fool.

Her lips parted as her tongue hit the top of her mouth, preparing the first of many fiery curses she was going to spit at Abaddon.

Before she could, he cleared the space between them with unnatural speed, slamming her into the wall. A sharpened nail scratched gently at her neck as every muscle stiffened. His lips brushed her ear, "Temper, temper. You dare think such wicked things about your creator? Remember who gave you that power. I own you; you would do well to be reminded one way or another if necessary."

Lilith sent fierce cold winds to blow through her mind, begging her body to embrace them instead of the fiery rage that initially burned.

Pulling her chin to meet her now red eyes, he watched the fire die back again.

"Good. I'll see you in a few days. There's business to address." He kissed her forehead and smoothly glided across the marble floors, out the door and down the hall.

She glared daggers through the back of his head as she commanded those icy winds to stuff her feelings back, down, deeper. He would be able to smell it if she weren't careful. The response would be far worse than his anger at visions of her melting his skin off.

Abaddon delighted in the fear. It was like heroin for him from other lesser beings that could be tormented, but not her. Fear of him was forbidden, she would be considered flawed, and she had given up too much to get here. To be considered less than, all her pain for that failure.

His reactions had scared her again, but she had learned to conceal it well. One day she would kill him, or he'd kill her, but she knew the dance between them would eventually end.

Shadow trotted along the dirt path, still uneasy with his surroundings.

All around us were fields, clearly belonging to farmers, although most I couldn't readily identify besides the peanuts. On my left was a faint glistening from a far-off water source, but the road was taking me back east.

If the sun operates the same way here, it is a double sun, I thought silently to myself.

We moved forward up a large sloping hill along the path. Suddenly I saw a gray stone tower emerge. Pulling Shadow quickly to a halt at the top, my eyes locked on a town in the distance.

Every muscle in me seized as my breathing quickened.

Sensing the change, my mount shifted uneasily beneath me, stretching out a hoof to paw the ground in anxious frustration.

Once more my view held a place I didn't know. It seemed like something out of a dark ages' history book and anyone who still lived like that in a time of technology couldn't be sane, at all.

My mind lurched from one question to the next, trying to compare the threat of what lay before me versus what lay behind me. Shadow had enough and started walking forward again.

"Whoa boy, stop it," I snatched the reins as he threw his head up in disapproval, no doubt from the pain of the metal bit slamming back in his mouth. "Sorry, I just need to think," I cooed as I dismounted to hold him from the ground.

The town was still far off. Doubtful anyone could make us out to be any more than a blob, but I walked back the opposite direction to use the hill as a block between us just in case.

We knew there were only fields and that cursed forest behind us. I toyed with the idea of wandering towards the water in the distance, but water had a habit of attracting more than just us. The other thought that leapt to mind was going through the peanut fields not too far back, but a sharp fear snagged that one away. Where there were crops, there were farmers, and usually they did not take kindly to strangers walking through their fields.

"Who even knows if there are people here. Maybe they are giants or dwarves, dark elves with a grudge against other beings." Shadow snorted as if to verbalize how ridiculous he knew I sounded.

He was right, that was silly, but ending up in a mystical forest being chased by a wolf-bear was equally insane. Turning us back towards the town, I tried to command my feet forward.

A primal fear crept up my neck, slinking into my head, something so intentional and knowing. All the hair on my arms stood up, and even Shadow turned his ears forward, tightening his shoulders in response.

We were not alone anymore.

I heard it first.

The silence in the fields was deafening, so any disruption was easy to pick up.

Wings, big wings.

They were coming from back behind to my right side, from the direction of the forest.

Everything screamed run, but my feet were cemented to the ground once more. I wanted to look, needed to look at what was coming our way, but maybe if I didn't move it wouldn't see us.

Fool.

The sound was getting louder and time had slowed.

Shadow began to prance frantically. I had to control him. If I lost him, we would both be in deep trouble.

Spinning him around, we faced the threat together clutching the lead rope on his halter tightly in an attempt to keep his feet on the ground.

Large wings hurled air my way as something large landed in front of us. I had to lift my arm in front of my face to block the blinding light.

Shadow reared and almost had me on my face, but I held on tightly. Moving closer to his chest I commanded he back up, which he did without hesitation.

Following his stare, I lowered my arm as my mouth fell open.

There, in front of us, was one of the most beautiful creatures I had ever laid eyes upon.

White feathered wings jutted out from either side of its back, stretching towards the sky. A horse, all white, dazzling, with a tail that dragged the ground stood proudly. My eyes followed a curved neck into a gorgeous, chiseled head, and in front of the ears extended an impressive rack of elk-like antlers. If I didn't know better, as I gawked at them, I would swear they were made of pure ivory.

Neither Shadow nor I moved as the creature stepped towards us, meeting those large amber eyes that matched the gold sigil on its chest. Four crosses emerged from top to bottom and left to right with a six-point star boxed in the middle of them. It was unlike any sigil I had ever seen.

It took another step towards us with head held high, those antlers spreading at least three feet out from its head on each side, a simply magnificent animal.

Trembling, I was so enamored with the beauty that fear for my life didn't even begin to register. Shadow, on the other hand, looked as though he might just drop dead if it took one more step.

"Hello dear one, welcome." My brain echoed with a soft female voice that moved like honey down the back of mind. At first, I wondered if it was simply imagined. "You, my dear, I'm speaking to you."

Slowly it registered that this enchanting animal was talking, not in the literal sense as her mouth didn't move, but somehow infiltrating my thoughts with hers.

As if the honeyed words contained some sort of soothing balm, I didn't flinch from fear or launch into manic laughter at the craziness of that understanding. "You've ventured far to get here, but you are welcome, you are safe. Would you wish my company down the road?"

Nodding my head, a blanket of comfort settled but no response could be uttered. For now, the anxious swirling of questions had fled me completely and I welcomed such peace.

Even Shadow seemed to relax as I mounted him and turned back down the road towards that stone tower that only minutes ago had me in utter terror.

Conceding my anxious feelings, I released the questions. There was this strange knowing that in time I would be made to understand.

So down the road we walked, black gelding following this enchanting white mare.

Miraculous.

No matter how many times he saw it, it was truly a remarkable sight.

Far off Cillian could see the Ivory Palace atop a tall hill, reflecting light in all directions. Soft, dancing light, not spotlights. Rolling down from the palace, the hillside revealed a sea of square-topped buildings, painted a swarm of bright colors that stretched in all directions as the land flattened. None stood very tall, most being only two or three stories high.

His eyes followed the sea of color as it changed from one street to the next, melting together like paints. Another beauty of polished ivory stone surrounding the entire city that shimmered in the sunlight was the wall.

From a distance it would seem there were no defenses, which was true. They weren't needed; not with Olam presiding, and the Law of course.

The Law, one of the only absolutes in this land, was reserved for the Shining City. Anyone was welcome. Open to all but only to reside; visitation was limited by Olam's power alone.

To reside, there were sacrifices. You had to offer up your most treasured belonging. It didn't need to be of high value, if it was of most value to you. With it you granted Master Olam full access in your mind, your entire life lived in full view. He would offer healing for the dark and broken pieces you held onto. If you refused, you couldn't gain entrance. Then again, if you welcomed such healing, you could live within the security of the city for eternity.

This city was sacred ground, a place of peace where people lived burdenless. Endless supplies, no one wanted for anything. Community relation with one another on a level that only happened inside these walls.

A beautiful sentiment, but just not believed by all. Some concealed a deeper darkness within, not easily brought from the shadows.

It had taken the better part of the day to arrive from the South Tower, even with Diadred's speed. They were both exhausted, moving slowly as they approached the barrier. Each entrance had one, a mirror-like shimmering extending across the entryway distorting your view of the other side. Cillian halted Diadred just before they touched it, awaiting passage from Master Olam.

Within seconds the shimmering split like a curtain, pulling back the thick mirror like water, and they both stepped through into the city.

Smiling faces, waves and looks of awe were thrown the mighty cat's way as he made his way down the ivory street. All Master Olam's creatures were held in high regard across the lands, but the people of the city truly admired Diadred.

Diadred picked up his chest proudly like a warrior returned from battle. Cillian knew it had more to do with how much they loved and respected their Master, less about how powerful Diadred thought he looked, so he simply rolled his eyes.

Street vendors were out trading their goods while children ran around playing tag with contagious laughter. Spices, pies, bread along with an array of meaty smells drifted through the air, enticing those who caught them to come partake.

The city was a melting pot of people from different regions and assorted colors. They all bustled around, enjoying the wonderful day.

To Cillian's right was a lady in a long-sleeve purple silk gown, with a gold sash at her waist and gold bands around her arms playing a tambourine. Her skin was dark as coal with braided hair that intwined a gold cord which swayed as she moved to the music. On his left was a gentleman crafting leather goods in canvas khaki pants held up by a custom belt that tucked in a loose fitted long sleeve white top. His hair that long turned gray and tanned skin that had spent many days under the sun contrasted a pair of fierce blue eyes.

Making their way further into the city, Cillian now held the Ivory Palace in full view. It was magnificent. He urged Diadred forward, faster up the hill.

The courtyard spread out in full welcome, more people just lounging in chairs near the center fountain, enjoying each other's company.

A young boy greeted them first, asking if Diadred needed special accommodations in the barn, which prompted a scowl with risen lips revealing a set of sharp fangs.

"Now that won't be necessary, son, we let our cats come inside around here," came a strong voice from across the courtyard.

They each turned to see Master Olam headed their way with his mouth turned upward into a large grin.

Diadred leapt over like a house pet bounding around his back and rubbing his huge head up under his Master's arm, nearly knocking him off balance.

"Good to see you too, old friend." He patted that scaly head before turning to Cillian.

Even though Cillian was tall, Olam had him by another five or six inches. One of the few people he had to look up to in his life.

Embracing him in a hug, he felt tension fall from his muscles. It was a reminder of how much relief was brought to the old man just in knowing Cillian was safe.

"Now, we have much to talk about, but first we eat. Come, join me in the dining hall, you look like you could use a meal."

Columns greeted them on either side as they crossed through the palace doors and strode along the tan marble floors into the dining room. The grand table was made of dark wood inlayed with gold engravings down the legs, the top held a large ivory slab with a roast turkey sitting in the middle. Potatoes, carrots and other vegetables lay silently steaming in small metal dishes. Towards the end were two pies, plus a bowl of fresh fruit; food fit for a king.

As soon as they were seated, different dishes began offering themselves up, a knife in the air prepared to slice and plate until the receiver denied any further. Olam gave a quick nod to the carrots after they had spooned enough onto his plate to settle.

A lump formed in Cillian's throat as he watched the spectacle.

It was always silly to him, using magic for fun or convenience. He believed it should be reserved for when it was needed, when it mattered.

"Sir, may I serve myself?" came the uneasy question from Cillian.

Olam lifted his eyes with a tinge of surprise, "Ah yes, not all are comfortable with dancing dishes, but frankly I find it fun. Please, go ahead."

Cillian began to slice the turkey and dish potatoes, eyeing the other dishes, carefully picking what called to his senses.

"Speaking of food, can you help me understand why the Gangors did not make you into such a thing? It's rare that anyone alone walks away from them, even skilled warriors such as yourself." The Master took a concerned tone.

Cillian reported the encounter back to Master Olam. He met his eyes to see a brow furrowed in frustration, not confusion, then turned back to the turkey that had gone cold. "It's never a good sign when dark creatures go against their design. I'm glad that you and Diadred were able to escape their clutches. It's been the most relieving news this week."

Cillian nodded in agreement. "Is there trouble in other regions, sir?"

"Not that I have heard, nothing of consequence, at least until today. We have a guest, and I doubt her presence currently is coincidence."

Cillian met Olam's eyes with a flash of curiosity as he finished chewing the large piece of potato in his mouth.

"You had more come through that waning spot along the border than just some simple deer, my boy." Olam stated before eating another bite.

"No sir, we saw the does, that's it. We watched the human and her mount turn around to head back from wherever they came from." Cillian replied.

"Yes, that is what you saw, but she came back."

"Of course, she did. Most do, but she couldn't have gained entrance." Cillian brushed it off before lifting his fork towards Olam. "That animal maybe, but not her, the wards won't allow it."

Olam continued. "Ah, but they did. The old power not only let her, but it led her."

Cillian almost spat his food back out as Olam drew out that last word with a smirk.

Olam's eyes lit up. "When all five Elders joined together to create a ward around our lands, it tucked us into a pocket of the outside world to keep us safe, hidden. Unfortunately, one Elder didn't want to help, Abaddon. He wished to go out and conquer their world, extending ours after he learned how weak the humans were in comparison to us. Since he refused to help close this realm off, there were only five of the six Elders left to create the ward. His lack of attendance allowed for the waning spots, where small sections couldn't be completely sealed. For his disobedience, he was banished to the far corner of the mountains. Instead of learning from his mistake, he chose to dabble in forbidden things, gaining evil influences of old."

Cillian continued eating. "Yes, Master, I know this already. The history of The Closure and how Abaddon ultimately began the Fallen."

Olam set down his utensils, catching Cillian's gaze with a hint of seriousness. "Humans may have been different than some of my past creations, but I cherished them. Centuries had passed, they had turned away from their original design; instead of cultivating, they conquered. We thought if they could see again, they would be able to become who they were created to be in the beginning. It was decided; I would fill our new world with humans from the outside. This would be the last realm of Starpathia that I would create, these lands here that you call home.

There were many that could see colors others in their world couldn't. Feelings of never being normal, emotions and empathy attached to everything, a life carrying more than most; it created a resilience. Their capacity for love was simply astonishing. I should know, I gave it to them. Here they healed faster than in their own world, here I taught them more than what they could see. Here I allowed them to learn how wonderful their minds were, I let them embrace the magic of this realm and created The Shining City as a place of rest for those who chose to stay in the end. Many did, and all could eventually be traced back as ancestors of yours."

Cillian listened intently to stories never told.

Olam's face shifted as a thin line sat on his mouth, the proud joy replaced with a deep sadness as he continued. "Jealousy can turn nasty so quickly. The other Elders were happy to share what mighty gifts they had with both young and old who found our lands...except one. Abaddon thought we had wasted more than enough on humans; he could never understand why I created realm after realm for them. He used his own power and ancient darkness to expose and twist the brokenness from them.

It was to protect the rest of humanity from this evil that The Closure was executed.

In days of old, humans could pass into this realm of Starpathia with ease, but there is a power here, a portal that can open more realms, older worlds. After his initial attacks on them, I knew I couldn't risk it. Their minds were just too fragile, so many humans there had no hope to cling to once the darkness overtook them."

"The Fallen," Cillian confirmed.

Olam nodded. "Yes, they are a result. Many of them are from the outside world before The Closure. They are old and tired. Centuries of twisting their pain and agony for gain. Power, he gave them such power and promise of revenge, his way of healing. Once they chose to pledge their lives to him, he simply locked them up, waiting, time to obsess over their rage until it consumed them.

The Gangors are the original Fallen, an army he wished to raise to send into other realms. They are so far gone that no part of them remains as human. Angry beasts, only able to do his bidding."

The blood had drained from Cillian's face. He was beginning to understand, as if puzzle pieces were clicking. "Those things were...once human?"

"I'm afraid so." The Master regrettably admitted.

"And we've been living for centuries using magic to grow flowers and cut roast." Cillian grumbled with the realization of what this meant. "Where does this girl fit?"

Master Olam looked gently on Cillian, carefully stepping around his words. "Lenora. There's an animal in that mind of hers, no doubt, but such compassion for others, hearing a song not everyone can. A gift she carries with her, unfortunately one born out of brokenness and pain, desperate to be heard. We need to get her before Abaddon does. Once he realizes she is here, he will do anything to have her." Olam sighed with a heaviness that allowed Cillian a glimpse of just how much he loved these people. "I'd like you to befriend her, help her hold on to the light, teach her how to stay away from him. I've already sent Ivoriene to protect her physically, for now."

Cillian had his eyes locked on Olam, he momentarily couldn't breathe as he rolled the words around in his head, 'teach her how to stay away...from him.' He hadn't been able to do that last time.

He'd failed.

How could Olam begin to ask something like this of him knowing what had happened? It was too much to expect.

"Cillian, I need your help." Olam pushed.

"No." He stood up, shoving the chair back as he bowed to extend some reverence after such quick denial. "I'll help you prepare others, your warriors for that hell that awaits them if Abaddon's creatures are unleashed again, but I will not babysit some human who doesn't know what she's up against."

"Then show her, you know more than most how to navigate Abaddon's attacks on the mind. Help me give her a chance." Olam had a tone to his voice that Cillian could have briefly mistaken as pleading.

"Why don't you help her? Send her home." Cillian wasn't ready yet, he wanted to hold tightly to the guilt that gripped him. It was comfortable now.

Olam breathed a sigh. "I can't send her home; this is where she's meant to be."

With that, Cillian held his gaze another second before turning on his heel to leave Master Olam standing alone. He could feel those eyes at his back as they followed him. He had to get away before he said something he would come to regret.

Chapter 5

"What is your name, dear one?" The soft voice purred into my mind again.

"Lenora, and yours?"

"Ivoriene, but you may call me Ivy if you wish," she replied as though a smile had feeling.

The grass swayed in the breeze as two sets of hooves clopped side by side on the dirt road; it was wider now, so Ivy had dropped back beside Shadow and I.

"This town, is it safe? Are there people there…like me?" I asked hesitantly, not wanting to offend my new friend.

Ivy nodded. "Safe, yes. You are far from harm, for now. These people are welcoming, simple folk. Like you? No, I'm afraid there hasn't been an outsider for a long time. Everyone you will meet today were born and raised here."

"Do they all look like you or that wolf bear, thing, I mean, animal-like?" I stuttered out my ridiculous question, trying to prepare myself for a town of animals.

"Goodness girl, no!" Ivy laughed with such intent that I found myself chuckling too at the ridiculous thought.

"Oh, I see – do they *look* like you? That is what you really wished to ask. Yes, they do. You share little physical differences, but humans here can use their mind to shape magic in or around them. A talent you have yet to possess." With that last statement she tipped her head, tossing me a look, but before I could object an image of the wolf bear found its way front and center to my mind, forcing me to lurch my head back in the saddle. "This is the forest guardian Balfour, whom you met with earlier. He is one of the great guardians of Starpathia, like I am. We are few, individually designed by our Master for a specific duty. Both he and I are the only of our kind."

"Is his duty to eat small women who get lost in the woods?" I responded with a grimace at the thought of that thing having a job.

"No, although I don't blame you for thinking that. Balfour protects the Southernmost border from…trouble, we'll call it."

Huffing, I responded. "I'm not sure I would define a girl and her horse as trouble."

"You would be surprised what trouble could have found you instead," her heavy sternness challenged my comment. "Enough about that for now. We're here."

In front of us, a quaint cobblestone town began to unfold.

"I'm taking you to an inn where you can get washed up, fed, and dressed in some warmer clothes for our journey tomorrow. Shadow can be turned in to the barn and you're welcome to go anywhere inside the town, just please don't leave. It's not safe for you after dark." There was genuine concern in those eyes as she turned to face me. I thought twice about asking what danger, deciding I wanted to sleep tonight and Ivy seemed weary of my questions.

Like lightening it hit me, prompting me to shout it out at Ivy instead of thinking it.

"Wait, I can't sleep here, who will feed my chickens?!"

Ivy had stepped back in surprise from the outburst, but her face softened, full of compassion as she replied. "I'm sorry, I cannot take you home. However, I can offer some reassurance. Time works differently here; you've barely been out of your world an entire second. You could spend years here and only be gone minutes there, so rest tonight. Your day has been long, my dear."

We walked in silence the rest of the way through town, and I reminded myself those free-range birds were practically wild anyway. They would be fine. What weighed heavier was the realization that there was little I had to return to; it was likely no one would know I was gone.

There was no concern shown by those we passed in town. She had told the truth when she said they looked like me, all simply dressed, farmers and trade workers. It was a small town like one you would see in the deep south. People selling fresh veggies, dogs even ran loose – so they did have normal animals too. Children played with sticks while mothers fussed about supper.

Very…normal, for a century ago. Add in a giant flying horse with antlers by my side…oh yeah, Lenora, this is normal.

The voice mocked inside, and I winced, wondering if Ivy had heard.

If she did, she showed no sign of it.

Tomorrow I would find out just how this whole telepathy thing worked, and if any of my thoughts were protected.

We stopped at the stables, and as I dismounted Shadow my joints burned in protest; I had been in the saddle for more miles than I dared consider. The stable boy led him away, while I was assured he would receive only the best care. Ivy then turned me over to a woman named Martha, who rambled about being a guest of their Master and she would tend to my every need.

Who that was, I didn't ask. My mind felt like sludge. With the comfort of safety also brought the weight of all my body had endured. Ivy let me know she would be around and would hear my call if needed. Martha watched me scarf down a large helping of chicken and dumplings before ushering me to a bath with the command to sleep afterwards.

The bathroom was small, containing a single drawered side table with a bowl atop it. In the back was a large metal tub that sat flat on the floor. To use the bathroom, there was an outhouse out back; I had visited earlier as I struggled to wrap my awareness around it.

After I eased into the hot water it dawned on me that there were no pipes, so where the water had come from and how it was hot remained a mystery. My body rejoiced in ecstasy as the heat loosened the tension from each muscle, with every passing second submerged there was less to care about, including the waters origins.

Slipping into a long sleeve cotton dressing gown I found my way to a single wood-framed bed and crawled under a heavy hand-stitched quilt. Within seconds I let the fatigue set in, closing my eyes and falling heavily into a wonderous sleep.

Abaddon had a manor carved into the side of one of the largest mountains at the Northeastern most corner of the realm. It was an impressive structure made of black marble, with large columns on multiple balconies that peaked over a large valley. Two kitchens were at the back, one for residents and another for the special dinner preparations. There was an informal dining hall, a library, and each household member's individual rooms. Underneath the manor was a supply basement, along with the servants' living quarters.

Only Abaddon, Lilith, and a few other commanders had the honor of living here. Another dozen cabins were scattered along the surrounding mountains, in addition to the dungeons inside the mountain that housed the rest of the Fallen.

Lilith hated that term; it was so depressing, but one day they would be the Fallen no more. Eventually they would rule over the Shining City, seated in the Ivory Palace; that was Abaddon's promise.

Watching as the last bits of red faded from the trees with the setting suns, Lilith smiled. It was nearly dark and there was promise of the first snow tonight.

Restless, Lilith twisted in the lounge chair she occupied on the balcony. Unusual memories flooded her mind earlier in the day, things she had no interest in giving much thought to. Being inside the last few days was suffocating and there was newfound desperation to stretch her legs. She was not simply some woman who wished to preside over the affairs of a household, nor did she wish for any company the filthy commanders had to offer.

No, tonight she would shed the silk green dress she currently wore, let her hair down and dance.

Tonight, she would fly.

Tonight, she would go for a hunt.

A wicked smile curved her lips as she stood, crossing the room to her wardrobe. In one snag of the bow on her back she untied the satin gown and it dropped to the floor. She carefully selected a pair of black pants with a matching long sleeve black coat. Not that she needed to keep out the cold, she loved the way it nipped on her bare skin, but this was more practical.

Eyes in the manor may feel the need to report her movements to Abaddon after their spat, and she couldn't risk that this evening. It would be unwise to walk out the front door, so she'd have to get creative.

Pulling on black boots, she let loose the thick long curls of ebony hair to fall around her shoulders before she strode back over to the balcony. Looking below, she estimated it was about a hundred-foot drop to the first ledge.

Closing her eyes, she envisioned strong cold winds coming to the mountain and shooting up from the ledge to the balcony in circular repetition. Focusing harder she pushed for more winds, faster they followed.

Satisfied, she opened her eyes and stepped off the balcony rail into the frigid air.

Initially the winds sent her up a few feet, but she slowed them, allowing her to drift down the side of the mountain and on to the ledge below. Her boots contacted the ground about the time the winds died, settling a calm through her bones as she took in the familiar scene.

Ice cracked quietly under her, overcast skies sent a promise of snow, the full moons trying their best to peek through them. Lilith took note that it was well below freezing once a breeze tossed her hair, licking the back of her neck that sent shivers down her spine.

This was her paradise, the darkness, the cold in her bones and the naked trees that appeared to shake in preparation of their impending white blanket.

A cold lady of the night, she smirked at the thought.

Abaddon believed she was made by fire, but it wasn't her first magic. It wasn't where her true strength could be found, but it was wonderful that he believed it so.

Fire was driven by passion, desire, or rage.

Those weren't at her mind's core; they were afterthoughts when she needed them.

Cold was what she was, who she was.

She had been reborn in ice, numbness and darkness. Any element that could chill your bones- wind, rain, ice, or snow- could be summoned to her side with a thought.

Abaddon believed he had broken her, not realizing even with his dark mind games that he was wrong. Her mind had been broken and numb long before he began twisting her. True, he had helped create the fire. It was a helpful tool in her mind's arsenal, but not as devastating as what she had been brewing the last century, alone in the cold.

He was the prince of darkness; he didn't need fire or ice.

Feelings or numbness.

He just needed your doubt, your fear, your shame or guilt. Those were first class tickets to a world of torment if he started digging through your head.

She'd banished all those footholds long ago, but the fear was still there.

Fear only for him, what he had done and what he could do if he were bored.

A large movement caught the corner of her eye.

Lilith stilled as she watched a great white wolf emerge on her left side, alone. Trotting along swiftly with his nose to the wind, tracking. Crossing her path, he stopped short. Human scent had clearly given away her position when his heavy gaze found her own. As if some primal respect passed between them, he turned back to the task at hand, one predator recognizing another out for a hunt.

Predator.

What she had become over time as the victim inside her died.

Once he was out of sight, Lilith sprinted as fast as she could, silently down the mountain. Bringing winds to the front, she removed branches from her path and air behind to push her forward. Within seconds her feet were hovering as the winds came under to carry her. She sprinted harder through the air, crossing miles in minutes.

Snow began to fall moderately south of their mountains. The ground offered no more steep declines, and off to her right was a small stream struggling to move chunks of ice. She hadn't come this way in years, but she knew Olam would have extra patrols in the mountains to the west.

Tonight, she required discretion.

With luck there were a few cabins just over the territory line in the southernmost glen not far ahead of her. No one ventured into the Fallens' lands anymore, but they used to.

Lilith recalled decades ago when silly boys would come over willingly on dares, but those days had long since passed.

Now if she wanted to meet new people, she had to find them.

It was a beautiful glen, one of many in the Norwood. The snow was falling harder now, and Lilith had returned to walking for the simple enjoyment of watching the magic as it softly landed on everything around her. As it danced in the air, the cold depths of her mind stirred restlessly, excitement leapt forward, moving to the dark song that echoed.

There, just fifty yards away, flickered a light, barely visible through the steady screen of white. Lilith moved in to investigate, picking up some winds to muffle any noise as she quickened gracefully over the colorless ground. Up ahead, nestled in the corner of this narrow valley, were two cabins, a larger stream dividing them.

No families would be found in either, children were never this close to their territory. They were outcasts to be so far away from any civilization. If luck went her way, they would be lonely men and not some old hags.

Moving around to the side of the first cabin she peered in the small wood-framed window. A roaring fire filled the fireplace, by the door was a small table with a bowl of bread and a single bed mat pushed up against the wall. The small wood rocking chair held an old man wrapped in a fur, sleeping with a bit of drool coming down from his chin. "Well, you are just too pitiful, shame," Lilith let out a discouraged sigh following her whisper.

Turning her sights onward, she crossed through the stream, letting water come up to her thighs, savoring the bitter cold as it flowed over her skin through her pants.

Minutes later she found herself soaked, approaching the second cabin. With bright eyes she looked through the window, heart racing at the sight before her. A lone man had just cleared his dinner plate, leaving it stranded on the dining table. He was middle aged with broad shoulders, large arms and brown tousled hair. His beard required attention and he needed a bath, but other than that, he was mildly attractive.

There was a chill that dashed across her full chest, one of the buttons had snagged itself free. Still dripping wet from the stream, she swept all her hair to one side, letting the curls bounce wherever they pleased. Stepping onto the porch she pushed on the flames already trying to tickle the back of her mind. "Not yet. Easy, my sweet." She cooed as she pulled in water to dowse them back.

Commanding her wind to come forward, she pushed and swung the front door wide open.

Standing straight ahead by the fire was the man, mouth open with astonishment at the sight that lay before him.

"Might I share your fire, good sir?" Lilith purred as she sauntered over to the fireplace, not waiting for an answer.

"I, um, sure, how…" he stumbled over his response.

She cut him off. "Why so alone out here in the cold?"

Moving closer to him, she placed both hands in front of her, pretending to need heat from the dancing flames.

He muttered something she didn't take the time to hear.

"Tonight, you drew a lucky card."

Stepping closer she cornered her prey; from her ice blue eyes he lowered his gaze to her chest now beading with sweat. The corner of his mouth tugged up into a seductive smile.

Lilith mirrored his with a sly grin of her own. Already she had infiltrated his mind, flashing pictures and suggestions to stoke his fire. She stood ready and waiting for him to make the first move.

Outside the winds howled as a snowstorm now descended upon the small log cabin. The door was still open, allowing flurries to roll in from the porch.

One large step from those long legs was all it took to close the gap between them. He grabbed her shoulders, spinning and slamming her back into the wall so hard it took her breath away. Within seconds he ripped her shirt completely open as buttons clattered on the wood floor beneath them.

Flames ran in circles, demanding to be set loose, her mind screaming as he pushed himself against her, pinning her arms above her head. With a laugh he seized her.

Time stilled as she iced over every bit of flame her misguided body tried to produce; she didn't move. Darkness seeped into every crack of her mind as she began to slow her breathing and close her eyes. Fear used to rise here but not anymore; the cold cocooned her instead.

She was in control.

He tore at her clothes like an animal desperate to devour its food. She started to wriggle her arms free, but he was strong. Her own natural born strength easily overpowered by his own. Tighter he gripped her delicate wrists together, pain shooting down her arm. Once more she snatched, opposing her weight to get away from him.

He leaned into her ear, hot breath on her neck as he growled, "You're not going anywhere."

Ice shot out in all directions, freezing over everything inside. Wind caught the door, slamming it shut, with a force that shook the entire room. Her eyes flashing a dark gray from the pale blue they had been only seconds earlier. Releasing Lilith in confusion, he stumbled back into the dining table, but it was too late.

He tried to run to the door, pulling frantically at the handle with all his strength, realizing immediately what she was, but the wind pushed back, keeping the door secure. Stumbling to put the small table in between them he got to his knees, tears in his eyes begging her to spare him.

"Please I...I'll do anything. What do you want? I can get m-m-money or jewels. I know someone in the Karakum who can access one of the royal families, anything. Please don't take me."

"Take you? Oh no sweetie, I won't take you. Filth like you don't deserve to grace our dungeons. You know what you are. This is your own fault."

"No, no, you m-made me." He shoved a finger in her direction.

"Me? M-made you." She mocked with a grin. "I did no such thing, you always had that in you. Those dark thoughts, that desire to take without asking. Curiosity. That place where you tear her clothes, you hold her down, inhaling that fear that flashes in her eyes, feeding on it. The struggle you require, so you take her again and again." Lilith balled her fist tightly as she swiped the air, baring her teeth.

He began to quietly sob, his head sagging into his hands.

Collecting herself, she shrugged a shoulder as she sat on the edge of the table. "I simply nudged you in the right direction, gave you opportunity."

"It's your fault, you asked for it." He spat; renewed strength and rage flashed in his eyes.

Your fault...asked for it. Those words reverberated in Lilith's mind, fanning the flame of a fire that no longer sought permission but propelled its way to the front, refusing to be concealed this time. Her hands smoldered, turning bright orange as she breathed flames that engulfed the table, turning it to ash.

Leaping back, the man smashed into the far side wall, hysterically swatting the flames that now consumed his shirt while he screamed. He turned his face just to see her charge him with arms stretched outward. A powerful force snatched the man from his feet and hurled him through the front door, ripping it from its hinges. With a heavy thud he landed in a pillow-soft pile of snow outside.

Lilith had heard the snaps as his bones broke. She calmly approached him, taking in the unnatural position of his twisted body.

Still alive, barely.

One quick thought brought the wind to her command, picking up a piece of the door to plunge through his chest.

"That was a rude thing to say to a lady," she said thoughtfully as she walked past him, careful not to step in the blood that now painted the white canvas around them.

Those blue eyes had returned as she hummed a simple song, walking along the stream.

With that, the snow stopped falling and the winds ceased.

Chapter 6

The shrill sound of a rooster crowing cut through the morning air and into my window as it pulled me from dreamless sleep. For a moment I believed to be back in my RV, home with my body objecting to get up and tend to the chickens all screaming to be fed.

Instead, my eyes caught the end table with the bowl atop, a simple hand carved wood piece that matched everything else in this room. Misunderstanding began to cloud until the memories flooded back, reminding me of where I was and that the nightmare was my reality, for now.

At some point Martha had brought me more clothes. They sat stacked neatly on a small wooden chair in the corner of the room. I swung my feet over to the floor and went to stand. Immediately my body reminded me of just how long I had been on a horse yesterday. Stifling a whimper as I straightened my back before gimping over to the clothes.

They were modest, like everything in this town. Green long sleeve shirt with a tie string across the chest and some sort of canvas pants that didn't look like I would enjoy a saddle with them on. Thankfully underneath were cleaner versions of what I had worn from home, so I wiggled into my jeans and layered the tank underneath the green shirt.

After finding my boots I wandered out of my room, taking in more of the inn than I had the night before. Something smelled divine as I crossed under a wood beam at the end of the hallway and into the dining room.

Martha was busy delivering food, laughing with patrons, and shooting stern reminders to a young bus boy. Once she caught sight of me, she practically jogged over, apron on and dishes in hand.

"Good morning, sugar! You look refreshed, green sure is your color just as I thought it would be," she winked as she ushered me to the bar. "How do grits and eggs sound, fresh out the hen if ya follow."

"That would be wonderful, thank you." I smiled. This woman truly was the definition of hospitality.

It didn't take long to consume everything she put in front of me, finishing to see most of the breakfast rush end. Martha swung back by to inform me that Ivy had gone out on an errand, but she would be back soon and not to worry. It was then greatly encouraged I go explore as Martha gave me a wave, walking back to the kitchen. One more reminder that I wasn't a prisoner, I alleged, pushing back the unkind thoughts that tried to surface about their intentions.

My attention went to Shadow now that all my other needs had been met, so I wandered out the heavy wood doors and in the direction of the stables. The gray cobblestones were rubbed smooth, I noted, a sign of many years of wear. Sun was shining and the warm breeze had me rethinking the need for the long sleeve shirt that covered my arms.

A nicker.

Shadow's black head hung over the stall door. Ears forward with hay in his hair, he rumbled that sweet sound in my direction again as a greeting. Warmth filled my chest as I realized this was the first time he had ever done that. The muscles in my cheeks started to burn from more enthusiastic smiling.

Entering the stall, I leaned into his mane, wrapping my arms around his neck to inhale the aroma: hay, horse, dirt, sweat, water and a hint of manure.

This was home to me.

"Good, you're ready," came a voice as I jumped out of my skin, anxiously turning to face whoever came up behind me.

"Please don't do that!" I squealed.

Ivy didn't flinch this time, clearly already accustomed to my dramatized reactions.

Nothing amusing was to be found in her voice as she asked me to quickly saddle up and then meet Martha inside for supplies.

"I thought you had errands and I was free to wander around?" I questioned.

Ivy seemed annoyed with my question. "I did, they were cut short, and now we have a change of plans. We'd rather you rode with me, but I already assumed you wouldn't leave your pet behind, so let's go."

"We – who is we, and where are we going?"

Ivy stopped to make eye contact. "My, aren't we full of questions this morning? Does the phrase 'make haste' translate in your world? I'll explain what I can on the way, but for now I need you to know there are scarier things here than territorial forest beasts."

With that, I suspiciously turned on my heels to grab my saddle.

Silently I tacked Shadow up, concerned to think too much, unsure if Ivy would hear me.

As I was checking the final straps of Shadow's bridle, Martha arrived wordlessly with a pack in one arm, the other stretched out to tap my shoulder.

My shoulders flinched at the light pressure.

"Jittery here aren't we, darling? This is everything I could scrounge up on short notice for the road. Fresh bread, carrots, apples and some dried jerky. You stick close to Ivy, you hear? Not everyone around is kind, and even some of the nice ones are dogs." Honest concern clouded that joy in her face momentarily, before her smile returned as she wrapped me in a big hug. This woman barely knew me and yet here she was, worried.

Leading Shadow out, I listened to his hooves clop on the cobblestones and set him up to mount. Swinging myself into my black suede-seated saddle, I pulled the reins up before directing him down the road after an antsy Ivy.

Martha watched us as she waved goodbye while my stomach filled with knots.

Something made me uneasy as we left the town we had just arrived in, like we were walking straight in the direction of chaos.

"Come on, Cillian, we both know how this is going to end. Save the trouble and just choose the winning side now. We can help you."

His mind was heavy, taking everything to drive out Abaddon's voice as it snuck around the darkness.

"You're wrong, you know. The Fallen are the real victims here, Cillian." Her voice rose with a sharpness.

Cillian pushed back at such a foolish belief. "You don't know what you're saying, Anara, this isn't you. Please come back with me. We can go home."

"Home? You know nothing of home." Fury flashed across her face as she spun around to lock eyes with her brother, tight brown curls falling loose from the bun atop her head. "Where were you? Mom waited, you know, believing she would see you one last time. Instead, you produced every excuse of why you couldn't come. She died still waiting... No, you don't get to show up now with delusions of home and demand I bow to them."

"This isn't a discussion; you are not well and I am taking you back now!" His heart was pounding as he snatched for Anara's arm. She returned by shoving him away. He'd already decided he'd drag her out if he needed to, even then though she would have to change her mind eventually. He simply couldn't lock her in a cage forever, although momentarily it didn't sound like a bad idea.

She trampled farther into the forest; they were awfully close to Fallen territory. Three days he had tracked her after receiving notice she'd left home. He had been a fool to leave her alone to mourn the passing of their mother. A coward, yes. Who knows how long Abaddon and his cronies had been selling her the promise of acceptance?

He had failed her once, but he wouldn't now.

"Anara, please, I beg you. I'll do anything, anything." His voice was full of fear as he jogged to her side.

Snow hadn't arrived yet, but the chill on the air promised it soon.

Briefly she slowed her pace, biting her lip, but then pressed on. Cillian knew with that look, she had made up her mind and no amount of pleading would stop her. There was no forgiving him for what he had done. Not in her mind right now, maybe not ever.

The light from the suns was nearly gone. If Cillian was going to act, it had to be now.

"I'm sorry," he whispered as he pulled the scarf around her auburn curls to gag her. He needed to carry Anara back down this mountain as quietly as possible to not attract unwanted attention.

Dropping her sack, she started to scream.

Cillian didn't want to hurt her; she was a very petite young woman, but he knew this was for her own good. Her brown eyes met his, flashing with ferocity at this sort of invasion of her space. She began kicking and thrashing about.

"Tsk, tsk, tsk. Oh, my boy, that was a foolish move." Cillian stiffened at the voice, the one that haunted his dreams, but it wasn't in his head this time. Standing in front of him was Abaddon, clad in black leathers, both hands in his pockets. Lilith was leaning against a pine, clearly bored, and two of his cronies were walking towards Anara.

"Get away from her," Cillian snarled as he snatched her back, putting himself in between them.

Abaddon lightly stepped forward. "If memory serves me correctly, sweet Anara arranged this meeting. That's why we're here. It might be in your best interest to let your sister make her own choices."

Rage boiled through Cillian's veins. "You'll have to kill me first."

"Now that could be arranged," a smile pulled at Lilith's mouth as Cillian shot her a look, wishing she'd try. There was a time he would have given anything for her to follow him, but she had made her choice long ago.

"Enough." Anara put a hand on her brother's shoulder and stepped forward.

"You promised, Abaddon." Anara held her head high, eyes narrowed and face set firmly in his direction.

"Yes, not a hair would be harmed on your brother's head by my command. My Anara is a smart one, made me take a blood oath and all, as if she didn't trust me to be a man of my word. Hurt my ego a tad, but for this girl I would take any oath she asked." His eyes were set on Anara as he drew out the last few words deliberately, carefully.

By the time Cillian had connected the dots in his head, Anara was already in Abaddon's embrace, staring up at him with the type of look reserved for more than friends. He was much taller than her, being an Elder, but nevertheless that look, Cillian knew it.

She loved him.

Anara turned back to Cillian; sorrow thick in her eyes as she took a step towards him. "Cillian, you're wrong. This is where I belong. Abaddon watched over me while you were away. He's not who you think he is. He takes care of his people; he wants a new world for everyone. Come with us." She extended her hand as she took another step.

Cillian thought he was going to vomit. This couldn't be real, time seemed to stop with the scene in front of him. The followers had stepped back, no longer needed. Lilith was picking her nails, still not amused, and Abaddon stood behind his sister with a twisted smile, eyes locked on Cillian.

There in front of them all was his beautiful sister. Anara had always been stunning. Growing up he caught all the jokes, but she was revered, coveted. Gentle and humble as she was kind. Auburn curls, big brown eyes like a doe, petite and tan with high cheek bones meeting a slender neck. He had always believed no man was good enough, and now here she was with the Prince of Darkness.

He would ruin her.

She loved Abaddon; it was apparent she would follow him but was naïve to his cause. Simply ignoring everything because she had been hurting so long, alone.

Cillian hadn't been there to hold her hand, wipe her tears.

Abaddon had.

He recruits those who are angry, aching, his orphans, and twists those feelings to meet his needs. What did he want with Anara?

"That is the question isn't it. How does it feel, to not know? To squirm as you fight the repugnance of what lay before you?" Abaddon's voice cut through his head.

Cillian struggled to thrust him back.

His temples throbbed, behind his eyes burning as that influence filled his mind.

"What will I do with my sweet Anara, why do I want her, how can she help me? Oh, there's that thought. That's it, you think I'll destroy her, turn her into another of my animals like Lilith? The possibilities, can't you see them, Cillian? You can't save her. How would it feel, to paint the forest in my blood, to rip off my head?"

His head felt like a volcano, the pressure building, the wrath. He wanted Abaddon's head on a plate. He knew though, that's what Abaddon wanted. Forcing back the intensity as it rose, he fought to keep the anger at bay. He could let it out later but not here, not now.

It won't help Anara, you can't beat him here, not yet.

Turning his focus back to her standing in front of him, he grounded his mind. That sweet smile, the light wind hitting his face, the sound of the nearby creek, the smell of sweat, the present. Abaddon's laughter faded while he resolved himself to settle, and although no one else heard his thoughts, the look on Lilith's face was a reminder of her knowing.

There was nothing further that could be done, so he turned and walked away.

Coward.

Cillian pitched forward, ripping the sheets from the bed, sweat soaking the shirt he was in. Outside the window the suns were up. Morning was here. He breathed a heavy groan at the memory that clung, the nightmare he had relived again.

Anara.

Stomach twisting, he put his head to his hands. He would skip breakfast this morning, buy just a little more time before having to see Master Olam again. Cillian had no intentions of helping him with this new woman.

Olam's last request had cost him his sister.

Chapter 7

"How does this thing work, I mean, you thinking words in my head?" I bluntly asked after hours of riding through rolling green hills.

There was a moment of silence before Ivy responded. "You want to know if I can hear your thoughts?"

"Well yes, wouldn't you?" I snapped sharply.

"Don't fret, I can hear nothing you don't allow me to. Promise."

"How do you do it?"

"It's a mental awareness, a gift; I was created with it by Master Olam. It's how I talk, in a way, but I can only hear what someone wishes me too." Ivy said.

Breathing a huge sigh of relief I gave Ivy a half smile, happy to crawl back into my head safely when I needed to. "You said the plans changed?"

"There were disagreements. Some here will be excited to help you. Others may not be so inclined. Originally you were to go to the Shining City, a place of safety, the center of our world."

"Where are we going now?" I asked.

Ivy was happy to answer my multitude of questions now. "Karakum. We're going to cross the rushing river and pass through the forest, into the black desert to reach the West Tower. You're in for a real treat, it's quite different from Temani. Those who settled that region were nobility from across great waters, I was once told. A royal people who loved the extravagancies their world had to offer. Magic is loved there as well, unlike in Temani."

"Why do they not wish to use magic there?" That seemed quite odd to me.

"Many of the original ancestors' first arrival here was not by choice, they were caught in a conflict. Instead of dreaming up new things, they use their gifts to pass down generational reminders of home. It's why it felt so comfortable there for you. Now, the West Tower holds someone we'd like you to meet."

"We?"

Ivy slowed, as if contemplating what to tell me. "My Master, he wishes to keep you safe. Your presence here will not stay hidden long, and once it is known, you will be in grave danger."

Hesitation caught her last words.

Reality had finally caught up with me as I truly processed what was happening. There were other worlds.

I was in one.

I couldn't go home.

I was in danger.

I didn't know why.

The heaviness I had held in my muscles began to release its hold. Quietly I let a few tears loose, embarrassed to ask more of the strange creature I willingly followed as we trotted down the path towards some river.

Approaching a large cobblestone bridge, Ivy began to slow to a walk. Rushing waters caught all our attention, separating around large boulders in various parts of the river. The water was furious, beautiful and fast. Shadow and I took turns admiring the craftsmanship of the bridge with towering stone eagle-type animals on either side, glaring inward to anyone who passed over. Our eyes wandered to the rapids, truly fearing the water below.

It was wide, much wider than originally imagined.

Part of me waited tensely for a troll to pop out, demanding ransom for safe passage. But as we made it to the other side, I exhaled in relief that no troll ever appeared.

Up ahead was something familiar.

Forest.

The same massive trees and uneasy feeling I had experienced when we entered this realm threatened me again. Shadow went on alert as he shortened his stride, ears forward waiting for a need to run. Something calming brushed my mind, as gentle as a feather, reminding me we were not alone this time. We had a friend, and I didn't believe Ivy to be some pet. Something told me she was closer to a warrior than a guide.

Upon entering the canopy of trees, we stilled, listening for any sound that could convey a threat. Even Ivy seemed more watchful, her wings were folded back tightly now as the trees and bush thickened. Many sights were the same, but I took note of plants that were foreign to my eyes. Now I couldn't say for certain if they were new or simply went unnoticed the last time, while we were running for our lives.

This time there was a clearly defined dirt road, not very wide, so we were single file as we weaved back and forth twisting further into the woodlands. In here there was a nip to the air that made me grateful to have the long sleeve shirt from Martha over my tank. We were still headed northwest at a steady pace, trotting again instead of walking.

Silence, other than the soft thud of hooves on the ground, my saddle creaking as I rose and fell with Shadow's steps, plus the labored breathing, reminding me again of how out of shape we were.

Ivy carried herself ahead with such elegance, floating instead of trotting, her tail up and arched over like an Arabian, a reminder of my sweet Raya. Those antlers had to weigh a ton, but she carried her head high, chest out and stride lengthened to balance herself smoothly.

"We won't be in here long; this part of the forest is lengthy but not very deep. It allows crossing for my Master's protectors to go from south to east along the Western border."

The words surprised me even though they came through soft and calm.

"I can sense your unease here, not in your mind but through Shadow. He's feeding off that anxiousness."

At once I was ashamed. My horse was fearful because I was; when he looked to me for confidence it simply wasn't there, putting himself at risk in his own mind.

"You have good reason. Balfour is downright terrifying, and I would rather you be on guard for now, although he isn't the enemy."

"So, who is the enemy?"

"It's best we do not speak of them here. Enjoy the ignorance and the safety it brings while you have it."

With that she moved into a canter, Shadow happy to follow, refusing to fall behind. Up ahead we could see a break in the tree line, the end of the wood again.

The sight that lay before us as we broke free of the trees was nothing short of breathtaking. How I longed for a camera, just to preserve the imagery and feelings as I first laid eyes on the vast black desert.

Rolling hills of sand dark as coal stretched far beyond the horizon on my right, further still was something tall and shimmering, or my eyes were playing tricks. Straight ahead the sand hills were calmer, more flat areas with occasional shrub-like trees and a recently walked path heading straight for another building far off in the distance. This one was large and wide, light gold brickwork that rivaled the simplistic gray cobblestones from the South Tower.

My gaze swept further west as the vast sea of black sand continued, backed by massive rock formations of all shapes and sizes. Many clusters of large green palms and a variety of other smaller green trees or shrubs glistened near a body of water. Moat, if I wasn't mistaken, in place of the wall I had seen around the last settlement.

It wasn't quite as warm as I would expect in a desert, but the suns were on their way down with nightfall mere hours away. Still, it wasn't cool either. Beads of sweat began to gather under my nose and across my forehead.

"Up ahead we will find welcome at the West Tower. The people here are different, there will be questions and expectations. Do not wander and do not go off alone outside the tower unless I tell you so. For now, we keep others on a need-to-know basis, which most will not need to know."

"What do I tell them if they ask where I'm from?" I didn't like the thought of having to lie. I'd never been particularly good at it, other than to myself.

"We simply state it is Master Olam's orders. Anyone who pushes after that is no ally of ours."

Before another question could be asked, Ivy started forward and my eyes caught small dots coming atop the sand dunes, far away.

Three of them. They were moving at a fast speed.

My mind went to camels given the scene, but that was only a guess. Ivy didn't seem the least bit concerned, and I knew she must see them, prompting me to keep my curiosity to myself. Shadow was equally intrigued, and he began to prance lightly, tossing his head, asking me to let him move in their direction.

Continuing over the hills of sand, it seemed like forever as the distant shapes began to take form, getting closer. Dust clouds were forming behind them as it became clear they were animals running. My depth perception was difficult to gage over the distance, but I squinted my eyes against the suns and drew in a small gasp.

Horses.

Not just any horses but Arabians, desert horses.

Those dainty dished heads, parrot noses and high tail carriage were a dead giveaway.

Shadow let out a whinny, calling to them, still excitedly chomping at the bit to run for a greeting. My heart raced as they drew in closer, aware now that there was only one rider. The other two horses were simply following.

Odd.

Only the lead horse had any resemblance of tack. There was a bay and a flea-bitten gray following behind him, all three horses matching a full gallop as their legs hit the ground in perfect symmetry.

Cresting the top of a dune, Ivy stopped with me slightly behind her. I was sure she held her head higher with proud eyes as the rider slowed their approached. Her stance was one that commanded respect.

Trotting up was a man dressed in satin, gold shirt and black pants with a matching dress robe atop them. The black turban around his head was secured with a gold crown matching the beautiful gold stitching that fanned out in an elaborate design covering his robe. Red and ivory accents were woven into the gold as it danced along the cloth, a striking contrast against the chestnut stallion he rode, who bore matching blankets that extended down the horse's rump in black and gold. Across the stallion's chest was a gold sash, beaded and trimmed with tassels. His head was rounded out showing a beautiful, collected carriage that boasted a matching gold bridle studded with black gems. The largest gem sat centered in the candle-shaped white blaze on his forehead.

Once they came to a stop, the man offered a small bow to Ivy. His skin was much darker than mine but still olive toned, with a clean-cut beard and bushy eyebrows. Soft brown eyes that were inviting crossed over me as he extended the same bow.

I blushed.

He turned his attention back to Ivy, and I imagined she was talking; it was going to take some getting used to being around others when I could not hear what was said.

"Thank you, Ivoriene, it is good to see you as well. Welcome, Lenora, to our land. My name is Shahara, and I'd like to escort you both to my home if you would allow me the honor?"

His voice was strong but delicate as he bowed again before turning his horse back in the direction he had come.

Shadow anxiously pranced, inching closer to the other horses. He was reminding me of Raya; she never could stand still. With the thought came a pang of guilt along with longing while my eyes held the beautiful Arabians. They were downright magical. Raya had been that majestic, such a lovely black Arabian mare.

It was not a time for memories, though, so I swallowed the lump in my throat.

Now was a time to pay attention, to learn and listen.

Something made me believe truth would be found here, soon.

"Go with speed and discretion." Olam commanded as Cillian mounted Diadred.

"Temani won't be so willing to help, you know. There are few there that even utilize or learn magic."

"That's their choice. No one is forced here, but I'm certain we can gather who we need. Remember, we aren't amassing a war party, just a defensive border. Take these; reminders of how costly The Closure was."

Olam handed Cillian four small amulets – suspended on a dainty gold chain with a six-point jeweled star at the center. They were like the one the Master always kept around his neck, each varying slightly with a different colored stone. Olam's was crystal clear.

"It's time they remember. For now, we do not need panic amongst the people, so let the Elders carefully select only those with exemplary gifts from each region. You can then send them into the Norwood to train, quietly. Elder Medora will be waiting."

"Won't that draw attention from the Fallen? Being so close, Abaddon will surely know."

"Precisely. It's what he will expect as well. Best keep him thinking he's smarter than he is. Turn his eyes away from Lenora in Karakum for the time being. Is that a problem, being so close?"

Cillian could feel Olam's sideways glance as he awaited his response. He wanted to be honest, indeed it was hard asking him to camp so close to them, to go back into the Norwood. Yet instead, he slipped into the role of the soldier he believed himself to be.

"No, sir." Cillian met his gaze, looking for some disdain, but instead he saw only concern. A part of him softened, realizing it was a genuine question. One more reminder of how much Olam loved them.

"Oh, Cillian keep an eye out. The body of a man was found outside his cabin, a piece of a door through his chest. It was one of the wanderers located just south of the territory border. Looks like someone is bored again."

Cillian's face tightened as he grimaced at the thought of what terror Lilith had put the man through before his demise. She liked to play twisted games with her victims. Killing was an art, she had once told Cillian, years ago. It was moments like these he wondered if the choice to spare her had been the right one...but as much as he hated admitting it, he knew there was more to her.

Cillian shook his head. "Abaddon's leash isn't working well as of late."

"I'm afraid he never really had her on one."

"Do you think there are more like her?" Cillian needed to ask.

Olam shook his head, looking up to something unknown in the bright blue sky. "I've been pondering the same, rumors from the Shadow Sentries. Who knows if they are like Lilith though...Abaddon keeps her close because she intimidates even him. He got more than he bargained for with that one. She had been tormented extensively, long before her feet touched our lands, and she's had a lifetime more with him."

Anara. It had been two years since he had seen or heard from her. His attempts at rescue had all been pointless. Not that he had given up, but it wasn't that easy; wards kept him from getting even close to their mountain, let alone inside. Cillian sometimes wished she weren't alive, that Abaddon had taken her life after she realized her mistake. A twisted but comforting hope. He doubted either of them could be so lucky. No one had seen a trace of her since the day she left.

An uneasy shift from Master Olam brought his attention back to the task at hand.

"Here's to hope, then. I'll visit Elder Dondi first. If we don't obtain enough help, you may want to think about making some more of Diadred here; he's better than people anyway." Cillian reached down to pet the cat while he appeared to smile, lifting a large head back into his hand.

Olam chuckled and sent them off. He knew they could do it; he would help them.

Upon Cillian's departure, a tall, thin man approached Master Olam, his hands folded tightly together in front of him. "Sir, you requested my presence."

"Yes, thank you for coming so quickly. I'm afraid it's time, Malachi. I won't stand by and let them do this alone. My people need us, now more than ever; it was always going to come to this."

With that, the gentleman bowed and made haste back across the courtyard.

Olam's face was solemn as he stared out towards his city. Of all his creations, people were his favorite and he needed them to trust him once again, for this time it was paramount.

Chapter 8

Howling echoed against the rock walls as Abaddon made his way down the long dark hall, the clicking sound of his boots adding to the symphony of madness. In between the wolf-like howls were screams that pierced the air, sobbing, grunts and manic laughter. This was his home, where he could feel purpose and desire wrapping him in the darkness. He didn't allow light in this part of the dungeons. Small flames danced in his eyes, aiding his vision amongst the utter blackness. On either side were rows of large, solid iron doors. He continued to walk past. Inside were nightmares of his own creation, each one special and custom designed for the occupant. It had been a long time since all the Shadow Boxes had been full. He had contemplated adding more but decided to take extra time with those whom he already had in his grip.

"Please, please, no get away from me!" Came a terrified high pitched female voice up ahead on his right; his most recent addition.

No matter how many times Abaddon inducted a new soul, it always surprised him at how easy it was to torture them. He never touched them, not in this stage. Simply being locked in the dark, alone with their own mind, was enough to start. All it took was finding those deep corners, the ones they tried to hide and make them re-live the memories on repeat. Sometimes he would add some color or flair, project small alterations to speed up the process. Even the kindest, gentlest souls have things they wish to keep hidden from others.

Humans. For as much as they ache to be known, they don't want to be *truly* known. Once he showed them who they really were, it became child's play to break them. All essential to ensure their first magic was full of fury, void of compassion. It made them powerful.

Everyone is guilty, carrying some degree of darkness with them no matter who they are, *except Olam*. The uninvited thought was a frustrating reminder of why he remained in power. There was no darkness in him to expose. It made Abaddon's attempts on his mind pointless, but all was not lost.

Taking Olam's precious pets and destroying them one by one would get the old man to move. He loved his people too much. These weak creations were more important to him than any of the Elders, the ones who had given everything to follow him, only for him to betray them. Creating some small world of refuge for these special beings...they were beneath him and the others, but Olam had commanded their protection.

Fools. All of them.

Abaddon had played his hand well, refusing to lay down his power while the rest of them sacrificed, losing every gift except their core magic. Of course, Olam was able to retain every bit of his supremacy as the "divine", but even that couldn't protect all his people. A century had passed and there were so many more than before. More fragile humans to add to his cause and too many for Olam to shield at once. Abaddon's patience would be rewarded soon enough. Olam underestimated the resources he now had under his mountain.

Knowing this darkness required people to *choose* first, to bend just a little before Abaddon could take them, put the smile back on his face. It tortured Olam to know they unknowingly but willingly walked into a world of terror. Every single one who passed over the territory line truly broke the old man's heart.

Crossing through the iron door at the end of the hall, he blasted an image of the angry father who'd beat his daughter every night for years. A woman in the nearest shadow box fell to her knees as she screamed out an unnatural cry, unable to escape as he attacked her mind. He'd only had her for two weeks, but she was weak. Tomorrow, he would move her to a new room; he noted briefly not to push too hard, or she wouldn't be of any use.

The door thudded shut, blocking the chaos behind him, so he turned his attention to the view ahead. Four bulky round tables sat in the middle of the room, surrounded by wooden chairs. There was a door at the far end concealing a small kitchen, and another door next to it that held a bathing room. Above him was the open second story with iron rails overlooking the dining area. Upstairs were ten small rooms, very modest, supplied only with a cot, small side table and single chair. Rock from the mountain made natural floors and walls of every area. No windows were possible this far into the mountain.

Three had come down from their rooms today, two men and a woman who all sat alone, eating with their eyes downcast.

Two servants caught sight of him, bread baskets fumbling in their hands as they quickly turned on their heels back through the kitchen door. There was something about his presence that could clear a room in seconds.

Abaddon tried to visit all initiates twice a week while they were cared for here, conditioning them to believe that although they were worthless now, they could become members of the Fallen. Not everyone passed, though, and many went back to the Shadow Boxes more than once before leaving this part of the dungeons. Those who failed found the pit.

Sauntering over to the woman known as Eydis, he snatched two glasses and a bottle from the long buffet table.

"Good evening, love. Don't you look ravishing tonight! Wine?"

Setting down the glasses, he poured a splash into each before sliding the cup in front of her. Knowing better than to refuse, she brought the cup to her lips, tasting the soured wine. He leaned in, noting the restraint she used to not to pull away from the brush of his lips on her skin.

"Are you doing something different with your hair? It looks less...pitiful than usual." He accented his words as he ran his fingers through the stringy blonde strands around her face. Darkness circled her dull eyes that bore little color, compared to the bright blue-green they had been; deep like the waterfalls where the people of Antola lived nearby. High cheek bones looked unnatural on the all too thin face that bore them. Her spine was visible through the thin gray shirt that draped fragile shoulders.

Both men stood up and headed for the stairs, quiet sorrow across their faces. They knew why Abaddon was here; he preferred the ladies, although the men weren't safe from his advances either, if the need arose.

Gulping down the last of the spoiled wine, she was barely able to set the glass on the table as her hands trembled.

"I'm sorry about that second round in the box, but it was necessary, you know." He searched her for any sign of reaction but found none. "Just to show you how important you are, I wanted to be here for your first night out again." Abaddon's smile spread out, showing a perfect set of white teeth contrasting his olive complexion as fake compassion for her tried to surface in those unnatural black eyes.

Standing, she allowed him to lead her upstairs into the 11th room, his room, with a large four-post bed covered in red silk sheets. Tears slid silently down her cheeks as he shut the door and bolted it, his dark silhouette moving hauntingly across the room.

Tonight, Eydis wished more than anything to pass his test, to get out of this hell, and she was determined to do anything for all eternity to keep from ever spending another minute in a dreadful shadow box.

Deserts like to play tricks on your depth perception, I quickly learned. What seemed not so far turned into hours of trekking across hot sands. My body continued to protest as we continued, very ready to dismount and sit on something soft. The shirt I shed earlier and tied around my neck was back on, simply because I wasn't sure if tank tops were considered indecent here.

Suddenly in full view of the West Tower, I could see it was vastly different from the south. Instead of a skinny cobblestone tower from the dark ages, this golden brick building was a large cylinder, tall with four small slender towers attached evenly around it. In the front was a square building meant to function as the entry, substantially larger than any house; it had me thinking of a small church instead of a tower. There was indeed a moat around the perimeter of the town. Beautiful vegetation grew along the banks, shades of bright green against the warm sand.

To my left was a sunset like nothing I had ever seen in my lifetime. It was a true spectacle watching the suns make their final decent, the bright orange globes sinking low beyond the horizon with a deep orange ring around each. Darkness had crept in as the cloudless deep blue wrapped around to meet the fiery ring, causing an explosion of reds, lighter blues, yellows and even hues of green all melted together but separate. To one side were rock formations—some tall, some short, all silhouetted against the magnificently painted sky.

The view put my wonderful sunsets over cotton fields back home, to shame. So many sunsets with so many memories. Times on horseback with Raya, moments in trucks with boys or sitting alone in tears wishing I could fly far away from home. A surge of emotions tried to sweep in, but before they could surprise wrapped me tight at the site of two beasts guarding the bridge ahead.

We had spent most of the ride in silence as advised by Ivy, but I simply couldn't hold in my thoughts any longer.

"No wonder you don't need a wall or gates. You have Butch and Brutus guarding the door!" It came out with every hint of sarcasm I imagined. I would have been terrified, but Shahara had already ridden ahead and the creatures bowed as he walked his horse proudly between them.

Sitting on either side of the bridge were two massive lions, each gold with two ebony horns that curved up and in. Protruding from the manes around their necks were black spikes to match those that ringed the front ankles. What I believed to be tails, were instead black cobras posted up with bright gold eyes, watching. Large black talons were fitting to the dark fangs extending on either side of their muzzle. A bright red sigil that sat branded into their chests corresponded to the bright red eyes that examined us as we came closer.

Shadow was not as nervous as he should have been. My guess, he wanted to be brave in front of the other horses. Yet as we began to approach the lions, his courage faltered. Shadow stopped, not wishing to go any further. I murmured to him, reassuring his safety before commanding him forward.

Nothing.

Everyone else had already passed, and now the snakes began to take a keen interest in us. That was it; up Shadow went in one big rear, kicking out his hooves in fear. By some miracle I kept my seat, and once we were back on the ground I relaxed. He needed me to be calm, so I stroked his neck, asking him to trust me. Finally, he took one step, then two before frantically scooting in between them to join the others.

Shahara was sitting quietly, eager eyes on me as we approached.

Light from the torches that were mounted on the archway near his face highlighted those sharp features. He smiled with his eyes locked on mine, before turning to bring us into the village.

Brushing off the heat that rose from my toes, I felt foolish. Butterflies found me like a middle school girl who had just touched a boy's hand for the first time.

More golden archways and tents filled the area. Fires were crackling as people stepped out to look as we passed. Some waved, some ignored us completely. Moving further into the village, the tents ceased and small square buildings began to appear. There were no doors but instead fabric curtains, simple colors but extravagantly embroidered.

In the center was the West Tower. An open balcony wrapped around its highest point with engraved pillars and satin fabrics flowing in the gentle breeze. Looking down was a beautiful woman, skin as dark as the desert sands, wearing a white sleeveless gown with gold trim who quickly vanished.

Shahara dismounted, handing his horse to a small stable boy who walked off, the other two horses following like dogs. A young girl came to take Shadow from me as Shahara spoke to her in another tongue, a beautiful language I had never heard. His English had been heavily laden with the accent he now used, resembling a middle eastern dialect from back home.

Ivy, who had been silent for several uncomfortable minutes, nodded towards Shahara. "Lenora, he will show you to your room, where you'll have handmaidens ready to prepare you for dinner before you meet Zubair. He's an Elder and a stickler for tradition, so please do as you're told and keep answers short. Unfortunately, you will be dining without me tonight, but I can still hear you if you need me."

"Would it be rude to skip dinner? Honestly, after a day's worth of Martha's snacks, I'm not that hungry. Plus, the idea of meeting people who keep death cats at their door by myself doesn't seem like a fun time to me."

Ivy's sweet laughter was a cause for my own chuckle as she gently shook her head.

"You'll be fine; you might even have fun. Much of your time with other people will have to be without me. Not everyone trusts a creature with my...gifts. There are some who believe Olam uses me to read private thoughts. Although they are wrong, it's best to respect their wishes if we wish to make alliances."

"Aren't those your Master's cats on the bridge?"

"Those are the Firnas; created by Olam but given to Zubair as a gift, so they answer to him alone. Enough questions though, let's not make him wait. Run along now."

Ivy turned to go back through the town. Where, though, I had no idea.

Shahara was waiting by the archway and only door I had seen so far, strong arms folded across his chest and a welcoming smile on his face.

Upon entrance we walked down a hall with stone-carved stools holding gold figurines and ornate, hand-painted jars. Torches were attached to the walls on both sides, burning brightly. Ahead were large gold and purple curtains pulled to the side with thick rope, opening into a massive open room. Potted palms spread out in different areas while large columns trimmed in gold paint surrounded them. In the center was a long table, low to the ground. No chairs, but pillows and cushions were in their place. Each one was more brilliant than the last with vibrant colors, tassels and trimmings.

Two women wearing simple white sleeveless gowns tied at the waist with a gold sash greeted us. Shahara spoke in that foreign language once more before motioning me to follow them.

They led me upstairs into one of the small, attached towers, and then behind another curtain. From their ushering, it was believed this was my room, complete with an open balcony looking over the vast desert. Inside, there was a four-post bed with sheer draperies on all four sides and more ornate pillows in a vivacious royal blue. Across the room and behind another drapery was a bathing pool that the women practically shoved me into. After my repeated protests about washing myself, they left.

Wrapping my now-clean body in a towel, I sat down at a mirror, finally. Multiple glass bottles of oils and lotions were at my disposal, all of them smelling divine as I carefully opened each one to sample. As if the scents called the mysterious women back, there they were brushing and fussing over my hair. It was yet again the foreign language, but it didn't sound promising.

They had me step into a long gold skirt slitted to just above my knee, beaded stripes of darker gold across the front. My hands went up as a long sleeve top was pulled over to match, gold with a white embroidered bodice, the sharp v-neck chest trimmed delicately in red. Each sleeve ballooned out from under my arm to below my elbow before transitioning into tightly covered forearms in gold sequins. The shoulders held no fabric, but more gold bead work laid across open skin, and about an inch of my waist was showing where the two pieces didn't quite meet.

To finish me off they painted my lips red, brushed my long brunette hair, keeping it down, and added a gold shawl over my head. The long silk fabric draped around my shoulders and was held in place by a chain sash across my forehead.

Looking in the mirror, a tiny gasp escaped my mouth. I looked stunning.

Modest but tightly fit, everything felt hand tailored for me. Three tiered large red jewels dangled from the sash against my forehead, joining my red lips in a fierce battle to be the center of attention.

We walked down to dinner barefoot, and as I entered the room nausea gripped me. There in front was Shahara, and three faces that I didn't know, waiting on me.

At once, the men stood and bowed, except the gentlemen at the head. Which quickly told me that man was in charge and must be Elder Zubair. On his right side was the woman seen standing on her balcony when we first arrived, now wearing an extravagant green gown. Earlier she had waved, but now she maintained a solemn expression, looking down. Shahara was on Zubair's left side, then two other locals. Shahara motioned me to sit next to a heavier set man even more elaborately dressed than I was.

Shahara spoke first, motioning to the head of the table.

"Lenora, this is Elder Zubair, he presides over Karakum and the West Tower."

"Welcome, Lenora. We can't help but notice our local attire suits you well." Zubair shot an innocent smile with his praise before his eyes became serious.

"Now, would you mind telling us who you are and why you've been paraded through my city by Olam's pet so we can share more proper introductions? One thing is certain, you are an outsider and that means you shouldn't be here."

My eyes darted around the room as my mouth went dry, panic written across my face while I fought back the urge to run.

Chapter 9

As morning began to dawn, the sun filtered through the heavy fog and wet forest within. Slowing the pace to revel a minute longer in the beautiful sight before them, they contemplated the stillness, as if each creature went silent to pay homage to something more than themselves. Cillian and Diadred had traveled through the night, deciding to take a more direct route. Just east of the Shining City the woodlands turned thick, the path straight to the village now overgrown, showing little use. Most would turn south, cross the river, and take the road northeast again to reach the East Tower, but that added another half day. Right now, time was of the essence.

So far there had been no sight of the local guardians in this region. Those ruffians were a nuisance. One day he would ask Olam why he had bothered with such barbaric creatures.

Far off they began to hear the roar of the waterfalls. They were close now. On the east side of the town was a large body of water that supplied the river. The water falling from the falls came from Elder Dondi's core; she supplied it as a calming gift to her people.

Further they went along, picking up speed at the promise of rest within the town. Rushing waters pushed forward memories of this place from long ago. He and Anara had spent so much time in the northeast as children, taking the mountain trail down to the top of the falls that bordered the northern territory where they had grown up. Those were such wonderful days, when life was grand, when his father had been alive and his mother had been smiling. Only a few years of childhood had been that way for their family before the Fallen laid waste to such safety and security.

These familiar lands had a way of bringing memories of when everything changed.

Cillian's father had been an iron worker in the mountains just over the territory line between the Norwood and Antola regions. There he took his wife and had two children, Cillian being the oldest and Anara just a year later. For quite some time they lived a simple life deep in the mountains near only a few other families who desired the same. Back then, the Fallen were treated more as bedtime stories to keep children compliant, seldom spoken of in their home.

His father would travel often to the city and create custom works for those who desired them, sometimes being gone a month at a time. No one thought twice when he was away one winter for five weeks, Cillian's mother thinking the weather had delayed him. The children were older, almost adults, more than capable of tending to extra duties to help her.

They never saw him again, not a trace.

No one disappeared into thin air unless the Fallen were involved. Cillian knew that now, but Anara and his mother never would consider the possibility. They had unwavering faith that his father was incapable of falling prey to schemes of common outlaws, convinced that's who the Fallen were, nothing more.

For a while his mother told people he had died in the snow, but that was impossible. Their father was also a skilled healer. When spring came and the snows melted, they searched but found nothing. New tales would be spun, stories they made up to explain it, each one as unlikely as the last.

His beautiful mother aged so much that year, stopped using her magic, stopped doing anything. Anara became her caretaker while Cillian left. The Fallen's recruitment were no longer bedtime stories to him. There were those who would train others willing to defend individuals who couldn't defend themselves.

Years of strict discipline had eventually made him the perfect informant...the first ever to infiltrate a member, and the last. They wouldn't make the same mistake twice; Cillian had barely escaped with his sanity, let alone his life.

Using his rare charm had caught Lilith off guard and rousing a relatable anger won her attention however misguided it truly was. He almost lost himself during those weeks in the boxes, but he never gave up. Watching her, he began to mourn who she must have been, wonder if she could be that woman again.

Towards the end of their dance Lilith shared that Cillian's father had never given up either, fighting long and hard against the darkness until he was used for another purpose. She never did tell Cillian how they got him there, only what they did with him once he was there. Deep down, he didn't really want to know that detail.

Sounds from above caught his attention as he created the bow quickly and knocked an arrow, swooping to his left.

Sharp blue eyes met his before they swung down, heavy thuds hitting the ground beneath them. Long blood red noses, with white and blue stripes on both sides, adorned their snouts. Behind the neck fanned out a large blue leathery fan to match the leather tail, sharp points that could fling small bone fragments covered in toxin. Sitting back on their haunches they were taller than Diadred, broad shoulders covered in dark gray fur with huge arms set squarely on either side of a narrow waist. Blue sigils were set into their protruding chests as they beat them a few times before walking off, making it clear that Cillian was required to follow.

The Mandros.

Guardians given to Elder Dondi from Master Olam, gifts to protect her and her region. What they lacked in discipline they made up for in brute strength. When they opened large jaws to reveal great fangs, it was over. Most would run, but in the forest it was pointless, as they could swing through the trees faster than most skilled predators could move on the ground.

Thankfully for Cillian, he was welcome here.

The forest started to thin as they entered the village. Many people were out wandering the area, carrying baskets with fruit or fish. Bustling around, it was clear they were preparing for something as brightly colored fabrics were strung from tree branches and flowers woven anywhere possible. A woman with long blond hair and sparkling blue eyes held hands with an equally handsome man as they walked towards the falling waters in the distance.

There were small huts spread around on all sides of the tower. Why they called it that, Cillian had no idea, other than the formality of it. This was no more a proper tower than Diadred was a mouse.

Set in the middle was what some may call a tree, but it was more than that. Its sheer size was impressive but instead of built it was woven. The tower walls were large roots that stretched to make the cylinder shape before branching off to create other small rooms, all covered in beautiful gold leaves with dark blue veins that never fell.

Elder Dondi came walking towards them as graceful as ever, her long red hair braided down her back, bright against the simple blue shirt and pants she wore. Barefoot, as usual, with arms stretched out in a warm welcome, matching the lovely grin on her face.

"Greetings, friend, it has been too long," came the soft voice of Dondi.

Small children had begun running towards Diadred, who happily went to play with them as Cillian dismounted.

"Some fearsome warrior." Cillian huffed as he watched his ferocious companion roll over on his side to welcome the climbing attacks of the little people.

Dondi embraced Cillian in a warm hug, her slender arms stronger than they appeared. Tall, he always forgot how tall she was until she hugged him. All the Elders were unnaturally tall, except Feldrid in the South Tower, a rumored side effect from the strain of The Closure. One Cillian believed because she was the only one who appeared to age, unlike Dondi here who glowed with youthful pale skin to offset those incredibly bright blue eyes.

"Come in, come in. Would you like some tea?"

They walked into the tree tower; it was as eccentric as Cillian remembered. Soft green grass grew all over the floor, short and fuzzy. Large windows allowed in floods of light to cover the flowers and fruit that grew everywhere. More roots wove together to create furniture and stairs leading up into the rooms above. Greenery stretched across a kitchen area were Dondi was pouring tea. Above her was a small balcony that housed an extensive library of books, vines wrapping in between each shelf.

In Temani, Feldrid was a rule maker, but here in Antola, Dondi was a rule breaker, dancing to the beat of her own drum no one else could hear.

Cillian took a seat on a bench that sprouted white lily-like flowers covered in orange stripes. He took a small cup offered from Dondi, questioning its contents and their effect on his mind, but decided that to appease her it would be worth the risk to drink.

"Cillian, how handsome you have grown. I always knew you would wind up looking like your father. You are tired though, I see it. As happy as I am to see you, it is unexpected. Nothing much happens in my small corner of the world, the quietest as I'm told. Whatever brings you to my woods cannot be particularly good, I imagine," her face searching his for revelations with a desire to know truth, not small talk.

It only took Cillian a few short minutes to get straight to the point and catch her up on the recent events, including Lenora. She listened intently as he laid out the plan from Master Olam. It was clear the danger to her people if Abaddon released his Gangors and all his followers, even more so if he was able to access other realms or The Shining City.

There wasn't an ounce of hesitation as she pledged to gather those that could be of use for training, however few they may be. "It will take me time; I need to think wisely on a list. Sending those you love off to an uncertain future is not something you do in haste, even if time is essential."

Dondi let loose a heavy sigh. There had been no sense of surprise from her. Since this land was one of the closest to Fallen territory, Cillian was sure she had lost many and knew one day there would be a reason for it.

"Tomorrow is the Day of Mayim; preparations are already underway, and it seems cruel to ask this of people before then. We should give those who may decide to join another day of enjoyment before we darken their world with this disturbing reality."

He wouldn't risk arguing, always knowing Dondi would be the easiest to talk to, another reason he had decided to come here first. At least he knew he could send some help north.

With an agreeing nod it was decided. Cillian pulled the amulets out of his pocket and placed them on the table between them.

Elder Dondi's eyes sparkled as tears welled before she gently selected the one with the blue star in the center. Her hands closed tightly around it as she brought it to her chest, and with a quick mention of where his room was, she excused herself.

Master Olam had instructed him to give amulets to each Elder regardless of their decision, but he could tell after the look on Dondi's face that whatever secret truth they held, it was a brutal one.

Outsider.

He knew, they all knew.

...need to know basis...

...scarier things than territorial forest beasts...

Run.

Cry.

Vomit.

Those were the current options my mind clung tightly too as I tried to process the scowl Zubair held firmly, like a father unhappy with the foolish decisions of his daughter and awaiting the begging of forgiveness.

But this wasn't my world, these weren't my people, and I truly had no idea how to respond or even if I physically could respond as my throat tightened.

Across from me the other man frustratingly raised his voice. "Do you know who you dine with, girl? You have been asked a question and we expect an honest response."

Voices raised as I began to shut out the extra noise, trying to curl up somewhere that wouldn't have me screamed at again.

It's not safe, we're not safe.

My mind frantically chanted the tune as it began to whip me into the all too familiar world of unrealistic panic, one that left me with little control. The hurricane inside me began to form, the emotions spurred on more flashbacks while terror flowed through my veins.

This was the impasse, I had mere seconds before the hyperventilating began, it was right there as I gulped in mouthfuls of air. My own eyes were closed tight as if I could just make it all go away if I couldn't see it. In the distance came the commotion of more voices.

The noises began to fade as I squinched my eyes tighter to keep them from opening. I felt weightless, as if I were flying. Shifting my concentration, I worked on my breathing for fear of not getting enough oxygen.

"Lenora, Lenora, Lenora..."

Cocooning myself tighter in the darkness I could feel shadows around me while I sucked in more of the thick air. It was so heavy as it drifted. At one point it was nipping at me, poking in search of some hole in which it could infiltrate, a vulnerability. The space I created in my mind was strange, nothing but everything all at once.

Something cold began biting up my right arm, my breathing began to steady. On my left near my ear was soft hot breath and whiskers.

"Lenora."

Opening my eyes, I beheld a different scene. The dining room was gone, replaced with an elaborate stable. Shadow's muzzle was in my ear, the smell of hay filling my nostrils. My arm was red, wet now and still cold. Looking up I met Shahara's gaze, those big brown eyes swimming with concern but softening as I tossed him a small smile.

"The cold will pass. I needed to bring you back before you went somewhere else on us, and it was the first thought that came to mind."

Below his hand were chunks of ice on the ground. The numbness in my arm began to prickle away as it came back to life.

"You did that."

"Yes, but only to get you back, no telling where you could have ended up if you did that trick again."

"Trick?"

The corner of his mouth twisted into a sly grin as pride flashed across his face.

"Well, 'gift' may be more appropriate. That magic, it's rare. So rare in fact I've never seen it until tonight, and by the looks of everyone else in the room, I'd say the same for them."

Confusion swirled around me as I tried to understand what was going on. "I don't have magic."

"You do now. I mean it's not surprising, a first magic is usually extraordinarily strong and comes out unintended."

My eyes went from him to my horse and all around, Shadow nudging my shoulder, clearly bored with our conversation. With that it clicked. I began to run through the last few minutes, all my thoughts and feelings on high-speed getting the perspective from inside my head plus outside my body all at once.

It was terrifying.

Climbing so far away from that room in my mind, wishing to be in the stable with Shadow, I had vanished from one place and arrived to the other.

"But that's not possible."

He chuckled, offering a hand to help me stand.

Knees were wobbly as I tried to find some balance, one hand on Shadow and the other held by Shahara.

"This must be what days without food or water feels like."

"I'm sure that took a lot out of you. Come inside and we'll get you in something more comfortable. I've already sent for Ivy; I'm surprised you didn't call for her."

"I didn't even think about it, honestly." I admitted, embarrassed that it hadn't come to mind.

"That was an impressive thing you did in there; you must have been pretty upset. I am tremendously sorry for the situation you found yourself in so soon after your arrival, but I'm not surprised. Master Olam and Ivy should know better than that. They should have prepared you better. I believed they had."

As we walked slowly back, Shahara was incredibly careful, never once letting go of my arm as he guided my steps along the road.

Anxiously I let him lead me back through the tower, but everyone had left to their own chambers, even the handmaidens who had helped me before.

All a true relief.

"If you need anything, simply ring this bell," Shahara said, motioning to the gold rope pull cord. "I had the cook leave you an assortment of food on your balcony table. Don't worry about tonight; we will all deal with it in the morning, so for now enjoy the view and get some sleep." He bowed and turned to leave before stopping to point across the room. "Almost forgot, there are some nightgowns in that chest. By the way, you looked exquisite coming down those stairs tonight." Tossing me a smile that made my heart jump, he fled the room with his robe swaying behind him.

It took mere minutes to scarf down the dinner and wine that had been left for me. Whatever happened had demanded much of my body. Wishing there had been more when I finished. Every bit of the food was delicious. Half of it I had never even seen, let alone eaten.

Balconies and outside porches had always been a favorite of mine, this one being no different. I enjoyed every minute in the cool breeze, sitting in a lounge chair gazing up at the stars while golden globes of fire danced across the sands. The nightgowns were right where they had been promised.

Ivy had calmly yet urgently tuned in right after Shahara left, it took quite a bit to reassure her I was fine and desired to be alone.

Exhausted didn't begin to explain how I felt.

"Understood. However, I need to see you first thing, before you speak to anyone else."

I'm sure she knew I had questions and she wanted to be the one to answer them.

Somewhere off in the desert something like a flute played, the notes riding along the wind until they reached my balcony. It was a serene, sad song. Thoughts of a lover mourning the loss of one who wouldn't return because she couldn't, or more simply, wouldn't.

Reflections took me back to my own lovers. I'd had many. Those thoughts weren't alone. Heaviness rippled through my mind as I was greeted by guilt.

Some of my years had been so dark, the anger that drove me to strip myself of any dignity I once had. Most of those men just wanted a release, and who was I to deny them? "Lovers" was hardly a fair term if I was being honest.

A familiar friend arrived with that judgment, riding the waves behind the guilt I gripped tightly...hello, shame. The one who used any and all we encountered.

The melody continued for a while, pausing at the end as if awaiting a response, looking for some hope but receiving none.

At least here, no one knew my story.

A new melody started, sadder than the first while pondering how long I could keep my past from infiltrating this world too.

Chapter 10

The Day of Mayim was in full swing, everyone was bouncing joyously around in their brightest colors. The smells of fresh fish and spices drifted his way as he followed the dirt path from the tree tower. Music filled the air with a contagion that urged on the people to stomp their feet and jump about. Different vendors had lined the streets, offering an array of fresh foods, crafts, or fun games in their booths. Cillian passed by an older man who was using magic to make water balloon animals, each of the children watching in amazement as they took turns guessing the creature before he finished.

"There you are," was all he heard before Dondi had him dancing in the street.

Cillian obliged even though he hated to dance, twirling and kicking about to the sounds of life that flowed around him. Dondi's face was glowing with each new partner, spinning around anyone who came close. Children giggled, sprinting among the adults who moved their bodies, some movements were graceful while others jerked about. Cillian's were less than fluid, but he smiled all the same, even the roughest hearts couldn't ignore such contagious bliss.

Dondi finally took a break, using an arm to motion Cillian over. "It feels like a lifetime since I've been here for this festival. I always thought it strange that at the end of fall you would celebrate the day of water. Why not spring?" Cillian gave her a pondering look as they walked towards the falls.

"Mayim means *water*. Water is most known for growing things come spring, true, but why?" She eyed him with a sly smirk.

Cillian paused before answering something he deemed obvious. "Because fall and winter kill back most of the vegetation. Warmer weather brings spring and life."

"Yes, but it's the water that feeds it back to life after winter's cold has taken it. Even the suns cannot bring life alone. Without water there is no hope of them coming back. Instead of waiting, why not announce our hope in the beginning? Celebrate what we know is to come at the end when it first begins. We celebrate the life the water will bring at the beginning of the death the cold inflicts to sustain that hope we have. Some winters are very harsh and long, some people need a physical reminder that there is a newness of life even after death. Therefore, we celebrate the new life as the leaves begin to fall." Dondi spoke softly as she motioned to the trees ahead with their magical colors of blue, gold, orange and purple. Leaves, one by one, gently floating to the ground.

"You always were one for sentiment," Cillian gently prodded his joke as Dondi returned with a smile.

"Go enjoy yourself, make friends, Cillian. More than just your cat." With that, Dondi spun back into the street to dance again.

With a deep sigh he surveyed all the color around him. It had been a long time since he had fun, and Dondi was wise. So, he did. He laughed and ate with people he did not know. Told grand stories of adventure to the children, played games, even danced again in the streets after some local tea eased his tension. Hours passed, and for a time there was joy in Cillian coupled with peace as the evening suns began to slip behind the trees.

A small horn sounded through the streets, beckoning those to heed its call. Sparkling orange hues bled through the forest and around them as everyone made their way to the waterfalls. It was time for Elder Dondi's water ceremony.

Hovering over the water was Dondi as the town gathered around, children scampering to the front or climbing parents for a clear view of what was about to unfold.

Cillian remembered making the trip with his father one year, just to see the spectacle Dondi would produce. His father had said she held true magic, not just in her hands but the gift of using her life to bring joy and safety to those she loved.

"Son, our hands should lift, not tear down, the character of another. We weren't made to destroy, but to build." He could hear the words echo as a small tear slid down his cheek. That had been just before the winter had fallen, the winter that brought his father's demise.

Dondi began spinning her hands, pulling the water from beneath her and twisting it all about. The small streams glistened, bouncing the warm rays of the sunset as it filtered through. Somewhere close by, a soft stringed instrument started a melody and all the people started to sing gently. It wasn't just lyrical words, but sounds of the heart. Something indescribable.

As Dondi continued to push and weave the water in, out, all around her growing the tangled web of beauty, the harmonies increased. It was a symphony of life, beauty, pain, sadness, joy, hope, all balled into this wonderful muse as it danced with the water.

Rising higher, the water and the song reached a crescendo with an explosion as the sound ceased for all except the water falling from the sky, tiny raindrops hit their faces.

Choosing to stand off on his own, for a few moments he allowed the feelings in, the longing, the sadness, grief in its mighty form to wash over him. More tears freely fell before something tiny and warm grabbed his hand.

Looking down he saw the clear blue eyes of a small girl, bright blonde hair and full of tears. She gripped his hand tighter before he shifted his gaze to watch the last of the light fade before him, returning the small squeeze with an acknowledging one of his own.

When it was over, the girl led him back to the crowd where a large man scooped her up, quickly apologizing for the disruption she may have caused.

Cillian brushed away the man's concern. "No apology needed. What is her name?"

"Kai. This is my daughter Kai. She has not spoken since her mother, my wife, disappeared." Struggling to push the words out, the large man hung his head, swallowing back what was sure to be immense torment.

"Thank you, Kai." Cillian's eyes met the girl's. He knew where her mother was, and that she would never see her again. She was so young. With that thought, his blood simmered quietly under his skin as he built the wall back up to dam his own emotions. He was needed here.

Everyone began making the trek back into town to go home, quieter than before but lighter and still joyful.

Cillian found Dondi, who appeared drained from the ceremony. "That takes a lot from you, doesn't it?"

"Yes. I'm not the spring chicken I used to be. In my younger years I would be able to do that with simple thought, but since The Closure, it takes everything I have." Dondi had a brief flicker of sadness before returning a smile.

He had wanted to ask, so he did. "Was it worth it? The Closure?"

"In a thousand lifetimes, I would do it over again. Without doubt it was the best decision I've made." There was no sorrow there, but fierce resolve. No matter the cost, Dondi didn't regret what had been done. "Now, let's go meet your new friends. I gave notice for them to meet us in the tower after the ceremony. Earlier I received some distressing news, so I think it best you all prepare to leave tonight. I'll have the Mandros escort you as far as the forest, unless you'd rather use my underground river."

Cillian's eyebrows raised. "Your what?"

It was silent except for the clicking of Lilith's heels as she walked down the hall and into the dining room. The black marble was dazzling as light poured in from the candles set on the table. He didn't even look up to acknowledge her as she took her seat across from him. Lilith was truly alluring in a midnight blue gown, one of his favorites, with her hair swept to the side.

She wasn't hungry but decided to poke at the dinner to amuse the eyes on her. Two commanders were seated at either side of Abaddon, but with a wave he dismissed them. Getting up from the table they shot wry smiles in her direction, sad to miss what was to come.

They knew.

He knew.

Abaddon finished chewing before speaking, "Do you know what we learned tonight, my sweet?"

"Something you wish to share with the class." Lilith replied drily.

He gently lifted a napkin to pat the corner of his mouth as he set the fork down. "We have a visitor. A newcomer, a girl, from outside our world. She's been sighted at the West Tower, and with your favorite creature Ivoreine at that."

Lilith froze, her eyes lifted to meet Abaddon's amused smile.

"That's not possible." Her voice came out in a hiss.

"Right you are, my pet, so how is she here and why does she have a bodyguard provided by Olam?" Abaddon rose from his chair and sauntered around the table coolly.

Lilith didn't feign a response, not just because she didn't have one but because she knew that tone and Abaddon wasn't looking for one.

"You know what's even better...it would seem the unfortunate thing got scared and vanished right from Zubair's own dinner table. Poof." His hands gestured the disappearance as he circled towards her chair, watching intently for any sort of reaction.

No, no one can ferry except...no, it's not possible.

Her mind was spinning while she worked to maintain some facial composure. He was toying with her. She needed to play his game, and soon, or there would be hell to pay. Hopefully, this was all he knew.

Relaxing her gaze, she went back to her food.

"What I would have given to see the faces of those morons," she huffed.

"Actually, I thought about sending you; a game of fetch, see how easily you could bring her here." He shot a sideways glance as he moved closer to her.

Without looking up she responded unconcernedly. "Of course, I would be happy too. I doubt she'd be any trouble at all."

"Mmm, yes, but then I had a different thought. That she might be trouble for you, and you know how much I love to see your life made easy here." He stroked her hair gently from behind.

She gripped the fork tighter as he leaned into her ear.

"That's when I decided to let our informant bring her home to us, by any means necessary. You know how to operate with no rules, too, don't you? Like your idiotic *hunts*." Lilith cringed as he snatched a fistful of hair, spitting the last few words.

He did know.

It wasn't what she did that was the problem, but the lack of control he had on her. The fact that it wasn't his idea or instruction that she had acted on.

"You know I could bring her here." She sneered through clenched teeth.

Pulling away, he nicked her cheek with a single nail. "You could, but not as effectively as he could. My bet is on her falling for a handsome savior, not some broken woman."

Broken.

He walked back out of the hall. Leaving her there with those words used to be more punishment that anything he could do to her.

He knew that.

For a moment she thought she may fall prey to the feelings, but that was a ruse. A ruse she used to keep him satisfied.

Once he was gone, she happily ate her food, unconcerned with his failed attempts at hurting her.

Broken. It didn't work anymore.

Yes, she had been once, but no longer. She was lucky, the darkness used the cold to forge her back together.

Interesting, though, this girl. Here now, and she could ferry through time. An old gift that hadn't been seen in many lifetimes. She needed to be found, her powers honed, and fast before those emotions set off chaos for everyone.

There in the front room talking on the soft grass, were five of Dondi's most gifted. Ranging in age stood four men- if you could call the boy who barely looked old enough to leave home a man- and one woman. The other three men were all young adults, not married or parents, related by the looks of it, but the woman was older than Cillian. She was petite, short curly gray hair and blue-gray eyes with a grimace set across her face, as if she wished to be anywhere but here.

"Here you are, Cillian. This is everyone!" Dondi motioned her arm over them as she added more excitement to her voice than was necessary. "Each of them is extremely gifted with magic. The triplets come from parents who have trained them some, so they are ahead of the game. Peeke here is young, but don't discredit him for it; you will need him. On the other hand, Relca is more mature, but her water abilities are only second to mine...barely."

Cillian took in the band in front of him, fighting back the urge to ask if there were more as he looked again at the pride on Dondi's face.

"First, I'd like to thank you for your willingness on behalf of Master Olam and..."

"We aren't doing this for you or your shiny city." Relca had taken a step forward as she snapped the words, and Cillian wondered what she planned to do with those tiny, clenched fists.

"Relca, please." Dondi pleaded, her face set towards a friend, not just some constituent.

Cillian took a breath and squared his jaw firmly in their direction. "Look, I don't need your allegiance to me, but I do need your allegiance to your people. I need your strength against the Fallen and I need your dedication to whatever it takes to keep you from becoming one of them in the process. Where your true loyalties lie is of little interest to me, as long as they are with the light and against the darkness."

No one spoke after that.

Preparations were quickly under way to gather supplies and get out. Cillian learned from Dondi that there had been whispers of the Fallen moving south from their borders. Regardless of whether they were true, it was unanimously decided not to wait and find out. The plan was for the group to take the underground river to the north while Cillian went south for his next meeting with Elder Feldrid.

Few knew about the river and Dondi wished to keep it that way, so they would exit at nightfall. Relca assured everyone her abilities with water would get them safely up the river in the small boat provided within the day. They would all travel on foot after leaving the boat, headed north to the tower where Elder Medora would be waiting.

Cillian and Diadred left under the cover of night for Temani, trusting Dondi to see the new recruits off and Relca to deliver them in one piece.

With luck, the next meeting would procure more support, although it was doubtful.

Chapter 11

Morning brought a headache, another blatant reminder of all my tossing and turning through the night. Not that the accommodations were a problem. This was the nicest room I'd ever been given to stay in, the bed was for sure. Strange dreams kept my sleep restless when it did come. There was a monster that couldn't be seen, a girl screaming and shaking a cage, and something else loose, somewhere. It was impossible to return to sleep after shooting up with the sensation of choking on dark smoke, chest heavy. Usually, I could remember details of my night terrors, but as I changed into more suitable clothes for the day, most of them were fog, far from me.

It took every ounce of courage to walk down those stairs into the dining hall. If not for my promise to meet Ivy, fear of seeing anyone from the night before would have kept me from leaving the room.

To my welcomed surprise there were very few people around the West Tower grounds, mostly servants or those I didn't recognize. No one seemed concerned with my presence. Passing quickly down the hall and out the door, I turned sharply in the direction of the barn as I ran directly into a young woman on the street.

"Pardon me, I'm so sorry." I stumbled back to meet eyes with one of last night's dinner guests, the woman in the green gown who had waved earlier in the day from the balcony.

Her thick accent held as she also apologized profusely for her 'clumsiness' while awkwardly pulling at her dress. This one, a simple day dress like my own, solid purple with a white sash gathered at the waist. Gold earrings were pierced all up her ears, ten or more on each with large hoops that hung from her lobes. Now that we were close, I was also able to see the elaborate tattoos she had across her chest and around her neck, the ink just barely a darker black than her beautiful skin.

"Excuse myself, my name is Urbi." She nodded with a welcoming grin.

"Urbi, that's a lovely name, I've never heard anything like it. Are you Elder Fubair's wife?"

"Gods, no!" she said with a mixture or horror and comedy.

Fumbling, I tried to apologize, "I didn't mean to offend, you're his family then?"

"In a way you could say family, but not like you think. Fubair is an Elder, although I'm sure he would love it some days if he weren't. Elders are not like us. They don't marry or have children; they are a different species entirely and are sworn to protect their regions as well as all within. My name means 'princess' in my ancestors' native tongue. They were royalty from another world, and I am the last of their line. Zubair keeps me close as a promise he made to my mother, one of protection; soon I will be married off, as is tradition. To whom I belong is yet to be decided."

Those last words hung heavy, a clear longing to be in a different position.

"Enough about me, though, welcome to our land. Please let me know whatever it is you need, and I will do my best to make your stay here much more comfortable than last night." With that, she grabbed my hand and squeezed it, eyes questioning but respecting what I wished to divulge or not.

"Thank you. It is refreshing to know that someone here likes me after my...last night," shooting her a slightly embarrassed grin while I returned the hand squeeze.

Shaking her head, she chuckled, "I'm not the only one here who likes you. Shahara looked taken aback when you came down those stairs last night, even more so after you performed such rare magic." Her voice was kind, but there was something unusual in her tone.

"Yea, he did seem pretty concerned." My cheeks were getting hot while my eyes shifted.

Looking over her shoulder, Urbi's voice dropped into a serious whisper. "That's a powerful gift. Be careful here. Not everyone will see it as happily as others. Some may view it as a threat. Keep close to your guardian, listen to her. Trust no one."

As if the mere mention had summoned her, Ivy was in my head again, wondering where the blazes I was. After quickly thanking Urbi I shuffled myself swiftly down the road and into the barn.

Some part of me expected her to be eating with Shadow, but instead she was waiting in the doorway. Yet my brain had me ask anyway. "Ivy, what do you eat?"

"After everything you've been through, that is your first question? Sorry, Lenora, we have more urgent things to talk about than my dietary preferences." She shook her head.

"Glad to know I could lighten the mood." Shadow's mane felt comforting as I dragged my fingers through it, unsure of what to say. Sure, I had a million questions, but I was also confused, scared and tired. Using humor to avoid serious situations was a specialty of mine.

Ivy must have caught on because she walked over to lower her head near mine. Those antlers were massive, they must be wider than I was tall. "Forgive me. Are you alright?"

Continuing to stroke the soft neck in front of me, I dared not lift my chin. "That's a loaded question. No. I don't think I have been since my arrival if I'm honest. Still processing this whole other world thing." Poking around in the buckets near the stall door, my fingers found a brush, an ornately carved one that looked to be worth a fortune. For a moment I felt bad about using a piece so delicate on my horse, but the need to use my hands won out.

"Nothing, the answer is nothing, by the way." Ivy replied.

Lifting my head, I looked at her puzzled. "Excuse me?"

"The answer to your question. I don't eat anything. Master Olam designed us to not require food or water. It would be an inconvenience in our purpose."

All I could do was laugh; Ivy chuckled too as I drew in a deep breath.

"You ferried. I still cannot believe you ferried." Ivy held the words with true astonishment.

"Ferried?" Baffled at such an odd word.

Ivy explained. "Yes, it's a rare gift, to ferry. Being able to move from one place to another with a simple thought... that is a power many would give anything for. You were already in danger with just your arrival. Now I fear you will be a target."

"My parents always told me I was trouble...I guess it's fair to assume that trait followed me here, too." Shifting my weight anxiously from one foot to another, I tried to laugh at the thought. Some kids say that just to say it. Some parents joke, but mine had always made it clear I was this complex, messy, difficult thing that continued to rouse chaos. The flicker of a conversation with an old friend ran through my head, one where they apologized for my parents. She had pitied me that day after witnessing some of the regular family drama, wrapping me in a hug while the words dug into my heart.

"No one has ever talked to me that way...I'm so sorry."

Surprise, then resentment had pushed to the surface as I replied.

"I've been talked to that way my entire life..."

The idea that people were respected in word by their parents was foreign to me. As I moved through life, I learned that it was much more common than the dysfunction that surrounded me for three decades. For a moment, staying here forever sounded like an answered prayer instead of something to fear.

Ivy had given me the time to trail off in my thoughts. Looking at her, I was grateful once more that she didn't have a front row seat in my mind. Briefly, I wondered what she would think of me if she glimpsed those caged beings inside, impatiently waiting for the day they would refuse being ignored a moment longer.

"Well, what do we do about this?" Standing up straight, I pushed myself to look more confident than I felt.

A calm voice came from Ivy as she held a tone of pride. "First, we need to teach you how to control it, so you don't ferry randomly all over the world. The problem is, there's no one around that has that gift or could begin to help you wield it."

I sighed, "Of course there isn't."

Ivy continued despite my remark. "Second, we need to see what else is lurking under your skin. In centuries past, those who had the ability to ferry could do much more than that. You need to tell me the moment anything else magical appears from your hand."

Crankily I added, "So far all I've done is piss off some dinner guests, but I'll let you know if that changes."

Ivy smirked, finally catching on.

"And lastly, we need to keep you safe. Shahara has been an ally of ours for a long time, but Lenora... trust no one completely. Regardless of who they are or what they do for you. There are shadows moving, and I don't know who they are. It's not as easy to tell friend from foe in our realm." It was a stern warning; one I had heard before.

Urbi.

Ivy's words echoed her own and it made me wonder if I could indeed trust her. "How am I supposed to learn anything if I can't trust anyone?" The words exited my mouth, and I meant them, but it would be easy for me to consider everyone an enemy. Years in my world had taught me that genuine love was hard to come by, and most love was transactional. It seems alternate worlds couldn't even change that truth.

"Listen to yourself, trust your instincts." Ivy repeated a well-known statement.

Rolling my eyes, I replied, "Ivy, that's fortune cookie advice."

"I'm sorry, what cookie?" Came the perplexed voice in my head.

Huffing, I waved a hand. "Never mind."

She snorted. "Just because I want you to be extra cautious, doesn't mean you won't learn. Shahara has been instructed to bring you the best teacher in these lands to at least attempt to help you control your magic."

"Great. When do I meet him?"

Ivy answered, "After lunch, you meet *them*. It would seem there was a debate on who was the best, so I told him to bring them all. At this point, I'll take any additional help we can get."

"Aren't we supposed to keep me hidden? Won't having more people know me risk whoever the bad guys are around here learning where I am?" It was hard to cover the fear laced through my words.

Ivy directly acknowledged that fear. "I'm sorry, Lenora, we're way past that now. The moment you ferried from that dining hall, everything changed. I mean it, everything. They will know soon if they don't already. Now, we prepare you. We train you to protect yourself. Most importantly, we teach you about the Fallen."

"Sit down, young man! You may be here under Olam's orders, but this is still my house and you will not make a show in here." Elder Feldrid's shrill voice cut through the room.

Cillian had risen to his feet after the ignorant remarks and utter refusal to even ask any of her people for aid in their mission. It had been going about as well as anticipated with the ridiculous arguments back and forth, but his patience was gone.

They simply didn't have time for this.

"With all due respect, we do not have time to argue." Cillian's voice was raw.

Feldrid dropped her eyes only for a moment as she rubbed the green stone in the amulet between her fingers. Her reaction had not been the same as Dondi's. Anger flashed in those emerald eyes of hers as she stared a long while before picking up the necklace gently. "You can do it without us."

Cillian slammed his fist on the wood table, surprising them both.

Feldrid lifted her eyes to meet his. There was a hurricane of rage and sorrow in them. "We don't have anyone, I'm sorry. You know as well as I do that barely anyone here has practiced or used their magical gifts for much more than daily chores. Generations of people are producing less and less magic, but here it's accepted, welcomed to not have anything but your own two hands to live your life with." Her voice had started with a snap but tempered. She was tired.

"That's not entirely true." Cillian held her gaze, daring her to look away.

She didn't.

You could have heard the whisper of mice as the room fell silent.

"How dare you consider them. You aren't worthy to know them, let alone decide what they will do. They swore off their positions long ago, traded it for a life of simplicity and peace. You cannot demand they do your bidding. Tell Olam the same!" Every word was bitten as Feldrid's voice raised higher.

Cillian calmly lowered his voice. "Not demand. Ask. You are right, but making this decision for them without asking is just as wrong."

Again, Feldrid's tone went higher. "If we ask, you know they will accept!" She dropped her head into her hands and spoke through them. "Why are you even here, Cillian? You could have gone to them; why get an old woman riled up?"

Cillian took his seat, looking at her with so much compassion. Elder Feldrid was not like the others. She was aging. Aging like a human or like something was draining her. "Feldrid, I wouldn't do it without your blessing. You are right. If we ask, they will help, but if we don't... This is your region; I have no authority here."

"Really? Well sometimes you darn well act like you do." He waited a moment and she began to laugh. "Olam knew what he was doing, putting you where he did."

"Well, I did try to march into the city all those years ago. I guess it made a good impression." Cillian continued the light banter.

"Alright, I will talk to them." Her voice was a bare whisper as she looked again at the pendant.

Cillian walked over, grabbed Feldrid's wrinkled hand, and planted a kiss on it. "Thank you. Please tell them to meet me at the North Tower. If things go well in Karakum, I should be there within the week."

Before he could turn and leave, Feldrid seized his arm.

He turned back to see her eyes gray, her face paler than before. She neither spoke nor moved while Cillian held his breath. He knew she was looking in a place she ought not be looking with her gift of foresight. It was something gained in darker years, she had told him before, not something many knew that she had.

Minutes ticked by slowly, and then her green eyes returned as she slumped over the table. At once Cillian pushed her back up.

She gasped a breath before releasing a shaky voice. "It might take you longer than you wish to arrive north, son."

Grabbing her shoulders Cillian searched her face. "What did you see?"

Elder Feldrid's eyes filled with tears as she met Cillian's. "Shadows are moving, I feel it. The girl, she can ferry. They are coming for her. There's a betrayer in the west, one that is not as they appear. You must help her, Cillian. If the girl falls, there will be unspeakable tragedy."

Lilith rapped on the door impatiently.

"Who is it?" Came a lovely voice from inside.

"Just your favorite, come to see how you're faring." Of course, Lilith could really care less how she was, but it was one of the few chores she had.

There was always hope that Abaddon let his guard down a little too much while playing house with this pet of his. Maybe one day she would get lucky, and these trips would have a benefit for her.

A surprised face full of joy appeared in the doorway. "Lilith! Come in, come in."

Stepping in from the cold, Lilith saw a large fire roaring inside, making it insufferably hot for her tastes. The door shut quietly behind her.

There in front auburn curls bounced around the room, piled on top of her head. A petite woman hurriedly cleaned up the round table, filling her arms with canvas and paints to put away in the closet. "I'm dreadfully sorry, I wasn't expecting anyone."

Lilith watched her make another trip before jumping in to help, remembering she had a part to play here too. "Here, let me get that for you. Abaddon sure does keep you busy, huh?"

Her eyes gave Lilith thanks, "Oh, yes! I love how much delight my paintings bring him. He tells me it's the best medicine to brighten the spirits of his followers, having someone make something just for them, full of color."

Lilith couldn't help but think how pathetically easy it had been to stage this false reality upon her arrival, then convince her to stay in a private cabin deep in the mountains, cut off from everyone.

Abaddon had been the grand designer, naturally. Lilith and Abaddon would visit, the guard who was never seen monitored the house, and one of the servants happened to have a gift that could loop magic in someone's mind to relive the same week over again. She wasn't really looping time; just erasing memory and keeping a fog around the cabin, so to speak. The loop was in place to keep her painting constantly and not ask questions or desire to leave. It had been well maintained for years without the slightest hiccup.

"Isn't this one just wonderful." Small hands held a canvas that had swirls all over of blues, greens and yellows. Each intricately wound around the other, melting together to create a sea of joy. In the bottom right corner was the artist's signature. Handing it over, she smiled. "I want you to have it. I was thinking of you when I was painting, so it seems only right you take it."

Carefully Lilith took the painting. It was nice, not her taste, but still nice. She mustered up her most grateful smile and set it down before wrapping the paint-covered woman in a big hug. "It's simply gorgeous. I'll have it hung in my room so you can see it when you visit." Lilith held up the painting, giving it a long stare before she brought herself to meet those big brown eyes again. "Thank you so much for the gift, Anara."

Chapter 12

In my mind I had pictured meeting these teachers on some open sand arena, where dummies and shields would be found waiting. There they would put me in a strict training routine, change my diet, make me relive middle school by taking laps until some new power spurted out of me. Instead, I followed Shahara onto a balcony porch like the one in my room. This one was, however, on the other side of the tower.

Immediately the mountains in the distance caught my eye. The small blurry images impressed me then; I couldn't imagine what it would be like standing at their base. Far beyond the stretching sand lay chains of pointed rocks. They had to be more colossal than anything I had seen so far, off in the north.

"This is the one who put Zubair's knickers in a bundle." The voice was sharp, clearly somehow offended by the mere sight of me. It belonged to a woman leaning against the rail of the balcony. If someone had told me she was a killer, I wouldn't have second guessed them. She wore loose pants with tight calf tall boots. Her shirt was tightly pressed against a mostly flat chest, with a wrapped sash in the middle that allowed the hilt of her sword to be seen. Her shiny blonde hair was pulled tightly into a bun, not a strand out of place. Dark blue-gray eyes drilled into me as I turned my own face away from her in sheer embarrassment.

"Now Signy, let's not upset the poor thing. Who knows where she'll end up." Shahara was glaring at Signy while the second teacher took a step towards me. She was an older woman with white hair woven into a braid down one side; her brown eyes were kind and the same tone as her skin. This woman looked out of place for the area. She wore a simple beige and homely tunic that was tattered on the edges.

"My name is Elise. I'm sorry, you'll have to excuse Signy; orphans rarely have manners or good dispositions." The small woman extended a hand and shot Signy a look that dared her to challenge.

Shahara cut in to introduce the third teacher, a man with dark skin like Urbi's and similar tattoos down his arms. He had been lurking in the corner when I arrived, but now stood next to Elise, massive arms across his chest. The man was without a doubt one of the toughest looking men I'd ever seen, built like those wrestlers back home. His ears held multiple gold piercings, as did his nose and eyebrow. Urbi had said she was the last of her line, but this man appeared related on looks alone.

"Jabari, I would like you to meet our guest, Lenora." Shahara gave me a smile and a nudge as I took in the three sets of eyes watching me. Each expression was different, but they all said the same, wondering who I was and why I was here.

Summoning up my Southern upbringing I nodded politely to them all. "Pleased to meet you all, thank you for taking time out of your day."

"See, Signy? Those are manners." Elise poked again, clearly not satisfied with the other jab moments earlier.

"Let's get started, shall we?" Shahara motioned me to my seat as everyone else took residence in one of the chairs circled around the balcony.

Once we were seated, Shahara shared tales of the beginning; the Elders, the Closure and the Fallen. No one spoke while he continued wrapping one story into another, asking that we hold our questions until the end;

by "our", he meant mine. It was kind of him not to single me out, but I'm sure everyone else knew what was going on.

As I listened to this new world's history unfold before me, I clung to every word, absorbing the information like a sponge. Abaddon would want me; he did not seem to be a very gracious host, and I had no intentions of becoming some bargaining chip for a mad man.

"Ferrying hasn't been seen in centuries. The last one to possess such power...well, they are only legend." Jabari looked at me with a vacant expression before the familiar pinpricks of fear slithered once more around my ears and into my mind.

Signy sat forward. "We all know the tales of that treacherous woman, and how the power she possessed disrupted her purpose."

"Did she die?" My voice was a mere whisper.

Shahara answered, "No..."

"Some say she ceased to exist." Signy cut in.

Elise added, "Others say she never existed, and some whisper she lives in the mountains of the Norwood with Abaddon."

Tingling reached further in my ears and as they began to itch, I tried to concentrate on my breathing.

"How are we supposed to help this kid if she can't even handle a few stories? Look at her." As Signy spoke, Shahara began to defend me; voiced raised in anger.

My arms began to go numb as my chest felt heavy, the air around me getting thicker with every passing second. Honestly, I didn't even want to try and fight the fear as it set over me like a blanket. Maybe wherever I went this time wouldn't be of this world. Closing my eyes, I began withdrawing back into the safe space in my head and for a moment it was quiet.

Seconds later, something like a woman's scream pierced my ears. It wasn't far off like the other sounds I had heard. At first I squinted tighter, wanting to retreat further from the sound, but something pulled me back down.

Slowly the sound came back before opening my eyes, I shuddered. There, not ten feet in front of me were the most terrifying creatures I had ever seen.

There were so many screams.

Shahara was on his feet. "Gangors! We're under attack!"

Elise stepped in. "Protect the girl at all costs!"

Frozen in place, I watched these strangers battle two winged demons for me. Shahara had mentioned them just minutes ago, describing them briefly, but no amount of detail would have prepared me for a faceoff with these things... No one had mentioned the nauseating stench of death they carried with them either.

Spears of ice flew from Shahara's fists while Elise used a force field to push them back. Jabari stood at a distance while he focused his hands in front of him. Chains found their way from his arms to the neck of the Gangor on the left, snaking around tightly as he held on with all his strength. Standing in front of me was Signy, a sword in each hand. She had taken a knee, stone still like a statue, watching every move. Something told me she was my last line of defense and for good reason. Taking extra time, I studied her closely for a moment. She seemed so human, but there was something there underneath her skin that made me think animal.

Me.

They were willing to risk their lives for me.

Why?

To our right, a third Gangor landed on the balcony. Within a millisecond Signy was on her feet, confronting the threat. I've never seen someone move like she did. The sheer speed was astonishing, a blur as she whipped around the creature, slashing her blades. Even the Gangor seemed surprised.

An unearthly scream ripped through the air as Jabari's chains finally severed the head of the first. A second cry rang causing me to whip my head to the left in time to see another land close by. It crawled towards me slowly, mouth open, dripping with black blood.

Jabari shouted something to someone, but I don't know what it was. They were running towards me. Maybe they could make it in time, but a feeling deep within doubted it as they battled the others. The creature stopped short and sat up; smiling, if that's what you wanted to call it. Echoes of screams poured from the monster's mouth, as if it were replaying the cries of those it had just destroyed.

Me.

They were here for *me*.

Innocent people had just died...because of me.

My anger rose, and with it my hands. I wanted to scream. Heat filled my body, my mind like lava, and for a moment I thought I would breathe fire. It was there at the back of my throat, simply waiting to be released. If I let it go, it would burn him away. There was no doubt of such power but just before I did, something stopped me.

A simple idea twisted around my head. Something inside rattled loudly from a cage before breathing life into the plan. Upon my acceptance, it celebrated at the contribution I'd allowed. Swallowing the lava down, my eyes fell once again at the Gangor. Anger had always scared me in my world, so I had mastered pushing it down, trading it for something else, if only for a time.

Fire was too kind for this thing.

Honestly, I'm not sure how I knew it would work, I just did. Lifting my hands, I pulled at the shadows, beckoning them to me, encouraging them to take form. They slithered from every crack, behind every object, from every closet near me, piling up on either side.

The Gangor perked up, watching with curiosity at what I was building. In an instant that curiosity morphed to confusion, and then terror. For on my left and right now stood my own Gangors, made of shadow. Satisfaction covered my face before commanding them forward. My shadows tore into it, shredding and spilling black blood all over, until only a last gurgle escaped the creature. Rotating back to me, they moved swiftly to my side, waiting for instruction. Moments crept past before swiping my arms across the shadows and they both fell away, back to the corners from whence they came.

Turning around I heard the thud as Elise pushed the last fatally wounded Gangor over the side of the rail, sure the fall would finish it.

Shahara looked at me in true disbelief and fear…fear of me.

If I didn't know any better, I would have thought Signy was proud as she walked over, sheathing both swords, speaking first. "See, she doesn't even need me."

Jabari's face never changed. It was still settled on the same look he had when I walked into the meeting earlier. Elise let her age show, more winded than anyone else as she moved closer.

It felt like ages as they all stared, waiting to see if more darkness would pull from the shadows.

"How did you do that?" Gone was the fear I thought I saw in Shahara's eyes, now replaced with something I couldn't quite identify.

Without the confidence I had briefly held in my creatures, the question prompted an uneasy response. "I'm not sure, I just did."

"We need more than 'I just did,' Lenora." Shahara's irritation was apparent.

Searching my mind for answers, I came up short again. "I'm sorry, I really don't know..."

He stepped forward, angry. "Not good enough."

"What this battle-fatigued knuckle head is trying to say, is we need you to walk us through what happened." Elise's calm voice cut the tension like a knife as Shahara softened.

"I'm sorry, Lenora, Elise is right. I'm on edge. Please tell us what you can before you forget it." Shahara took a seat next to Elise. I stood, unable to move.

Holding my gaze to Elise's concerning eyes, I tried to explain. "It's hard to put words to it. At first when I get overwhelmed, I want to hide. That's what happened before ferrying the other night. This time, the screams, they kept me here. When I was watching each of you, ready to die for me, something inside changed. That Gangor touched down, it was taunting me. I'm not sure why or how, but I could hear the people it killed, hear their dying cries. It enraged me and then..."

Trust no one.

Right, they don't need to know I think I can breathe fire; they didn't see it.

"...I reached for the shadows; I wanted it to be scared like those people were. That thing needed to experience their pain, to understand how horrible it was. It was all a feeling, I wasn't intending to create my own Gangors, it just happened."

"Incredible." Elise just stared at me.

Looking at the group, I dared a question. "Could the other person like me do that, with the shadows?"

Shahara replied. "No. I've never seen, heard, or read about anything like that except...well, it's not relevant. Something like this is above any skill level that I know of."

"Are your gifts the same? I mean, do your feelings have some sway on how your magic works?" I asked broadly.

Everyone was silent for a moment before Signy spoke. "Yes and no. Magic can be born in intense emotion, like fire, one of the more powerful elemental gifts but also one that is tough to manage. It's quite common for magic to unleash as a protection, too. It comes out as a simple reaction, unintended, when the user is in danger. My speed did this when I was running from harm for the first time. It seems when you ferried you did it, though unintentionally, and yes, there was a desire to get away, but you weren't in any physical harm."

Elise nodded in agreeance. "My shields came out when I was extremely afraid. My understanding with these shadows is that you created them, intentionally with a choice. Even if you are unsure how, it was no mere emotional reaction. Now, if you had just screamed and thrown fireballs, that would be different."

The hair on my neck stiffened; that's how I was going to react, but I didn't.

"Your emotions and those of others, will have a huge effect on how, where, and why you use your magic. Controlling your emotions will help, but you have a better handle on them than you might believe." Jabari barely moved as he finished talking. The man looked like a statue, eyeing me intently. Hopefully, he was speaking from experience and not thinking I had withheld anything.

More commotion came from inside the tower, and Shahara stood as Elder Zubair hurried over with two men close behind. It seems odd now that I think about it, us talking about our feelings while covered in blood, the once pristine balcony trashed with curtains torn and multiple Gangor bodies in pieces.

"What is the meaning of all this, Shahara?" Zubair's eyes swept over the macabre presentation around us.

Squaring his shoulders, his eyes swept to me along with his finger. "They were here for her."

"At least they failed on that front. A pair of them attacked people in the city, there are multiple wounded and more dead than I care to acknowledge. Did any escape?" His tone held more statement than question. If any had escaped, there would be consequences.

Elise answered, "No, not a single one that we saw."

The Elder released some of the tension he was holding. "Good. They may still know where she is, but there would be hell to pay if we allowed any of them to crawl back home. I'll give you each time to get presentable, and then I want everyone to meet in the dining hall. No doubt this will be the first of many attempts at bringing her to him."

"They can't just take her. You know that for him to contain her in the mountain, she must cross over the territory line willingly. She has a right to know more about who she's up against. Someone needs to prepare her mind for the darkness that is sure to surround her, if it's not already playing tricks in her head. The longer you silly boys dance around that, the more you put us all at risk." Signy had taken two steps towards me, clearly exasperated with whatever information was being withheld from my knowing.

For now, I didn't think there was anything darker in my mind than the usual, but then I had always had strange corners in there.

Shahara shook his head while Zubair tried to recover from the tone of insolence she used against him, an Elder.

Weakly, Elise stood. Moving forward caused her to stumble, and in one move Jabari grabbed her arm to steady her. "Signy is right. We need to find someone familiar with Abaddon's mind games. It's only a matter of time before she has a run-in with them. Having her caught off guard would be setting her up for failure, not only endangering her but the rest of us as well."

"It's not that simple. Very few have been under Abaddon's thumb without falling prey to his influence. Do any of you have the experience required to teach her such things?" Slowly Zubair passed a glance over each in attendance.

Shahara took a long look at me, until I started to feel uncomfortable. "There are a few things she could learn that are better than nothing. I will help her. Let her rest tonight while we meet."

Something about how he looked at me while saying that...I wondered if I really wanted his help.

"Then it is settled. I expect to see everyone downstairs in an hour, except you, Lenora. You are excused for the night. Sleep while you can; soon you may find it a luxury you are no longer afforded." Heavy red eyes full of despair met mine, and with that he turned around, giving orders in their foreign tongue.

"It's good to see an old friend. I'm surprised, but grateful. After your meeting with Olam, I thought you had sworn off helping the girl. You know, no one blamed you for not wanting to." Ivy trailed off.

Cillian looked away, clearly uncomfortable, "If I'm calling others from retirement, the least I can do is something I don't want to. How are you,

Ivy? It's been too long. You don't look a day older for the wear; I must remember to ask Olam how he does it." Cillian smiled.

Ivy tossed her head, "I wish I could say the same for you, my friend. You look downright dreadful, and much older than last time."

Chuckling, he tried to brush off her concern. "Isn't that what serving is supposed to do?"

"Depends on who you ask, I imagine. You know, a spot has been open for you in the Ivory Palace for a while, Olam would welcome your presence in The Shining City...you've been through enough." Ivy's eyes were soft, matching her voice as she reminded Cillian what he already knew.

"You know me, peace and all that. Not ready yet." Cillian tried hard to convince her of such truth. It was a truth she already knew; as long as he had family still alive, he couldn't give up trying to save them.

"I wish I could give you better news than what I have, but I'm afraid it's escalated here. Gangors have already made an attack on the tower," Ivy stated bleakly as they passed over the bridge leading into the city.

Cillian spoke with more concern than he expected. "Was she injured?"

"No. I have not been to see her as my help was needed in the town. For now, she's resting in her room. It would seem she produced impressive magic earlier against a Gangor, but I have no real details of what she has done. Are you thinking of taking her and leaving?" The white mare questioned.

Cillian took a minute to think as Diadred walked with Ivy further into the town. "No. There is someone here I have reason to believe is a member of the Fallen. We need to know for certain who that is. Until we do, we stay and train Lenora while learning all we can."

"So far, I don't have the first lead, but the resonating theme is me telling her to trust no one." Ivy replied.

Cillian slowed his pace before turning to face her. "That's a start. I'll meet her in the morning after I poke this hive with a stick at dinner tonight."

"You do that, you'll be staying in the barn." Ivy warned.

Laughing, Cillian patted Diadred. "I'd rather hang out with this guy anyway."

"Just don't get in too much trouble before you have an opportunity to meet Lenora. I'm looking forward to finally giving her good news." She scoffed.

He tossed Ivy a questioning look as they arrived outside the tower. "Oh yeah, what's there to tell?"

Pausing for effect, she lingered in the silence before responding. "That I've brought someone she can trust, at last."

Chapter 13

"Master, we have received confirmation that Elder Feldrid has indeed sent help north. Her sons are on the move." Malachi's eyes narrowed as he lowered his voice for the last few words.

"Those two have been tucked away for far too long. Their absence won't go unnoticed." Olam sent him off before turning back to his book. He longed for this to be over, wished that he could simply fast forward through it all and deliver each of them safely to the other side. That isn't how it was done though. Sure, he could do it, but it would require taking free will away, something he simply wouldn't do.

He would, however, continue reaching out, sending aid and providing his strength where theirs faltered. Most of the time they had no idea what measure had been gone to in assisting their walk towards the light, what darkness had been illuminated before they could even see it.

The girl.

She was special. Then again, they all were. Each so different and vastly the same at once.

Lenora needed support. She needed to know there were those who could be trusted, to learn a better way than what she had practiced for so long, even though it was all she knew. This outsider yearned to do better, to learn, to change but she needed more time before confronting herself again. Here she would continue her journey and this time she wouldn't be alone.

None of them would be alone.

Getting up from his chair, he walked to the balcony on his room. Outside the air was crisp but not yet too cold. He closed his eyes as he leaned onto the rail, simply whispering to the wind that danced and wrapped around him, yearning to follow its master's voice.

Light flowed from his mouth, giving the once invisible wind texture and presence. Once he finished, he commanded it south, gusting away high in the sky towards its destination. "Oh Feldrid, thank you. I know your fear, but take heart in these dark times. Light will burn again."

Staring down at my hands, I kept turning them over, anticipating strange markings. Why, I couldn't say. What I had done earlier was impossible...wasn't it? Of course, I had also crawled so far from the last perceived threat, I ended up in the barn. If running away or lashing out mentally could produce such effect, what would happen if I voiced things?

At the continued urging of the two ladies whose names I still did not know, I had finally bathed; it felt surreal washing the dried blood from my skin, all of it black and gummy. Dressed comfortably, I was ordered to rest with the promise of dinner to be delivered. Some may have thought it a kindness, but I was no stranger to being talked about. They were leaving me out on purpose because I scared them. There had been clear terror in Shahara's face after I produced those things.

Fear makes people act rashly. What will they do with you?

My own conscious was mocking me, trying to rouse the anxious need to run.

Run fast and far before they leave you, or worse...you're too much Lenora. Those emotions were always going to get you. You're dramatic, crazy, just save us the trouble of dealing with you.

"Enough!" I screeched louder than intended.

Standing up, I took three quick strides to my door, knowing they were meeting any minute. Leaning in, I placed my ear to the cool surface but could hear nothing.

We could leave, you know. With that power I'm sure we could protect ourselves now, go home.

That was a decent thought for once from one of the many obnoxious voices in my head.

No. That's rude, we don't need to upset our new friends. Besides, we don't know anything about anywhere in this unknown world. Staying would be best.

Ivy said trust no one. For all you know, you just did something forbidden and they are going to kill you...I mean, what you did...

My palms started to sweat while I backed down from the door. Truth was I had no idea what was going on, and I'm not sure I wanted to wait to get in trouble, which was a common theme in my life.

Within minutes I had found a small fabric pouch, placed a few items in it that could be useful, and changed into my old clothes that had been washed earlier that morning. The convenient thing about all these balconies was the massive curtains that hung around. Pulling two of them down, I knotted them together, then tied one end onto the rail. Leaning over, I peered down at the ground below; it wasn't a far drop, but I would be on the edge of the porch attached to the dining hall. If memory served me correctly, there were large potted palms and other greenery that blocked the view of the far corner.

Of course, there was a large chance I was wrong.

It was a chance I had to take. Looking back, I did a quick inventory around the room to make sure I didn't miss anything else that could be of value to me. With a gentle hand I slowly lowered my curtain rope over the edge. Even if it didn't make it all the way, it would get me close enough for a safe jump. Climbing over, I shimmied myself slowly down the curtains, praying no one would notice.

Once I had passed the first story, I opened my eyes to reveal a grateful sight; I was blocked by a corner wall, many columns and trees. However, I could hear raised voices drifting out into the evening air. Agitated voices.

Jumping down quietly, I crouched down beside the column. They were further away than expected, to my relief. I could have made a dash down the alley towards the barn, but curiosity nipped at me. It wouldn't hurt to move onto the porch and listen in a little. Maybe I was wrong. Creeping forward, I moved onto the marble floor, across the first section of porch and up against one large blue potted palm. Straining to listen, I was finally able to pick out multiple voices, but I dared not venture to peek around for a look.

"Confound it all, that's not a gift, it's a curse." Zubair bellowed.

"Just because you've never seen it, it scares you. I get it, but it doesn't mean there's something wrong with the girl." Elise snapped in my defense with a little more ferocity than expected from her.

"Can we be certain she's not already been taken by Abaddon?" It was Shahara...he was indeed scared of me, with what seemed like good reason.

"Sit down, you are such an instigator. For all we know any one of us could be acting as a spy?" Signy cut through the night with her aggravation. "I mean seriously, you think Ivy would be parading her all over the world if that were the case? You think the Gangors would have shown up if that were the case? No. She'd be in the mountains, planning to bring down our entire world with that snake. Not here, cowering in bath water and ferrying when your authoritative impudence overtakes the conversation, scaring the daylight out of her."

I genuinely was beginning to like Signy.

A new voice began, a man who's voice I did not recognize. "Regardless, we need to keep a close watch on her, maybe put a guard outside her door for both her protection and our peace of mind."

Shahara spoke first, to my heartbreak. "Agreed, we don't know truly who or what she is."

So that was it. In a matter of minutes, I went from guest to prisoner. Black sheep in my own world and untrusted in this new one, *aren't you par for the course.*

There was nothing more to learn, I backed out into the small street and took what I thought was the way back around the tower, towards the stables.

Approaching the entrance I slowed, peeking in carefully to ensure Ivy wasn't around. No one had really seen me; it was dark, and there were very few people out on the streets after the attack earlier.

Shadow's saddle was right where I left it. As I heaved it onto his back, he barely moved, content to eat his hay and oblivious to my urgency.

"Can I help you?" The hairs on my neck rose in response to another unfamiliar male voice. From where I was standing, he must have already been further within the stables, because I had my eyes on the door.

Dread filled me as seconds passed by without words or a breath. He found me speechless, and my mind was swimming with nothing useful to explain my presence here.

Maybe he's just a stable man or a weary traveler who is simply offering to help.

"No, thank you." My shaky response was less than convincing as I forced myself to tighten the girth and not turn around.

"It's a bit late to be going for a ride. Not very safe out there after those attacks earlier, I would imagine." His voice slowed, almost laced with concern.

"We are just going for a stroll, you know, clear the mind. It's needed right now, blood and all that scary stuff," came the stupid, stuttered response from my less than brilliant mouth.

"Ah, no need to explain then, I know a warrior when I see one. Carry on." His steps receded, and I caught the side of him as he walked out of the stables smiling.

My mouth was open, absorbing the tone of ridicule he had revealed. "Shadow, I do believe that man just mocked me."

Let's be honest though, I didn't really care. He let me leave.

Snatching up the small pouch I had packed before stuffing it inside the saddle bag, we headed out. There was little food, and I was poorly prepared. No part of me wanted to be alone again. I was scared, but I was not about to be someone's prisoner...again, there had been enough of that in my own world.

One of the tower scribes walked into the dining hall quickly, bowing at the waist before the table. "Elder Zubair, pardon my interruption, but Cillian has arrived on behalf of Master Olam."

Each of the six people at the table looked disgruntled as ever, clearly once again not agreeing on whatever they were meant to agree upon.

Cillian had walked in casually, observing everything down the hall, and quietly waited, standing behind the scribe.

Surprised, Elder Zubair responded. "Cillian, we weren't expecting you."

"No sir, I imagine you were not. Am I interrupting? Looks as though you're planning a war party by the scowls of your constituents." He briefly studied each of the current guests.

A small smirk pulled at the corner of Zubair's mouth as he motioned for Cillian to take a seat. "Not at all, Cillian. Praise Olam you arrived here tonight. We need some help; I'll take it regardless of its source. But why are you here Cillian? Surely the Gangor attacks haven't reached the ears of Olam so soon."

"No sir, but don't be surprised if he does know. That man has eyes and ears everywhere. Even I am not privy to all the ways he sources information. I'm here for an urgent matter entirely separate, although undoubtedly intwined in the chaos you have unfolding around here." Cillian's calm presence eased the tension for the Elder, at least for a moment.

Compassion filled Cillian's heart as he studied the weary ruler. "It's best to wait until morning. It would seem you have enough on your plate for tonight."

"My lord, could we move on." The gentlemen on Zubair's left pushed to change the subject.

Zubair raised an arm in his direction. "Cillian, this is Omar. He is the head commander of our local forces."

Cillian questioned them. "Forces?"

"Since the Fallen have been growing, so have we." The man was large, face set firmly with shoulders back and sharp features of stone, exactly the carriage you would expect from a military leader.

"Olam never mentioned an Army." Cillian's eyebrows raised in the direction of Zubair.

Reluctantly the Elder began to explain. "He wouldn't have, although I am sure he knows what we've been doing. I never asked. Respectfully

I disagreed with his peaceful treatment of the Fallen. It may not be massive, but we have an elite group of gifted men and women who have been trained in combat for the day Abaddon decides not to remain quiet any longer."

Cillian released a huge sigh of relief; this was what they needed. He imagined the morning meeting would be quick and successful.

Shahara's patience was waning as well as Omar's while the two got off subject again. "With all due respect, we have an immediate issue that requires your decision, Zubair." Shahara leaned into the Elder with a soft yet stern voice as his eyes locked on Cillian, clearly showing their disdain.

"The girl needs our protection, but we also need to protect our people. Who knows what she is capable of and when it could show up? I move to vote on her removal from the tower to the northern mountains of the west, with armed escorts, until we can understand her more. We cannot afford to place our people in danger. Her mere presence was enough to incite a full-blown attack, the likes of which have not been seen in decades."

Cillian took time to read the room, garnering what information he could. It would seem Omar only had Shahara on board with this plan. The rest were clearly not, and Zubair was not passing his judgment, yet.

"You lock this child up and you might as well kill us all. She's not some animal to be caged." It was Jabari who finally spoke, boldly, in a tone that demanded the room's attention.

Shahara sprang from his seat. "Look, I don't like it any more than any of you, but you saw what she did. What if she creates those shadows things again and sends them at us instead? You can't kill shadows!"

"If she's going to do that, locking her away won't stop her. You'll only give her more reason to hate us." Elise sighed.

Cillian cut in. "Might I ask why you are all so frightened of this girl?"

A small laugh came from across the room. "The boys are upset this small woman is more powerful than them. Can't have that. Not only can she ferry, but while facing down a Gangor she created shadow creatures that copied it, and on her command tore the thing to pieces. She is brilliant," Signy answered, using the knife to pick at the cuticle on her fingers.

Cillian tried to hide his awe at the news, he'd have to play his hand wisely here after a stunt like that. "Well, Omar, your problem is already solved; this girl of yours is gone."

Shahara's face went white. "What did you say?"

He smirked gently while he met Shahara's shocked face. "She left, on that black horse of hers right before I came over."

"You let her leave?!" Omar was on his feet with Shahara, shouting orders.

Raising his voice to match the level in the room, Cillian stood. "You won't catch her like that. You go running after her, she'll get scared and ferry to who knows where." Cillian turned to Zubair, "Sir, let me retrieve her."

"My lord, you have to let us..."

Zubair cut Shahara off. "Cillian has a point." He nodded towards Cillian. "Go, bring her back quietly."

No one spoke against the Elder, but it didn't mean Shahara was happy about it.

Everyone stood to take their leave. Cillian paused, turning to face Zubair. "Sir, the girl is not your prisoner, correct? Master Olam has given Ivy and I the role as her guardians. It would complicate things if we weren't all on the same page."

Zubair held Cillian's gaze as Omar and Shahara drilled dagger-like stares into him. The three teachers watched the exchange intently, wondering where each would land in power.

With a deep breath Zubair spoke firmly, "No, she is a guest here."

Signy snickered.

He continued with eyes set straight ahead. There was no lightness in his tone. "Cillian, I do need to protect my people. I expect you to take full responsibility and answer for any mishaps while she is here."

He nodded respectfully, "Of course, I will accept nothing less."

Cillian left the room with the others, making a quick move for the stables. Once he was sure no one was following, he entered. Walking down the aisle he passed all the stalls and took a left at the end. Once he laid eyes on them, he released his breath. He never really trusted they wouldn't go after her. Letting her get close to the mountains without him was even more dangerous.

There in front of him near the hay stall was Diadred, Shadow, Ivy, and Lenora.

Shadow lifted his head as Diadred stood on guard. Footsteps were approaching.

A man rounded the corner. He was strikingly handsome. Not in the hero way but in the realistic manly way. No knight in shining armor, more hippie lumberjack kind of guy. He was tall, lean build but not small. His head was full of deep brown hair that matched the brown full beard. Coming closer, his smile lit up the dreary aisle in the back part of the stables.

He nodded at Ivy. I assumed they were talking.

As he looked my way, I caught my breath; his eyes were a stunning, emerald green with a light dash of freckles across his nose. He made his way into my space, hand extended. "I see you've met Diadred. Hope he hasn't been too much of a handful. I'm Cillian." It took much longer to respond to his handshake than intended. My hand awkwardly met his. It was weird, the comfort I found in a simple handshake.

Apparently, although he had let me leave on Shadow, he had also contacted Ivy to send her after me. I had not gotten far before being intercepted by Ivy and his strange cat-like creature, Diadred. To my surprise, as I waited for my punishment, none came. Ivy had been astonished I hadn't tried to run off sooner. She may not have understood my feelings, but she made space for them.

Now as I stared at this man, I wondered if he too would do the same, or if I would receive a lecture on how reckless my behavior was...

He stepped back, "They scared you pretty good, huh?"

"Would you want to be someone's prisoner?" I snapped.

"No. No, I suppose I wouldn't." Cillian watched me as I shifted uncomfortably from one leg to another.

Ivy excused herself to tend to some concerns with the few informants she had, something Cillian sent her off to do. It didn't take me long to learn he would run this show from now on.

She swore I could trust him with my life. Time would tell if that were true...

Cillian tried again, "You ready to go back to your room?"

"They were ready to lock me up..." I reminded him.

Locking eyes with mine, his tone was no longer casual but serious, "Not anymore. I have it on good authority they won't try that again."

He was waiting, listening, leaning up against a stall door.

You could hear Diadred's breathing while the horses munched hay. Continuing to rub my arms anxiously, I acknowledged how uncomfortable I felt in my own skin after what the shadows had done; not that I ever had felt comfortable before. When you spend your life hearing how difficult you are and always will be you don't ever settle into confidence with yourself.

"They didn't scare me, the shadows. It wasn't triggered by fear, not like the ferrying. It was intentional. Those things, they killed innocent people. Then they made me listen to the sound of their screams as they were slaughtered."

Tears silently slid down my cheeks as the weight of the day unraveled. "Who, what does something like that...those people lost their lives!" Unintentionally my voice rose with anger as my tears continued to fall. "Did you hear me? They killed a family just to replay the sounds!" Falling to my knees I held my hands in front of me watching them shake, then fall. Grabbing my face, I leaned over and let out the stifling cries that had been held in too long.

It took Cillian's long legs only three strides to get to me. After a moment he knelt and wrapped me in an embrace while I continued crying on his shoulder, he simply held me without saying a word. Small red orange orbs were leaving my face to hit the ground below, a few lit small patches of hay near my knees.

Pushing back, I looked up at him with swollen eyes. It took me a moment to notice the fires around me and the holes in his shirt. Terrified, I shoved him away in fear that my fiery tears would cause more harm. Immediately I stood up desperate to stomp out the small flames around us.

"Lenora, I'm fine, see; no burns." Cillian showed me the holes. His clean shoulder was not burnt. Grabbing my own face in confusion, my eyes searched for understanding.

"The fire you possess here, many others share." He lifted both hands as they produced flames. "If you have fire magic, you can't be burned by it."

In my momentary relief, the weight of another day felt heavy on my shoulders.

"Can I sleep in the barn tonight? I'll go back in the morning, but I really can't right now."

Something sad flickered in his eyes as he turned his gaze to meet mine. "Lenora, you don't need my permission. You are an adult after all, and I'm not over you."

Something about that stunned me, it was foreign.

"I'll bed down over here with Diadred if you need anything. Won't be the first time I've shared a night's rest with this cat."

Grabbing some extra hay, I walked into Shadow's stall. "Thank you, Cillian, for being so kind." Fixing myself a place to lay in the corner, the exhaustion leaked into my bones, settling like lead.

Cillian shuffled his own space around before he replied. "I didn't do anything more than anyone else. Goodnight, Lenora."

But he did.

He had treated me with more respect and kindness than any man had shown me in a lifetime. I had almost forgot what being treated like a human felt like.

Chapter 14

Abaddon moved further into the cave, the damp cold dripping around him. This part of the dungeons was unknown to everyone except him and Lilith. The pit, where those who failed to be useful would find themselves. It was also where he would retreat for wisdom from the Masi, a darkness maker as she called herself.

The Gangors had riled things up a bit, it's why they were good. It was a shame he couldn't create more; the Closure had cost him that ability.

What was more concerning were whispers of a new power from the girl, rumors, and none of them very consistent. The only truth he had learned was Cillian's early arrival, an extremely determined and skilled opponent. He could have simply killed him long ago, but slow torture suited his tastes more after all the complications that man had caused.

Stalactites hung from the ceiling before the small corridor opened into a large room, expanding on the caverns below. Repetitive ticks of water dripping into the small pools softly echoed across the large formations forming from the floor.

A flash of fire came from his right hand as he rolled the ball around to illuminate the darkening space. Unnervingly he moved deeper, not daring to make a sound. She already knew he was here. She had her purpose, but Abaddon did desire on occasion to throw her back to the depths of hell from which he was sure she crawled out of. It had been her who lured him into this mountain so many centuries ago with her whispers. In here the first shadow box had appeared, his own. Only once had he dared an attempt on her mind. Only once had a mind opened to him that he wished never had, instead pulling back out as quickly as possible in response to the repulsive darkness that would have happily consumed even him into madness.

Sometimes she would make him wait hours, moving around in circles with his fire while she watched. She craved the conversation he would bring, however brief; feeding on his own darkness, even though it paled in comparison.

He never knew what form she would take. A shape shifter of sorts, she could be anyone or anything you could imagine. Unpredictability was something that twisted Abaddon uneasily, it's why he loved humans. They were always predictable on some base level for survival, but not this creature. They were a match together in every way, except the one that made his stomach knot, for she was far more powerful than anything this world had in the darkest ways. Not that she had ever produced anything to make him believe, but he could feel it when she arrived, his own darkness quivering in her presence.

"You've been away so long." The siren voice echoed all around him at once.

Abaddon had learned to challenge his own discomfort, morphing it into respect. She would not speak to someone who sulked or quivered. No, those who did fear she devoured. It's how he kept in her good graces, so he liked to believe, by feeding her the failed humans. There was something she respected in him that stroked his ego just enough to dance with this devil.

"Traffic, love. You know how it is, pure madness out there." He smiled broadly.

Small rocks around his feet vibrated as the voice came again at once. "I would very much love to learn your world. You will take me there one day, Abaddon, you will."

Not a question, a statement. She always said that; he doubted whatever it meant was anything beneficial for him.

"There should be some visitors for you this evening, I hear this man has lived quite the life." Stories, she loved consuming stories lived from the minds of those they threw into the pit.

"You want something...you always want something." Her voice purred down seductively as he stood in silence waiting for her revelation. "The girl has unique power and a strength she draws from unexpected places; you don't like it."

Abaddon responded blandly, "Oh really, you think I don't already know that?"

Emerging behind a stalagmite, a mirror reflection of himself approached. She had chosen to taunt him today; he was quite amused. "Well, don't you look handsome, you sexy thing."

"The answer you seek is comfortable for you, a place you know well but don't understand. With them she will rise, without them you will fall." She leaned in closer to the fire than usual. His mirrored reflection began to melt and twist into black smoke before departing.

Moments of silence fell as he waited, garnering impatience but not daring to speak.

Finally, a whisper licked his ear. He could feel the hot breath on the back of his neck, heavy and moist. What could only be described as an icy fog drifted around him. His skin pulled at his bones, begging to retreat. She had changed to her true form as she always did before giving him a riddle, and he dare not turn to look as she spoke.

"Follower of man

Dark as night
Completely silent
Stalking after the light
Who am I?"

They were never too hard, the riddles she required for him to walk back out, but they both knew the answers wouldn't truly save him. It was a game for her, like a cat with a mouse. "Shadow," Abaddon whispered.

With that he felt the dark heaviness pull from the room, her presence retreating further into the labyrinth of caves below.

This was a most disheartening visit; she was never wrong and the words she spoke beat throughout his head with every step as he climbed back out of the cave below.

"With them she will rise, without them you will fall."

She had something he didn't, and that would just not do. It was time to investigate other avenues, he didn't have time to wait for the girl to curiously wander his way.

Keeping guard through the night had kept sleep far from Cillian. He would only allow himself the luxury on occasion when he forced Diadred to wander the stable aisle. Even though Zubair had reminded everyone Lenora was a guest, he knew there was at least one person who wouldn't pay that any mind. Now who that was remained unknown, but Cillian was beginning to have some ideas.

She was beautiful.

The most beautiful woman he could remember laying eyes upon. Her long brunette hair, olive skin and those eyes. Eyes that didn't hold any one true color, but many. Watching her tend to Shadow with such intention, he saw she loved that horse, and with the way she checked in on Diadred told Cillian she likely used that level of care with all animals.

Balancing that rough exterior with the extreme fragility she held from whatever life had taken must be tiring. Cillian imagined she had done this survival dance for some time and only now the complexity their realm had brought was forcing her to look at herself. He had to help her there. The others had a right to be nervous. She very well could be dangerous if not given direction by the right people.

"Are they angry with me?" Lenora had meandered over cautiously, twisting her fingers together over again, her long hair pulled and braided to the side. The jeans hugged her tightly and even the loose shirt complimented her well. Although not a large woman by any stretch of the imagination, she held a woman's body.

Getting to his feet he brushed the hay from his pants. "No, not angry. Like I told you last night, you have nothing to worry about. You are a *guest* here." He accentuated the word again, hoping it would bring some calm to her nerves.

Looking around, she anxiously rubbed her thumbs together. "People can say one thing and mean another, you know."

Cillian watched her, guard up with uncertainty, as if one misstep would be too costly to recover from. "You don't trust them, do you?"

"It's not like I did much before, but now…" Her voice trailed off before picking up laced with sorrow. "You didn't see how they looked at me, like some monster."

"We will just have to watch them closely then, won't we? Now, I have a meeting with Zubair this morning. Try to stay out of trouble while I'm gone, and don't light anything on fire." Cillian winked and tried to send a reassuring smile her way before moving in the direction of the tower. He needed to figure out who was the betrayer among them, and he wouldn't learn it camped out in the stables. As much as he wished to tell her, he wouldn't risk setting her further on edge. Who knows what she might do. She didn't need any extra reasons to worry. There were more than enough for both of them already.

It had already taken me over half an hour after Cillian left to work up the courage to walk outside the barn, let alone in the direction of the Tower. Both Ivy and Cillian were off having meetings. I had considered riding Shadow, but the last thing I needed were people thinking it was another escape attempt.

Not a prisoner, a guest. I tried to reassure myself, but I still didn't buy it.

The barn had gotten stuffy and no part of me wanted to go inside anywhere, so I just walked wherever my feet took me. And wouldn't you know it, those feet walked me once again smack dab into Urbi around a corner. She was dressed beautifully as usual, this time an orange gown hanging off her ebony shoulders adorned with a delicate necklace to match with bead work that hung down her back.

Shock was plastered across her face as she stumbled through words to apologize. It was quickly clear by her lack of eye contact and anxious demeanor that more than their run in had surprised her. My first thought as I fumbled myself for words was her having a fear of me.

"Urbi, I'm sorry, I was looking at the ground."

"No, no, no. The fault is mine." She glanced again over her shoulder as if someone would pop out any second and take her to a dungeon.

The odd engagement continued to be uncomfortable and I was trying to put my own mind at ease that it wasn't because of me. "It's a beautiful day. Would you like to join me for a walk, maybe show me around?"

Finally, her brown eyes settled in my direction, the fear in them softened, and I could have sworn compassion or even pity had moved in as a replacement. Without so much as a warning she snatched my wrist so hard my shoulder popped as she dragged us to the other side of the street, down an alley and behind a small outbuilding.

There was an obvious part of me that wanted to fight against the hijacking and demand an explanation, but there was another part that knew I could trust her. The look she cast was as much for her own safety as my own. Further we moved away from the Tower, I knew this as tents started to come into view, not running but definitely in a hurry. Just before the buildings ended, we took a sharp right turn and then a hard left through a purple curtained doorway.

As my eyes adjusted to the dimly lit room, Urbi released me to speak with an elderly woman sitting alone on a cushion, once more in their foreign tongue. There seemed to be no one else in the small space. Meticulously organized baskets full of colorful fabrics lined the walls. A small cot-like bed was laid out in the corner across from what I could only imagine was a makeshift kitchen area.

"Come, sit." Urbi motioned to a few other cushions as the elderly lady paid a smile before leaving to step outside.

Urbi leaned over, grabbing both of my hands with tears welling in her eyes. "There's no time for formalities or backstories, Lenora. I am sorry, but you must leave, for you are in grave danger here."

The snarky part of me wanted to blurt out 'tell me something I don't know' but the terror in her face made me think better of it. This woman hardly knew me, but for some reason she was terrified for me.

Calm came to the rescue as my voice stayed low. It was as much for her as it was for myself. "Urbi, I need a little bit more than that, you just drug me the length of the city into a hut." Gently I squeezed her hand and gave her a small smile.

"There's little time. This is what I know, they are coming."

"Who is coming?"

"The Fallen." Her voice fell to a whisper, but a stern one. "Not just Gangors but some of Abaddon's own. They will tear this place to shreds, more of my people will die." No longer was fear there but anger and a defensive posture. She wasn't just doing this for me. That face wasn't some prize princess, but a queen protecting her people. Spitting into the ground, she held her head high and released my hands. "Shahara, that pig. We're courting per tradition because he is one of my suitors. These insolent men, when will they learn. Why I can't just rule my people under Zubair without a husband is beyond me...but I digress. After you arrived, he began acting very strange. Shahara's obsession with you after the Gangor attack even had Omar looking at him outlandishly, and that astounded me considering how ignorant that man is. It's why I gave you the first warning after you ferried."

My fingers began to tingle while Urbi continued to talk quickly, trying to meet all her points in this rundown of information.

Urbi stood up, pulling at her dress and taking a deep breath like she needed to get on with it, no turning back now. "I've heard of them, but I've never met one that I knew or really understood how they operate. It's rumored that Abaddon has members of the Fallen that don't live up north. They reside among us like spies, feeding info and sowing chaos when needed. If it were me, I'd place those people in trusted positions of power amongst the Elders. Unlike the dark creatures that are twisted into weapons, they are carefully selected for intelligence and promised power or revenge if they have a chip on their shoulder. One of the many reasons Master Olam warns us about those things."

Nausea filled my stomach as the knot tightened in my throat. Some part of me *knew* where this was going.

"What happened this morning...he didn't know I was headed to his room. Ever since you created those shadows, I've been trying to use my influence to understand what's going on. Zubair was keeping me in the dark...I need to keep my people safe. Shahara thought no one was around, it was incredibly early, I've never heard dark chanting like that with such unspeakable words. It wants you; Abaddon wants you. There's something about you, I think he's worried, which makes him ten times more dangerous. Shahara must be one of them, it's why he's so bent on containing you somewhere and using dark magic to communicate with things he shouldn't. You need to leave, please, not just for your own safety but for my people. This is not their fight." Her voice was straining. Tears once more slid down her cheek as she looked at me from her knees. She was pleading. "Please, I beg of you, don't lead him here."

Cillian was on his way back to the barn feeling a bit lighter than yesterday. The meeting had gone well and he had the full support of Zubair's unofficial army. Tomorrow there would be a team headed north to rendezvous with Dondi's group, who had hopefully arrived and settled in with Elder Medora. What concerned him currently was Ivy's abrupt departure; she was being summoned back to the Shining City.

No matter, his skills were enough to keep Lenora safe.

The barn welcomed him as he entered, one of the few buildings with actual doors. Diadred was lounging about on his back in the hay as soon as he walked in.

"Lazy, worthless cat. What have you done today?"

With the sound of Cillian's voice, Diadred rolled over, yawned and let out a big stretch with rump in the air, tails going everywhere.

Shadow was pacing back and forth in his stall, something Cillian had never seen him do. The hay bag was untouched and his head was held high while he anxiously moved about.

Lenora was nowhere to be found, which wasn't truly odd, but something churned his stomach uncomfortably as if danger was close.

"Diadred, find her." It was all that had to be said to turn the lazy barn cat into an attentive warrior. He stood up and leaped for the door, but before he could push, it swung open from the outside.

In stepped Lenora.

Her face was set firmly in their direction with no ounce of surprise to find them there. Cillian could tell something was wrong. Her eyes were serious, but no sorrow could be seen. Shoulders back and head high, she walked past him and continued to Shadow's stall, reaching for his nose with a calming sound. Within seconds she had thrown the saddle on and grabbed her things. There was something in the air that kept anyone from speaking as she continued tacking up the horse. Turning, she looked at the two of them. "I'm leaving."

"Really?" Cillian questioned. "To go where?"

Her tone flattened, "Away from here, anywhere. I doubt you'll let me leave alone, so grab your stuff and let's go."

Eyeing her cautiously, Cillian did as she asked. She was right, he would follow; it wasn't as if restraining her was wise. Plus, if he had any hope of learning what this was about, he needed to let her know she could trust him.

Within minutes they were mounted and headed north out of town. As they crested a sand dune on the outskirts, Lenora stopped her horse to take one more look behind them. Gone was the nervous woman he had left this morning, and the woman there in her place felt immensely more dangerous than before.

Chapter 15

The trip to visit Anara had not yielded anything useful. Lilith would have to look for information elsewhere. None of the commanders would know anything, Abaddon always played each move close to the chest with her being the only one ever privy to his plans. Lately though, even she was being kept in the dark. The chatter, be it unreliable, was that the girl had vanished from Karakum. It brought joy to her that the fool Shahara would be in for a wakeup call and Abaddon would be stewing.

Shame.

Oh well, it was his own stupidity and his loss, not hers.

Taking the long way around to avoid the Shadow Boxes, she climbed another flight of stairs moving higher inside the mountain. Today she would get to blow off some steam with a few new recruits, one in particular she was charged with to clean up for an actual outing.

When she opened the heavy door, her eyes burned from the bright sunshine of a clear day. It took a minute for them to adjust to outside after walking the dark halls of the dungeons. A whiff of fresh air hit her with a hint of pine, the cool breeze biting coyly at her face. Stretched out ahead was a large training field on the edge of a cliff, high up in the mountains. A cascade of falls poured over the side where a small stream cut through the land, falling far down to the river below. Far off in the distance were more mountains and a deep forest, stretching until the end of the edge of their world. It wasn't much farther where you would find the walls from The Closure keeping them all in, for now.

There were a few of the Fallen practicing small magic across the area, mostly fire. It was what was easiest to create in hurting people. Abaddon had a thing for fire. He was skilled at coaxing it out of even the sweetest of humans, and it was effective. Some still retained magic they had prior, but not usually. The fire really was all consuming, eventually...

Off to Lilith's left, near the bridge that went over the stream, was her target for the day. From what she had been told, this one had been tough to work with, holding out for the hope of seeing her family again. It was explained, in gruesome detail, the lengths Abaddon had gone to twist her; he always did pay special attention to the strong-willed ones. Lilith couldn't remember the last time a torture had gone on so intense for so long, other than what had been done to her. For a fleeting second, as Lilith approached the withered frame of what truly was a gorgeous woman at one time, she almost pitied her...*can't have that.*

Life is cruel, you just get over it.

"You, come, let me get a look at you." Lilith snapped her fingers and motioned the woman to stand.

She did as she was told, moving faster than expected. Her feet had been in the water and the rippling caused Lilith to believe it might have been reviving her strength. Good, she would need it.

After circling her, Lilith used her hand to lift the woman's chin from one side to the other, noting the welts and bite marks that covered her. Every inch of skin that she could see was marked, and she was certain the skin underneath her clothes was hiding the more hideous cuts, burns or bruises.

Lilith reached in the pocket of her pants for a small length of fabric to hand the woman, "Tie your hair up, it will get in the way. I'm told you're called Eydis. Is that correct?"

"Yes," came the monotone, almost dead like voice of Eydis while she did as Lilith directed, tying her stringy hair on top of her head.

Reaching around to pull her gloves off, Lilith set them aside before quickly flinging fireballs at the targets across the stream. Motioning for Eydis to do the same, she stepped out of the way, waiting to see what she would be able to do.

Eydis was barely able to produce sparks as she kept trying to coax the fire into her open hands. Lilith watched on, annoyed. This woman was supposed to be ready, and clearly couldn't even produce a simple fire ball. Weighing the choice of just sending her back or continuing, she decided it wouldn't be best to pick a fight with Abaddon now.

"Dig deep, get angry. Those targets over there aren't going to give you the chance to sit here and practice. Remember, they want you dead, they ripped your house to pieces after realizing you had been taken, there's no going back!" Lilith sneered the words towards her, getting closer, her own fire burning around her wrists.

Nothing, no reaction.

Eydis didn't respond. She had closed her eyes and tilted her head towards the sky, hands draping by her sides with palms open.

He had broken her.

They said she was ready, but he had pushed her too far; he ruined quite a few good talents that way. Once again, his own lack of self-control was evident. Breaking one's spirit down was a game for him, he lived for it. But wisdom required restraint, and after that, you needed to redirect the anger within.

Abaddon favored a commander, Damion, who could read visual memories. He was used regularly to harvest necessary information from humans. After the Shadow Boxes and anything else required, he would learn of their last hope, whatever they clung to so Abaddon could shatter it. Most of it was smoke and mirrors. On occasion there was some truth, but generally lies. In this case, they had described the death of Eydis's husband and daughter at the hands of the Mandros as punishment for her joining the Fallen. They told her the command of such cruelty came from Olam himself. Those who made it this far were never close to the Master, so they had little foreknowledge of who he was. If they were, they never would have dabbled with such danger.

Lilith once again used her influence to blast the details of such torment into Eydis' mind, leaving nothing to the imagination. Making sure to highlight how desperately the little girl had called for her mother, begging her for rescue. Upon those last words, Eydis' eyes flew open, burning bright blue as her head straightened, both arms lifted, and to her side came water from the stream. The water passed through her hands and exited her palms as burning blue fire that crackled and sparked. Gazing upon the sight before her, Lilith stood stunned, even taking a step back as Eydis let out a primal howl before hurling the electric blue fire at a huge boulder on the edge of the cliff. Within an instant, it was reduced to ash.

It took everything out of her. Eydis slumped over to fall, but strong arms intercepted her. Lilith stared at the high cheek bones with astonishment before lowering her to the ground carefully.

This was new.

New was never good.

Although the desert south of the West Tower had stretched on forever, the desert north was much shorter before butting up to rocky, barren mountains. This area was not as alive as previous places in the Starpathian realm had been, and I wondered what could survive, or want to, in these mountains. Cillian had told me that few went this way, the terrain was hard and supplies were limited. He did promise that beyond them, to the east, lay a forest and the North Tower wouldn't be much further. There, we would meet the group that had been amassed to defend the rest of the world from…whatever Abaddon was planning.

We had just reached a flat area that seemed defendable and suitable for rest as darkness fell. Shadow's black neck was no longer visible, it would be unwise to continue further for now, so we stopped to dismount.

After minutes of awkward silence that had already plagued most of the trip, I finally spoke up. "You want to know what happened back there, I imagine?"

Cillian was still moving random things around to make a comfortable spot to lean while he muttered his response, "I figured you'd tell me when you're ready."

He couldn't see my scowl. Why it bothered me that he respected me was idiotic, but it was foreign, and I still didn't know how to behave.

Taking a deep breath, I recounted Urbi dragging me across town, pleading for the life of her people and revealing Shahara's true allegiance. We hadn't risked a fire, still being in the region of Karakum, plus by now everyone would know we were gone.

Darkness kept me from seeing Cillian's reaction, if there was one. Silence crept around us as while anxiously awaiting his response. It took him much longer than I deemed necessary, a lingering silence that made me want to scream.

Cillian finally cleared his throat, and spoke, "I'm sorry that I didn't see it sooner. I thought Omar and Shahara were up to something, but I didn't have enough straightforward evidence to call out a member of the court. Lenora, forgive me."

In that moment I wanted to grab his hand, tell him he didn't need to apologize; but I didn't.

"Hopefully, that small army will only be a day behind us, if it will still be sent." Cillian was no doubt concerned that Shahara would get the Elder to change his mind, but I was hopeful.

"Signy will come, and the other teachers. I had Urbi give them a message."

"Well, I'm grateful Urbi got to you in time. Get some sleep, I'll take watch."

My heart hurt, he sounded as if there was something he could have done to prevent this. That was simply untrue. Instinctively my mind wanted to plan, but my exhaustion won out again and I found it easiest to lay down, drifting into sleep.

Master Olam had just received news that Elder Dondi's troupe had arrived in the Norwood and settled in well. He had sent additional provisions Elder Medora's way for all her new guests. The winter there would be bitter, no doubt, with Lilith fuming in the mountains. There had been confirmation of a small army supplied by Elder Zubair. He always knew that man would have one, but hadn't heard from Ivy or Cillian yet.

Elder Feldrid had sent her thanks after receiving Olam's blessing on the wind. He knew how hard it had been to send her sons off to war. She would need her strength, and his gift bought her some more time. Feldrid had secretly taken a husband and had the twin boys long ago. The cost of such a thing was her immortality, but Olam had been buying her extra time to see them grow up. Even though she had gone against their code, he loved her dearly and needed her to know it.

They were all coming together, one by one. Each day pushed them all closer to what felt like an ending, but it would truly be a wonderful beginning. It was a plan that had long been set in motion after The Closure had gone awry. The Elders had all taken vows to rule with love. Each of them had handed over a part of their power to protect this realm and the portal that would lead on into eternity.

Abaddon always was too greedy, always wanting more and pursuing things he never needed. Olam knew after the Gangors appeared that Abaddon had chosen, he would never give up or turn back. One day there would be a cost much greater to protect all the realms and people within.

Olam picked up the book, treasuring the words he needed his people to understand, "Love has no fear, because perfect love expels all fear. If we are afraid, it is because fear involves punishment, and this shows that we have not yet experienced perfect love." He read it over again each morning, preparing his heart for the days to come, and reminding himself of how important this was.

Chapter 16

My neck burned as a reminder of the rock I had used as a pillow for the mere hours I was able to drift in and out of sleep. The night had been void of noise, which I still found much more unnerving than the usual music of a wooded forest floor. It wasn't the only silence around, though. More descended on the trip as Cillian and I made our way through rocks jutting from the ground. Shadow was tiptoeing with clear discomfort over the sharp terrain, but he continued onward. Our water was almost gone, but thankfully the temperatures stayed mild even as the suns beat down upon us. I had caught a few glimpses ahead of green trees, the promise of a forest, as we made our way down the steep paths out of the mountains and into the Norwood.

Every attempt at conversation I had made was met with short or no responses. Cillian was genuinely beginning to irritate me. Much of the morning had been spent wondering what I could have done to upset him. Finally I dared to ask such a question and was met with a curt, "Nothing, I'm fine."

I scowled.

It wasn't unusual for silence to be uncomfortable; it had been used on me on more than one occasion as a punishment. Talking came naturally to me. Even when I was nervous, I would just speak faster instead of holding my tongue.

Diadred had taken Cillian ahead, bounding down the rest of the way until his paws found flat ground in front of more massive pines, just like the ones I had first seen upon my entrance to this realm. These trees were even more enormous as we turned further north into the forest, noting the temperatures drop again. If that continued to happen, this shirt wouldn't do much to keep me warm.

Sensing my discomfort, Cillian spoke up, "It won't be much further now. We can move faster in here, there should be a sentry outpost soon. Once we arrive, we can get you something a bit warmer, a proper meal and sleep that isn't on rocks."

"Is the outpost the North Tower?" I questioned, hoping that meant no more travel.

"No, there are three outposts around the North Tower that are used by any weary travelers needing rest. Right now, winter hasn't fully moved in, but when it does this place will be covered in snow, ice and bitter winds. It makes travel difficult, to say the least. We need keen eyes to attend in case of any run-ins with the Shadow Sentries."

"Shadow Sentries?"

Cillian paused before continuing, "Yes, the Norwood guardians, well in a way. Very few people like to stay in the north for the obvious harsh winter and proximity to the Fallen. Long ago these Shadow Sentries served no one, rogues to no cause. There was a battle before The Closure, one that banished Abaddon and his first followers deep into the north. Master Olam and Medora led the charge, the Sentries intervened. Olam was concerned Abaddon would gain mastery of their unique gifts, so he challenged them and won their servitude. Given there is little to rule, Medora convinced Olam to allow her to keep them in the Norwood, acting as a barrier between the Fallen and the rest of the regions. These guardians are information gatherers and intimidators at best. Medora doesn't allow them to kill unless another life is at stake. Hopefully, we'll get lucky and they won't be around when we arrive."

Diadred sped up his pace and I pushed Shadow into a canter to keep up. Desperate to continue the conversation, I raised my voice to be heard above the noise my saddle made. "Why wouldn't we want the sentries to be there?"

"They are odd creatures; they can be downright terrifying when they want to be and they aren't of this world."

I scoffed, "What could be scarier than what I've seen so far?"

Cillian slowed Diadred down to a stop and Shadow copied him. "Lenora, don't be fooled, there are much darker things here. The closer we bring you to Abaddon, the more chances increase for your worst nightmares to come to life. You are right, the Shadow Sentries are nothing compared to what Olam is trying to protect you from." His voice was stern as he finished his warning.

Kicking Shadow forward, I quickened our pace deciding then to keep quiet, irritated. Fear had been far away most of the day, but the further we moved into the forest, the faster it began to reacquaint itself in my mind.

As a distraction, I urged Shadow into a canter, not because we had to, but it was nice to enjoy something exhilarating together. The ground was soft, and Shadow lengthened his stride, trying to push ahead of Diadred. Within seconds the two boys found themselves racing headfirst into a challenge. Pushing my hands forward, I shot a sly smile Cillian's way before lifting myself slightly out of my seat to square my weight more over Shadow's shoulders. He took the cue eagerly and moved into a gallop, swerving in front of the surprised cat. Trees flew by us, far apart, thankfully. This part of the forest had little to no underbrush growing anywhere.

Diadred let out a strange half growl, half purr as he came up on Shadow's flank, clearly annoyed with the maneuverer. Cillian laughed as I moved Shadow back and forth with the intent of keeping the pair behind us. I'm not sure how many miles we went on this way, but it was marvelous. I wished it would have lasted longer.

Everything happened so fast, I barely had time to register it all.

Something moved at us from the front with unnatural speed, a blur of black wings. My first thought were the Gangors with us being so much closer to their home. Shadow reared as something came at him from beneath the ground. I didn't stand a chance of keeping my seat as I tumbled backwards out of my saddle. My back hit first, knocking the wind out of me, and I did my best to scream Cillian's name. Strong hands had me by my upper arm, half dragging me to stand on my feet.

Looking around, I got my bearings; Shadow was rearing again, but I still couldn't see what had him spooked and Diadred was chasing something from tree to tree, actively slashing bark with his sharp claws. Cillian had put his back to mine, speaking calm and low with a sword drawn that required both hands to wield. Where the large black blade had come from, I didn't have the slightest idea, but I marveled at the engravings that seemed to glow.

"Stand down, we are here for rest and are headed to meet with Elder Medora."

Silence. To whom was he talking?

"Olam has given us protection and sanctioned passage. Stand down."

A sneering whisper caught my ear, sending chills down my spine as I instinctually formed balls of fire in my hands.

"How do we know you are friend and not foe?" the voice echoed through the forest as if they were multiple, all around us.

"You know." Cillian's words had a bite to it that time, as if he were daring the voice to challenge whatever authority he seemed to have here.

We had both been slowly scanning all around, alert to the presence of something moving between the trees. Truthfully, I did not see anything until it was there. Not thirty feet away stood what could only be the outpost, a modest building, like an old cottage which was much more than I expected. As if it had simply apparated from thin air, it was there.

Shadow seemed as baffled as I was, calming enough for me to grab his reins. Cillian began to relax his shoulders, loosening his grip on the hilt of his sword and calling for Diadred. We cautiously walked towards the building as smoke rose from a cobblestone chimney. There was a hitching post out in front of the porch where I tied Shadow, loosening his girth. Stepping inside, we were greeted by warmth from the fire as well as the aroma of potatoes. The promise of a warm meal suddenly had my belly begging for food. There were two beds on either side of the big open room, a dining table that housed bowls full of steaming something and an open cubby with what appeared to be animal fur coats.

"You are welcome here for the night, yet don't move further on your quest until the crest of morning light." Spinning into the eerie voice, I almost smacked Cillian square in the face. He was not as startled as he should have been. Something told me he was waiting for it.

Every bit of the terrible voice matched the hooded figure before me. It was draped in all black robes with huge, tattered wings tucked behind it's back that must have spanned the width of this cottage when they were open. I could not see a face through its hood, and the creature seemed solid but also made of smoke. The corners of its cloak faded away leaking into the shadows of the room, as if being beckoned to return. Large black-boned hands with clawed knuckles gripped the hilt of a sword, and surprise seized me as I realized it was the same sword Cillian was still wielding.

"Thank you, we will." Cillian replied.

With that it melted back into the shadows outside. Not a trace of the creature remained. Looking to my left, I caught Cillian also do a disappearing act with the sword he had been using. Briefly wiping his hands on a nearby hanging rag, he made the short journey to a dining table.

It took me a minute to unglue my feet from the floor to follow his lead, however strange it might have been.

After giving time for a few bites of what appeared to be brothy potato soup, I questioned him. "Shadow Sentries, huh?"

"Yep." He replied with a mouthful of soup.

"Why did you have a matching sword and how did you make it go away?"

Cillian took the time to engulf his soup, finishing the bowl completely before answering.

"That is their sword. They know if you wield it, you are a friend. There are other ways to grant safe passage, but that is the fastest and with them you don't get a second conversation." The look on his face told me he may have attempted one of those 'second' conversations before. "One of my gifts is weapon creation. I can manifest any needed weapon from my hands with a thought."

"Of course you can." I scoffed obnoxiously before correcting at his look of surprise. "Well, I mean, it's beneficial...for you to be able to do that." *You just mocked the man.* "Are they alive or...I mean...what are they? Also, I thought Medora won't let them kill?" I stumbled around my words.

"They are living, each individual but one single entity. I'm not sure what they are made of, but shadows are involved, they use them. You can ask Medora more when we get there. She'll know more about her creepy critters. As far as killing goes, you're right, but there are still many other things that can be as bad, if not worse than death."

Something tugged at my mind unnervingly, something familiar yet foreign. Once again, I looked at my hands, the hands that had pulled from the shadows, created things. They were my hands, nothing special, yet they weren't. There was some new knowledge they came into that I don't believe they were ever meant to know. "Those shadow creatures I made, are they the same?" My throat tightened as the words left my lips.

Cillian swallowed, "No. At least I don't think so. This would be the closest thing to them that I've ever seen, but you pulled from the shadow, created something. These guys just use them to slink around as a camouflage or a portal. It's different."

Those green eyes of his found mine. He could see the oceans of anxiety and for once I could see his own worry swimming around. He didn't know, he was guessing, and that bothered him. These mysteries were foreign to a man who had lived who knew how long and seen most everything this world had to offer…except me.

As if he sensed my heart rate increase, he reached across to squeeze my arm that sat on the edge of the small wooden table. The worry hadn't gone, but honesty surfaced. He was ready to level with me, no more kid gloves. "Lenora, this all must be very unnerving; I'm surprised you are holding it together as well as you are. Understand this, the further north we go the more danger you are in and the less you can trust your own mind. No one can call on shadows that I know of, not even Abaddon, so keep that to yourself."

Chapter 17

The trees were bigger here, much bigger, if that was even possible. As I continued to guide Shadow forward, my neck craned back trying to see where the tops of the massive pines ended and the sky began, but I simply couldn't. They appeared to stretch on into the heavens. Trunks that shimmered, taking on a silver hue, unlike anything I had ever seen passed me on either side. I bet it would have taken ten people arm to arm to wrap around the base of these enormous living things. Only the gentle crunch of Shadow's hooves on the dead ground could be heard. Even as soft as it was, the sound seemed to echo through the forest floor. Diadred in his feline stealth was silent, as was Cillian. We had agreed to ride in silence. Not only were Shadow Sentries around, but it was always possible that members of the Fallen were scouting the area.

Turning my attention back to the trees, I marveled at the wonderous sight. Although the trunks and branches shimmered strangely, the needles were a familiar deep green. Not one breeze had drifted in since we entered. The stillness was comforting here though, and the fur coat that hugged my shoulders tightly warded off the bitter cold. Shadow had traded fancy Karakum garments for fur blankets and even a new saddle. The odd cottage had supplied more than food and dreamless sleep. We all were clothed more appropriately, footwear included. Fleece lined boots that had been a perfect fit hugged my calves as they swung with freedom in stirrups with thinner leather straps, allowing a much-needed pressure release in my knees. Shadow's new saddle reminded me of the Australian ones back home, but even then, it wasn't the same. Whatever it was, I was grateful for the supple leather and fur-topped seat full of comfort that rivaled anything I had ridden in before.

We must have gone close to ten miles by now, if I was gauging our distance with any close accuracy. It had not been a casual stroll either, this being the first lengthy rest at a brisk walk through the ethereal pines. It was much needed for Shadow as his heavy breathing could be clearly seen in the frigid air. Splotches of white appeared on the ground up ahead, a sign of snow. Diadred seemed to never tire as he trotted up ahead of us while Cillian mumbled something about being close to the outer boundary of the North Tower.

Further in there was more snow. What had only been small patches turned into blankets, and little of the dark earth remained visible. It was old snow, there was none in the trees, and it wasn't powdery but icy and solid as Shadow's hooves punched holes with loud crunches. I thought I saw a glimmer, like glass, a sheer screen that blurred the rest of my vision ahead. Cillian had dismounted and was now walking, waving me to hurry forward. We had fallen behind quite a bit.

After moving Shadow up, I stopped at Cillian's command feet away from the strange shimmering curtain that blurred the rest of whatever lay beyond. "What is this?" I questioned softy as Cillian approached it cautiously.

"We're here." He had already called the sword of the Shadow Sentries to his hand while he walked along the edge of the curtain.

Here...it was supposed to imply safety, but none of Cillian's posture said that. Something was wrong, that much I knew without asking.

Urging Shadow forward to follow behind, the hair on my neck stood up. It wasn't the cold that caused it, either.

Cillian was looking for something. What, I didn't know, and it didn't seem to be the time for questions. His ear was turned to the curtain for some reason. After another thirty yards, he stopped short, stepping back again. Reaching his arm in, he vanished.

Diadred snatched his head back, appalled and confused. Shadow approached cautiously, snorting, not wanting to get any closer to the curtain that just ate their friend. I knew there had to be more to it than that. Within seconds a head popped out, Cillian's.

"Found the door, just follow my path in the snow straight through." He attempted an encouraging half smile before retreating in.

Diadred went first, then after lots of sweet talking, Shadow risked stepping through.

It felt like walking through door beads, except they were wet and mildly electric. On the other side was a clearing with many cottages stretching towards a large mass of rock jutting about one hundred feet out of the ground. Atop the mass was a small, dark gray stone castle, something simple that seemed to be exactly what I'd seen in Scottish travel ads as historical bed and breakfasts.

Cillian had sprinted with Diadred towards a group of people gathered around. I dismounted Shadow and was walking towards them when I caught the sound of crying, not just mild crying but tears of mourning.

As I stepped into the circle, the sight laid before me caused me to cover my mouth with a hand as a small gasp escaped. There was a young man on the ground, small bushes growing where his eyes had been, and lack of movement told me he was no longer with us. Vines extended from his arms, weaving into large branches that lay broken near him. His legs were tightly bound and were being cocooned by the same vines.

On the right a young boy, barely old enough to be a man, kneeled with hands out, begging him to rise again with chants I didn't understand. Behind the boy stood a ridiculously small elderly woman with curly hair facing Cillian's direction with a hand on the boy's shoulder. To her left stood two other young men who I could have sworn were related to the deceased. One quietly sobbed while the other tried to maintain composure for who I could only assume was a brother, whether by blood or in combat.

"He's gone, dear." The older woman tried to pull the young boy away from his frantic attempts at healing. He finally dropped his arms as if in defeat and hung his head.

My heart sunk as the others all bowed their heads in reverence, except one.

A woman, extremely tall with skin white as snow and hair black as coal. She was strikingly beautiful with steel gray eyes that I thought would pierce my very soul, peeling back all that I held. She stepped up to the other side of the older woman, placing a large hand on the boy's shoulder. We all stood silently for a moment before they began to quietly hum. The tall woman lifted her hands to the sky. "From dust you were made, to dust you shall return." Her voice commanded reverence from the very trees.

A minute later the woman started quietly giving orders to prepare the body for burial, who I believed to be Elder Medora.

Cillian stood frozen, face locked on the young man lying lifeless on the ground. A sharp voice rose shrilly when a quick movement caught my eye. The woman with curly hair had started towards us, shaking her fist in our direction. "This is all your fault, you and your foolish Master. Olam should know this boy's blood is on his hands!" Fury raged in her face as tears welled in her eyes. Within seconds she slammed both fists into Cillian's chest, collapsing into his arms.

He let her scream, this small old woman, releasing her fury onto him. There was water pouring from her face as she cursed us all. Every bit of me wanted to comfort her. I had no idea what had happened, but it was heartbreak, and heartbreak always needed someone to blame. Silently, I determined in that moment that if I ever needed to be that person, I would take it.

Cillian spoke softly. "Relca, I am so sorry."

What could you say...nothing that would bring their friend back.

She stepped back to gain composure, "Sorry? You aren't sorry. Did you even know his name, Cillian?"

She waited.

He didn't, that much was obvious.

"No. I didn't think so, and you don't deserve to clear your conscious with the knowledge." She spat at his feet as she walked away. Something in me surged, the fire rose. I knew she was hurting, but how dare she disrespect him like that. In a simple second my feet moved from the ground as the heat boiled beneath my skin, begging to be released, surprising even me as I lurched forward.

"Let her be." Cillian had reached an arm to block my trajectory.

Taking a deep breath, I asked the animal in me to subside. Reluctantly it did.

"He died saving us, you know," came the sweet voice of the boy who finally had stood at the Elder's insisting. He couldn't have been more than seventeen, a handsome kid who'd clearly been to hell and back.

Medora used her same commanding voice, except with a salve of empathy to send him back to the castle to rest. He listened without question, quietly dragging in the direction of the rest of the group.

Those deep gray eyes met mine, not as warm as I was secretly hoping for. She then settled her gaze on Cillian, who was desperately trying to put his own face of stone back in place. Reaching out, she forced him into a hug. "Don't take what the old nag said to heart, she's just hurting."

"I know. What in the name of Olam happened here? I haven't seen your shield up in decades."

Medora sighed. "They came under attack after a training mission in the forest went sideways. The young man, Silas, he held them off until his brothers and Relca could get the boy to safety." She shook her head gently as she continued. "From what I gather, there were too many Gangors and Fallen, but what made them retreat...there was a woman. This woman had a power I've never heard of. It seemed wise to raise the shields until we can reassess."

"What was it?" Cillian questioned.

"Honestly, I don't know, you'll really have to ask one of them for a better description, but it overtook everyone quickly." She shifted her gaze back to me, "So this is her, huh? The one everyone is outraged about?"

"My name is Lenora." I held my hand out. She took it and smiled.

So, she can smile.

Medora held the warmness for a moment before letting it droop. "You don't look like much, but you really have my Shadow Sentries concerned...and only Abaddon does that."

Lilith sat waiting in a velvet chair, casually tapping her nails on the side of the small marble table. Fire crackled in the fireplace of the study, an insufferably warm room that she wished to be rid of as soon as possible.

She knew Abaddon was making her wait purposefully, another method of control, just because he could.

No matter. Today she would enjoy this meeting.

She heard him before she saw him enter, dressed in a dark blue suit. He was in a pleasant mood, which made it even more enjoyable to ruin it.

"What news do you have for me?" He walked over to kiss her on the cheek before moving to a matching chair near the fireplace. There was a bottle of wine and a goblet waiting for him on the side table; he went to pour first.

Standing, she walked over to the window, pushing apart the drapes to allow the frigid air to trace her cheeks, washing over her face. Today she had chosen a dazzling red gown that slit up to the better part of her thigh, another favorite of his.

"Silence doesn't befit you. I haven't seen you in days, there must news to share with me?"

A smirk pulled at the corner of her mouth as she crossed the room to pour herself a glass of wine before speaking. "Well, Eydis was almost worthless, thanks to you; but I fixed her. Now we have a wonderful new weapon to terrorize whomever, in the name of avenging her daughter." She watched Abaddon look her over, that smile plastered to his face.

"Well, that's vague. Sorry you don't approve of my methods but thank you for cleaning up my mess. Who knows, maybe I rely on you for just that." He shot her a wink before taking a long sip from his glass.

"Thank you for the faith. Well, at least she's useful now. I took her for a spin earlier, I thought an attack on the North Tower would be a clever way to get some air." Lilith watched him spit his wine back as she took a long sip of her own, pretending she didn't see.

He was too good to snap back. He needed control but she could feel the heavy stare. Her eyes met his as she played coy. "What? I mean, you almost ruined her, I needed to see what she could do; and boy, did I see a lot."

"The Towers and Elders are off limits without my approval. You know this, there are rules." His words were slow, intentionally so.

"Well, you weren't around to ask." She shrugged as she crossed back to the window.

He was fuming, but there was little he could do to her, and he knew that.

She pushed him further, "Had you been in the area or given me insight as to where you might be, I would have asked. Lately I can't find you anywhere. You aren't sharing anything, so why should I? The most important thing is, she did marvelous; she's both powerful and useful. Something that has become quite rare around here."

"It was a foolish risk; I'm not ready yet. We still don't have Lenora, or have you forgotten that?" Abaddon used his nail to scratch the glass while he spoke.

Annoyed, Lilith continued and avoided his question completely. "Don't you want to know what she did?"

He paused; he knew she wouldn't just say that for any reason.

Lilith excitedly looked his way, as if she were a child bringing in something to show a proud parent. "I don't know how, but she channeled water into fire into electricity."

Lilith knew he would want to know more.

But he didn't say anything.

Walking over, she met a now-standing Abaddon eye to eye, "We can do it, we can take Olam. Kill off the Elders, take the Shining City and gain control of the portal. Between the three of us, we stand an excellent chance. What's the point of Lenora now? We don't need her!"

Turning his back, he slammed the goblet down with anything but pride or approval on his lips. "You truly are a fool. We do need her. We can't advance with 'an excellent chance', we need assured defeat. On another note, you just took something new and revealed it to the enemy." Seething, his tone burned, but his voice never rose. "It took half a century to hone you. We can't just run in with some powerful toy that has no allegiance to me." He shook his head. "You must get rid of her, we can't risk it. Send her to the pit and remember to whom you answer. Lilith, you are not in charge."

Lilith couldn't believe it. Well, she could. He was anxious, intimidated, almost unsure. There had been too much *new*, things he couldn't control or predict, but there was something else there too. Secrets being kept from her about Lenora. Every cell in her body wanted to tear him apart here. Lilith knew her days were numbered, anyway.

Tactically, he had a point. She had known the risk when she'd done it; but if he had any faith in his own methods, in the plan Lilith knew, he'd utilize Eydis.

Unless there was a different plan.

New. It was never good. It hadn't been for Lilith. She thought with such a superior gift he would be glad to use Eydis, even as a simple distraction.

He saw her mind wandering. "You will do it; you know I'm right." He had walked over and gently stroked her cheek with his thumb. "There's only room for one special lady around here, and I don't see you ever stepping down. You see, we need to get Lenora; she is our focus, not this defective woman." He gave her a smile.

In a blur, his claws were out as he slashed the side of her cheek wide open. Red streams of blood dripped down to her neck as she went to snatch away. It was too late. He grabbed her chin with his hands, hard.

"To remind you just how much you mean to me, why don't you stay with me tonight. It's been years, and I've missed you. I'm thinking we go for a new record, test some of your pain tolerances, eh?" Turning on his heels, he walked away, out the door and down the hall, footsteps slowly receding.

Ah...*that* was it. He wouldn't risk another version of Lilith around. No matter how powerful Eydis was, he had learned his lesson already.

His request wasn't anything of the sort, it was a silent command. One she couldn't ignore, no matter how much she wished to do so. Tonight, she had misjudged him. Each day she seemed further from him. He was the fool, Eydis was useful, more so than he would ever be. This could be salvaged though, and the more she thought about it, she realized this could work in her favor.

Eydis was not likely to be controlled. Befriended, possibly, but she was explosive. Bombs were useful, though, and she would make sure to detonate this one carefully.

Chapter 18

"Ivoriene, thank you for your help." Olam greeted the beautiful creature as one did an old friend. "Has the girl been worried?" he questioned concernedly.

"I'm sorry, sir, she's too close now. They must be deep in the Norwood. No longer can I see or hear her. I could join them in the north; you know all you need to do is ask." Antlers lowered, she bowed gracefully, as one does to a King.

"Not now. We can keep them safer if we stay away. I'm calling a meeting of the Elders, they are already on the way. I'll need your help keeping the city safe."

"Isn't that unwise, Olam? Abaddon will suspect an attack is on the horizon."

"Yes, but he won't move yet, he's not ready. Ivy, I have need of you here, it's time. I'll be leaving soon, and you shall assume residence in the palace alone, for now." Olam turned to place his hand on her head, stroking her regal neck once more. "You have served me well, dear one. Now I leave you to serve those I love."

Closing her eyes, Ivy heaved a big breath, letting out a nicker and leaning her muzzle into his hand. "We can only hope she makes it back...are you sure it's all worth it, Master?"

His white eyes lit up as his mouth turned upward into a contagious smile, one full of heart. "Always. In every realm and every lifetime, it will always be worth it."

"We thought we made it; we were so close to being back." One of the brothers, Kristo, took a deep breath as he recounted the story to Cillian. "The Gangors had fallen back...except her. Lilith rained down powerful winds of fire as Relca shielded us with water, her own. Elder Dondi wasn't lying when she said she was powerful." Looking over, he shot the woman a small smile, who returned with a nod to continue. "Trevir was injured, a Gangor had shredded his arm and he was losing blood fast. We couldn't retreat further while we waited for the boy, Peeke, to heal him." Quiet sobs were coming from Trevir, no doubt feeling burdened with guilt, but his arm didn't show the first sign of injury. Cillian couldn't help but be impressed by whatever healing abilities the boy had, but he was equally furious that Lilith would attack a tower. It told him she was growing increasingly bold and he needed to do everything he could to buy Lenora time.

"Go on." Medora urged him back to the story.

Drawing another breath, he began to tremble. "She came out of nowhere, with magic I've never even heard of...I can't."

Cillian put a hand on Kristo's shoulder. "What did Lilith do, son? We need to know."

His face went blank as he met Cillian's. "It wasn't Lilith. It was another woman, a woman from Antola. She was one of us, but...no longer one of us."

Color drained from Cillian's face as Kristo described the death of his brother Silas.

"She pulled water directly from Relca and turned it to blue flames that engulfed her arms. From the flames she threw lighting. Silas stepped in front to shield us, sending vines from the ground her way to build a wall, but it was too late. The lighting hit him and he fell, his magic going haywire, vines everywhere as if rebelling against him. It was so fast, then the bushes grew from...his...eyes." Kristo looked like he would be sick. Medora gently ushered the boys back out of the small meeting room we were in, commanding they rest again.

Cillian's mind was reeling. There were more of her; this was a nightmare. Lilith on her own was dangerous enough without having an attack dog. Lenora was anxiously tapping her foot on the ground. Relca still hadn't bothered to look at him, but she would have to get over it. There wasn't any time to tap dance around each other's feelings. They were all in very real danger.

"Relca, who was she?"

Silence.

"Relca, did you recognize her? He said she was of your people?"

Nothing.

Cillian was losing patience.

"R..."

"Relca! You will speak when spoken to right now, by the suns. This is no time for pettiness. If you care about any member of your troupe dying out there, you will tell Cillian everything he needs to know, now." Medora had reentered the room, eyes darkening. This woman could command armies with that voice. She looked the part today too, with the sleek black hair pulled back in a tight bun, her black pants, black tunic, black boots and a blue belt that sat above her hips holding a black sword on her right.

Relca's face dropped only ever so slightly before turning to Cillian. "I don't know how she's doing it; I've never seen or heard of anything like this. She is from Antola, one of the kindest women in our region. She was on a trek, to clear her mind from problems at home. Her daughter Kai hasn't spoken since she left."

Cillian thought learning would be helpful. It wasn't. A picture of the precious girl who held his hand during the Day of Mayim flashed before his eyes as his heart sank...

"Cillian," Lenora was on her feet and by his side before he knew it. She gently touched his arm. "What is it?"

Knowing what had to have been done to the woman to push her here...Anara's face slammed into his mind, it was too much.

Will you find her here too, Cillian? Maybe she's waiting just further north to tear you to pieces...could you do it...could you kill her? If you justify killing this little girl's mother, surely you would have to put Anara out of her misery... Even though Abaddon wasn't here to torment him, his mind created the rabbit hole on its own...he couldn't answer it either.

Soft hands squeezed his arm again, pulling him back to the room. He looked down to meet Lenora's worried face, full of concern, for him. She had pulled herself close, desperately looking for reassurance that he indeed was going to be fine. Flashing her a smile, he turned back to Medora and Relca.

"I met the daughter, Kai, on the Day of Mayim. The father told me. It's simply hard to imagine the girl never getting her mother back, even though she's alive around here." Cillian took a deep breath and locked Anara back in the box she belonged in. "Nevertheless, we need to secure the perimeter. Medora, how well can you maintain the shield?"

"Easily. The shield works well, but it's not perfect. My powers allow me to choose who gains entrance but once you've gone through, you can come and go as you please. Sometimes it can't discern if someone has passed through, so you can potentially walk strangers through."

Cillian cut in. "I doubt we have anyone who wants the enemy here."

"Let's hope. We're well stocked on supplies thanks to Olam, so we can wait them out awhile here. Along with the shield, I have my Shadow Sentries at our call, and my sword." She patted the hilt of the large blade on her hip.

"Karakum might be sending a small group of their people, trained in combat. I'm not sure how many." Cillian tried to put the hope back in his voice for Lenora, but he was doubtful anyone else would come.

"Relca, can you take over equipping every able body here? We will need everyone we can get, no matter their age. Their ability to protect themselves may be the only thing that keeps them alive in the days to come." Reluctantly, she agreed.

The millions of stairs from the castle to the ground were at least easier to climb down than up. Town didn't seem to fit; it was, more simply put, a cluster of cottages around the base of the rock mountain that held the Tower. The North Tower itself only had about thirty who lived there year-round. Most were warriors like Medora, other than a few who tended the grounds, cooking and cleaning. If you came to live here, it seemed a lonely life but rewarding, knowing you were a barrier between those who would cause harm and those who could be harmed.

It had been a lovely tour of the grounds. They were quite simple, all stone and wood. Fires burned in every room, with no color to grace the halls. There were no windows because of the bitter cold that resided outside in the deep of the season.

Temperatures had dropped again, requiring a heavier coat than I had been provided earlier. Shadow was currently put up in a barn that had a hole in the middle which allowed smoke to rise out from a large stone fireplace, keeping the animals warm at night as the temperatures fell further.

Night had descended as I followed Cillian back into the forest. We were staying within the shield, but Medora had stretched it further north to give us a place to train without curious eyes watching. The tree trunks glowed in the moonlight of the seven moons, now sitting high in the sky. One sat larger than the others in the center with six positioned around it creating a star shape. Wonderous didn't begin to describe the sight. Awestruck was more accurate and surprised I had been here so long without witnessing their beauty.

A small snap pulled my head down and back to Cillian, who was still moving deeper into the forest. He was adamant that we get as far away as possible to work on some of my gifts, specifically my shadows, which required discretion. I jogged to catch up. There was a small clearing encircled with pines and a massive oak-like tree in the center. He seemed to know the place, because we headed straight for it. I had thought the pines were magnificent, but while they were taller, their beauty was nothing compared to this tree. The trunk stood wide and white, smooth too with small, stretched lines of light gray that twisted around. The leaves were small, oval shapes and they were everywhere, a deep yet bright red. Its branches were mighty, stretching their thick arms outwards. I was surprised to find how bright it was, thanks to the light from the moons. The tree bark was glowing, too, from its own light.

"Cillian, this place is simply breathtaking." I meant it, every word. Each time I thought these lands couldn't surprise me anymore, they did.

He came to stand next to me as I continued to stare, mesmerized by the tree. "It's the only one of its kind, protected here. I always forget to ask why Olam didn't make more, but he is known for his love of things that are extraordinary."

"It sure is that." I reached out to touch one of the leaves that I imagined would be like velvet, but something stopped me. Not an invisible force field, but it was as if to do so would defile it or cause great harm. An even deeper of a truth tickled my mind; that this tree had already caused more harm than I could ever imagine.

Odd.

Cillian had been watching me ever so closely before speaking. "Well, at least that part of you is like the rest of us. Can't touch the tree."

"Pardon?"

"No one can touch it, and no one can really say why. I asked Olam about it once, a long time ago. He said it wasn't for me to know."

"Well, that's frustrating. You didn't ever ask again?"

"No. There are some things that aren't meant for us to know. I trust Olam, he didn't want to share, end of story. Still, I was hopeful you could touch it."

There it was again, that mutual respect he demonstrated that attracted me to the man even more.

Turning back to the tree, I heard a small breeze move the leaves. The sound took my breath away. I had heard it once before. Recognized as the same music that played upon entry into this realm of Starpathia, the seductive sound I had followed through the tears in their world.

Cillian was talking, I thought, but there was no way to pull my eyes from the tree as the branches continued to dance in the wind, the song getting louder. Staring intently, I let out a small shriek when a dark black snake moved up the trunk. As it slithered higher, the white bark began to turn black, and powder fell from the tree. Like a disease, the darkness spread as the snake grew bigger, going higher in the tree. The leaves began to wither and fall, turning to ash. In a simple minute, the entire creation before us had been tainted, a naked burnt trunk with feeble branches in its place. The snake had risen and wrapped around the top, waiting, watching.

Something heavy touched my shoulder. "Did you hear me?"

Whirling around, I locked eyes with Cillian.

He frowned. "What's wrong?"

Panicked I pointed back to the tree, "The snake, he..."

There before my eyes was the tree, restored back to the beauty I saw when I had entered the clearing. "What...but it..."

"Lenora, what snake?"

"No, he was there, and the tree..." Puzzled, I studied the leaves again. The breeze was blowing gently, but no music could be heard. Whatever had just happened, it was apparent it had only been seen by me. Cillian was wrong, I'm not the same. I may not be able to touch it, but something told me that vision meant something. The last thing I needed to do was add to Cillian's stress level, and I wasn't convinced what I saw was something I needed to bother him with. "Well, it's gone now...maybe the day is just getting to me, or weeks, ha."

Flashing a sweet smile his way, I stepped away from the tree. "Teach me, oh great one." I laughed; a bit more than I should have. Cillian didn't seem as amused, but I swatted playfully at his arm, trying to lighten the mood.

"This is serious. We need to run through what you can do, and I want you to call on each gift. They won't be as helpful if you can't control them. Let's start with fire, it's easy enough to bring up."

He was right, I had a lot of it, and it didn't take much to do the easy things. Pulling my gloves off, because I was unsure if I would burn them, I closed my eyes tightly. With a few simple thoughts of home and the Gangors, my hands were covered in flames. I threw a few balls around into the ground to keep from harming the trees.

"Good. Do you feel confident you are mastering it and it's not mastering you? The Fallen are all angry. The more it consumes you, the more uncontrollable your fire gifts can become. I don't want that for you, so be careful. It's one of the easiest ways to get lured in."

Rolling the fire around my hands, I wondered when anyone would elaborate more on Abaddon. I felt like I knew his history but virtually nothing about what I was supposed to be fearful of that he could do.

"Now, the shadows."

My hands dropped the fire, "Could we ferry instead?"

"No." he said sternly. "It's too dangerous, you could end up outside the shield. I can't help you with that gift, no one can. You should only use it if you have no other choice."

Let's dabble with darkness and play with shadows...but no, we can't work on the one thing that will keep me safest. My mind mocked the decision, but I knew it was no use to argue it now. It had always been about the shadows. Intrigue, fear, or both drove him to want to know more. As for me, I was bothered that I was excited, and not afraid at all to call back out to the shadows.

Hours ticked by. Finally, I flopped onto the freezing ground to stare up at the moons. They had moved, and only three were still visible above the treetops. No matter how I tried, I couldn't pull at the shadows, nothing, nada, zip. Cillian shared my frustrations; we recreated all the feelings, tried everything he knew to try to help, but it was useless.

"Maybe it's gone?" I resigned, leaning my arms on my knees as the cold laid heavy around us.

Cillian shook his head, "No. Power like that doesn't just show up once to disappear. It's still around."

"It wasn't emotional, it was intentional, but these hands aren't doing anything." Lifting my palms to flip them back and forth, I let them drop in frustration.

"Well, it's no use staying out here all night to freeze. Let's go sleep, and we'll resume training first thing in the morning." Cillian offered me a hand to stand up. I took it. But my foot caught a root and I stumbled forward, falling into his strong arms. He gently pulled me up. As our bodies came together to touch, something like a small spark shot between us, then I met his eyes with mine. He didn't let go, and I had no interest in pushing away. The freckles across his nose were barely visible in the low light, but those green eyes sparkled. For a brief second, I thought he was going to kiss me, but instead he stood me back up completely and we made our way to the Tower in silence. A comforting silence we seemed to mutually share, one I enjoyed increasingly with him. In my own world I couldn't ever sit with silence, but with him next to me I'd do it eternally.

Chapter 19

Hiding her would be near impossible. Killing her was out of the question, but maybe she would stay on her own accord. Lilith had kept her word; she was the only person who seemed to be advocating for Eydis. It was risky, very risky, but she didn't have a better plan. Not that Lilith cared if Eydis went off to wreak havoc on unsuspecting nobodies, but she would be so much more useful if she did as she was told.

Walking through the door of the small shack near the river brought back memories of her last hunt. Since then, the older man had left and the area abandoned. It was highly unlikely that anyone would wander this way for a long while. The location was far enough south of their mountain to keep Abaddon or any commanders from nosing around, and the last thing anyone would think is that Lilith just let the woman go.

It smelled musty, and it was ice cold; perfect for her, but she wanted Eydis to be alive when she returned, so she went over to the fireplace to start a fire. Once it was burning hot, Lilith unpacked the sacks of food, clothing, and blankets, and set them up around the cabin. Eydis had asked to go down to the river. Lilith was hesitant, but if Eydis wanted to run, nothing could stop her. Lilith's hope was that in giving the woman her freedom, she would choose to stay.

"Thank you." The soft voice startled Lilith, and she turned to see the still too small frame of Eydis in the doorway. Her feet were bare, and the bottom of her pants wet. Lilith smiled; she had chosen to stay, and by the looks of it, found the water. "It's beautiful here. The cold, the ice in the river, the silence. I feel so dead, but the pain from the cold makes me feel…"

"…alive." Lilith finished the sentence for her. "It does. I will never understand the people who can't appreciate the cold. There's more food over on that shelf. I'll be back in a few days. It's not wise to leave, but I promise when I return, we will avenge your daughter." A small ping of guilt hit her as she left Eydis to head back to the mountain, something she hadn't felt in a long time. Quickly, she dismissed it. Now was not the time for sentiment. No, she had waited far too long for this, and she would finish it.

Cillian had decided to let Lenora sleep a bit more, and as dawn approached he moved quietly down the castle corridor. It was always dreary inside. He had told Medora before to find someone to decorate or put out a few plants, anything to add some life. Headed to the dining hall he passed quite a few servants, no doubt there would be others up early getting breakfast before they started to train. This building always did bring back so many memories. He had stayed here, training, after his father went missing. It was comforting to be back around the familiar grounds and the comfort of the cold. Entering the hall, he scanned the long wooden tables for a familiar face. It didn't take long for his eyes to find the two he was looking for.

"Well, look who the cat dragged in." Cillian's voice was full of joy as he walked up behind the unsuspecting men.

They didn't even need to see him to know. Each turned around, pushing away the stools to hug their dear friend, exclaiming how wonderful it was to see each other again.

Cillian pulled up a seat as he listened to small talk and stories of what had been going on in their quiet corner of the world. It always amazed him how the two brothers couldn't look more different; Eleazar had deep brown skin, brown eyes, and thick black hair, while Osten had blond hair, fair skin, and blue eyes. Their statures were different too, with Eleazar standing tall and lean while Osten was shorter with broad shoulders and big arms. Studying their features closely, he marveled at how little they had aged. Cillian had been granted long life from Olam for his service, but these two, their mother was Elder Feldrid. Elders weren't supposed to age, yet Feldrid always had, as long as he could remember. Cillian assumed it had something to do with breaking the Elders' oath, but these two seemed to have inherited that anti-aging gene. They were over one hundred now, yet Cillian at fifty looked older than they did.

"Enough about our farm life, how's our favorite wanderer?" Osten tapped Cillian's arm with the back of his hand to urge him on.

"Nothing worth talking about."

"What you really mean to say is, staying nowhere long, eating horribly and still sleeping with that cat," Eleazar teased as they all let out a few laughs.

"You got me, not much has changed." Cillian sighed a bit heavier than he intended, although it matched the heaviness in his heart.

"Your new travel companion seems to be quite the important one. Do we really think she's safe here?" Eleazar asked.

"Not at all." Cillian was sure she was always in danger with Lilith and Abaddon after her. "I'm sorry you two are back here, having to face him again."

"We're not the only ones having to visit old nightmares; I know this can't have been easy for you either, after all this time. Between us, Olam should have let us destroy him last time, not just drive him back into the mountains." Osten lowered his voice and leaned closer to Cillian. "Have you taught her how to protect her mind?"

Cillian's eyes fell to the floor in embarrassment, "No."

The brothers didn't do much to hide their shock.

"She should have known, *yesterday*." Eleazar firmly stated.

"It's not like I didn't want to, we simply haven't had time," Cillian snapped back before lowering his own voice. "I'm going to do it this morning, but I haven't gone back to those memories in a long time. Honestly, I'm not sure what's left in there, which is why I need your word that if I fail, you two will protect her."

Osten grabbed Cillian's shoulder with a nod, "We're in this together, you know. Between us, the chatter amongst the leaders is if she fails, we're toast."

Cillian's brow furrowed, "Fails at what?"

"Killing Abaddon, of course." Osten chuckled.

There was no laughter in Cillian's eyes. He knew she would need years of training to ever possibly be able to succeed. He also knew Olam would never expect such a thing...*would he?*

Abaddon let the door slam behind him as he entered a corridor on the east side of the dungeons adjacent to the Shadow Boxes. At least Lilith finally agreed with him. He expected more out of her, but then again, it was the part he couldn't control that made her a force to be reckoned with. A few years ago, her impatience had really started to show, and she'd been acting out ever since. Getting fooled by Cillian did a number on her, and almost cost them a lot more than would ever be worth risking. They were both tired of sulking in the mountains, having to live so carefully and only getting the scraps of people foolish enough to wander too far, or simply too broken to even enjoy toying with.

Olam had it all, had taken it all. Lilith always shared that with the Elder, a vision for more. The portal linked every world Olam had ever created, and no one knew how many realms of Starpathia there were. Abaddon had seen many, in his early days when he had been foolish enough to serve Olam. Lilith was the one who inspired him to take it all for himself. He deserved it. He wondered if, one day, she would try to take everything from him. It was unlikely, but never off the table. Never had he been so foolish as to believe he was safe from her wrath, if she ever was emboldened enough. However, he could still end her if the need arose after Olam was gone.

It had taken half a century to gain her compliance, devotion to their cause but never fully to him. As much as he hated admitting it, he needed Lilith and always had. Abaddon had power, but he was always going to need more power to destroy Olam.

There was the prophecy, the one she didn't know about, the one he'd been wrong about before.

Lilith had been the only one in one hundred years to show something new. He had worked hard to keep her ferrying ability a secret. It's how she'd escaped the dungeons so long ago, the first time. There were two now that Lenora had shown up, two to ever ferry. Each one the same; after they ferried, in poured more gifts, some unique, some common but immensely more powerful than others. It was a shame he was out of time, but obtaining Lenora would be more important than trying to control Eydis ever would be. He couldn't risk letting the one thing that could destroy him stay in the hands of his enemy.

Pulling open the cool iron handle, he listened to the heavy door scratch the stone floor as it slowly opened. Screams could be heard across the room. They were tired ones, hoarse, no doubt from enduring hours of agony. There was a torch bound to the wall near a large man who stood silently. The light bounced off his ebony skin, and his dark clothes made him almost blend into the room. Turning, he met Abaddon with a small nod. "Damion, thank you for coming on such short notice. Have we learned anything helpful?"

Damion stepped aside, revealing a man slumped over, chained to the wall. His wrists held large shackles, and he could barely hold himself up. "He held out longer than I expected. I went through every memory without finding much. The girl and Cillian ran, headed north. It would seem there's a small army on its way to the Tower as well. Nothing impressive, but enough magic among them to cause inconveniences."

Both legs were bent unnaturally to reveal many broken bones. His clothes had been stripped off him and there were gashes across him chest, arms and thighs. Abaddon walked over to grab the man's dark hair, pulling his head up to see his face. "Ouch. Shahara, I must say I don't think the ladies will look at you quite the same as they did before. Such a shame to mess up such a pretty face. I do apologize, but I can't have my spies failing now; it wouldn't be good for business." Shahara let out a small groan as Abaddon released his head to roll back forward.

"An army, eh? Well, we all knew they'd come for us eventually." Abaddon lit a small flame on his finger as he watched the fire dance.

"*Army* might not be the best word, my liege," Damion clarified.

"How many?"

"From what I could see about one hundred strong, maybe more."

Abaddon took a few steps forward, then back again. "Do we know where Lenora is?" He gave Damion a more serious look.

"There hasn't been any visual confirmation, but we are certain she is holed up in the North Tower. Medora has her shields up currently, making it impossible to know anything else."

"Unless someone gets in." Abaddon corrected.

Damion cleared his throat, "We also received word there is an Elder meeting being held in the Shining City tomorrow."

Abaddon furrowed his brow in offense. "No invite for me? Now that is rude." His mouth curled in a sly grin.

Walking back to the door, Abaddon pushed to leave but stopped short. "Damion, I do believe I have an urgent need for some extra expertise. After you take out the garbage, why don't you meet me upstairs. Send for Lilith, too. It's time for a family reunion and a field trip."

Dragging myself downstairs, I made my way for the front entrance to the Tower. The night hadn't treated me well and the few hours of sleep I did find where choppy at best. Opening the door, I caught a glimpse of the first few rays from the dawn. Being high up on the rock mountain allowed me to see past the trees and into the east. Colors of soft blue, purple, orange and yellow swirled as the light cut through the trees, spreading onto everything it touched as I made my way down the long stretch of stairs back to the ground. Each stair had been carved out of the rock, only wide enough for one other to pass around you on the side.

Cillian hadn't been in his room and I had quickly jumped at the chance to get away for a while on my own to ride Shadow. I couldn't stop thinking about the tree and what the vision had meant. It was exciting, to feel a part of my adventuring spirit return as I continued to practically run down the stairs. As I reached the bottom, I took note of a group across the snow-covered ground who were training with magic. Sometimes I had to pinch myself to remember where I was, and that this was my life, for now. I wondered if I would ever go home, but lately it didn't bother me as much when I contemplated never going back.

Shadow was happy to see me. Someone had blanketed him, for which I was grateful. Even with the fire roaring in the middle of the circular barn, it still was cool from the frigid air that drifted in. No matter where we were, the smells of a horse barn are the same, invigorating to my soul and more comforting than anything in the world. It had always been my safe space, a place of peace. Some people ran into the arms of their mother when they needed them, but I always had run to the barn, to throw my hands around the sleek black neck of my crazy mare when my world was falling. Tacking my boy up took a bit longer than usual with the extra blanketing required, but the growing anticipation to visit the tree pushed me.

Walking Shadow out, I was relieved to have not had anyone question me. People had passed by, but most barely even acknowledged my existence. These people seemed to keep to themselves. They had a job here, to keep evil away and that was that. I placed my foot in the stirrup and swung myself into the saddle while trying to keep Shadow still. It was cold, and he was trying to prance off. It had been a while since we had just been normal or had fun, so I gave him his head and we galloped off north, into the forest.

The pines were stoic, there was almost no breeze, but I swore as we went further the cold came in heavier. It took much less time to make it to the tree on horseback than when Cillian and I had walked. Even though I knew what to expect as we stepped into the clearing, the vision still took my breath away, especially as the snow began to lightly fall around us.

We walked closer to the magnificent oak. Shadow and I were breathing heavily, the smoky puffs from our exhales easily seen. The run had gotten both our blood pumping, warming us from the inside out. Something about the tree bothered my horse. He was on alert, snorting like Raya used to do when she assumed there something was dangerous.

"Shhhhh. There, there, boy, it's just a tree." My soft voice and pats on his neck helped ease the tension as I felt him relax some, but not completely. Clicking Shadow forward, I walked him around it entirely, noticing how wide it was, a grand oak for sure. Coming back to where we started, I faintly heard the sound of tinkling bells. It reminded me of fairies playing as the wind picked up through the trees, blowing the bright red leaves around. Shadow anxiously began to stomp his feet when the music became louder. "Can you hear it, too?" I questioned.

It was the same music as before, when we entered this world. I had heard it last night, but Cillian hadn't. Slowly, my view changed and the tree became what it had been in my vision from last night; black, barren, but this time the snake sat motionless. Today I wasn't scared, I wasn't even sure it was real; more like a vision of a past story, like a walking dream. As I watched, the tree returned to its normal, beautiful self for a moment before switching once more to the destroyed creation. This time, the snake was on the ground at the base of the trunk. Startled a bit, I backed Shadow up a few steps to add some distance between us.

The snake rose as the leaves began to grow back on what few remaining branches there were. Deep red leaves started dripping red liquid onto the snow-white ground. Some poured more, causing red to run down the branches like...blood. A metallic tang hit my nose as I realized, it *was* blood. The snake still didn't move. Wherever the blood went on the bark, the black was washed away and the beautiful white was restored. Branches started to regrow, more red leaves, more blood until the tree was more white than black, and over half of it returned to beauty.

Hissing hit my ears as I snatched my face downward; the snake was trying to retreat up against the trunk as the blood dripped onto him. It was burning him, like acid, until the snake was nothing but ash. In mere moments, the tree became fully restored, blood ceasing.

Shadow was stomping again, trying to turn us back in the direction of the Tower. I said no, desperately wanting to try to touch the tree again as something pulled at me. There was something here, something special and important that I didn't yet understand. Kicking him, I brought us forward, "Just a few more steps, come on Sha..."

The scream pierced my ears. It was blood curdling, it made me realize the music was no longer playing. It came from outside the shield.

Again. A second time, more horrifying than the first, it tore through the forest.

The shield boundary was right through those trees. I couldn't go through it; Cillian made me promise. I should go back for help first...

...they'll be dead by then.

Remember the last screams you heard...the Gangors already killed them, because of you.

The voice was right as the screams from Karakum rang in my ears.

Kicking Shadow, we ran through the trees further north, stopping short of the murky curtain that protected me from whatever was on the other side.

It could protect this person too.

Shadow stood like stone. Neither of us wanted to take another step. I could see a blob of movement coming towards the shield.

What if it's one of my teachers? What if it's someone come to warn us?

A third shriek let out but was cut short. The blob was no longer moving.

Did you just let them die? What kind of person are you? You're no warrior...

Putting my lips together I let out a shrill kiss as my heels dug into Shadow's side, a concise command forward. The same weird feeling washed over me as we galloped through the curtain, leaving the shield's safety behind. In seconds, I had my confirmation. Up ahead was a woman lying in the snow, which had begun to fall harder. She couldn't have been more than forty feet in front of us, as we ran to her. Grabbing my lead line, I practically jumped off my horse onto the soft ground, stumbling a bit before standing up fully. The woman was in a beautiful blue velvet coat with a fur hood. I had never seen her before.

"Ma'am, can you get up?" She let out a small groan as she turned her face to mine. She was gorgeous; I would say royalty. Pulling her hand from her stomach revealed a dark, oily spot on the coat. The red stain in the snow below gave away the bloody injury.

"Come on, I need you to get up and walk. I can get you to safety." Grabbing her shoulder, I threw her arm around me and heaved her up, thankful she was not a larger person. Anxiously, I looked behind us as we turned towards the Tower. The snow was falling even faster now giving me limited visibility. Hopefully for our sakes, that would be good, keeping us hidden from whatever attacked the woman.

We only had to make it about fifty feet to get to safety, but she was moving so slowly. It took us a lifetime to get there, but finally I felt the strange sensation of us crossing through the curtain onto the other side of the shield.

As soon as we were fully through, I sat her down against one of the large pines to assess her injury, hopeful I could leave her to get more help.

"Thank you, oh, thank you." The woman reached out to squeeze my hand, breathless. Her skin was ivory and her black hair fell around her face with a pair of stunning, ice blue eyes. She began to look frantically all around her, "Where's Anara, oh no, where is Anara?! Did another girl come through, my little sister?!" The woman screeched as she grabbed my arm with her bloody hand, tears streaming down her face.

"No, ma'am, I just saw you, I'm sorry. Let me get help and we'll send a search party for her." I tried to console her as she began to sob.

"We must get her, she's all alone, the Gangor will kill her! Please, I'll do anything, anything. There's no time." She tried to stand before falling back as she cried out in pain, clutching her side as fresh red blood ran down her dress.

Pushing her back down, I commanded her to stay. "You are in no shape to walk; you must stay here."

Pausing, I tried to think. There was no time, my mind was scrambled and the woman was frantic. Cillian would kill me, I needed to get him.

You have fire...magic, Lenora, you can do this...

"How many Gangors are there? Were they alone?"

"Yes, just one. It was a rogue. We were on our way to the North Tower for food. Our brother was taken by the Fallen, and we live high up in the mountains. Oh please, don't let her die, she's all I have." Reaching out, she grabbed my coat edge as I stood up, pleading with me.

Adrenaline pumping, I knew I had to retrieve the girl...or what was left of her. The snow had almost stopped, so I could see better as Shadow and I went back through the curtain. Our original tracks were gone, covered by the white powder. I dared not risk calling for the girl as we moved quietly through the trees. Thanks to the blanket of new snow, our movements were muffled, but there were no signs of a girl, or a Gangor.

Up ahead on my left, I thought I saw movement behind a tree. Goosebumps trailed across my skin as I cautiously turned Shadow in that direction. Clipping my reins to the small loop near my thigh, I called up fire into both hands. We had done no training on horseback, so I had no clue if Shadow would freak out, but it was worth the risk. Turning to the tree, I prepared to fire, but there was nothing.

No signs anything had been there either.

A scraping of bark came from behind, as I spun around to see a Gangor scurry up a tree, but before I could react, something solid slammed into the back of my head. In a matter of seconds all went black as Shadow jerked from beneath me. I felt my body go cold before slipping into an abyss of darkness.

Chapter 20

"Hello..." My voice came out scratchy as I dared to speak to the darkness ahead.

It didn't respond.

The grim hall seemed to go on forever. It was damp, and the hard rock felt cold beneath my bare feet. Leaning to one side of the wall, I let my right hand guide me. The blackness was all consuming, and I feared I would fall. Far ahead I could see a small light, just a dim glow from the ground, a space beneath a door.

Wincing, I touched my head again. I couldn't remember how I had gotten here, where here even was. Trying to remember just caused more dizziness as I gently massaged one of my temples to help with the pain, not stable enough to take my shoulder and weight from the wall. Stretching one foot in front of the other, I refused to stop. Forward was my only option. Some part of me knew there was nothing behind me. It was as if I had awakened while walking, there was no memory of my departure or arrival, simply waking up and walking this long hall.

Just a few more steps...yeah, right, you thought that ten minutes ago.

As if the light knew my hope was failing, it moved closer. Two more minutes and my long fingers met resistance, something hard but wood. Sliding both hands in front of me, I moved them across the grain, down and over until they felt something cold. My heart skipped a beat as my knuckles met to squeeze an iron door latch.

Click.

There it was. As I pushed with all the energy I had, the heavy door moved outwards.

Light flooded the hall, hurting my eyes. I threw my arm up in front of my face so they could adjust to the newfound space. Blinking back a few tears at the strain, I could begin to make out the scene. My feet had found soft ground. Pulling my head down, I looked at the bright green grass between my toes. Birds chirped all around, happily singing as if rain had just fallen. A soft scent of wildflowers drifted on a gentle breeze to meet my nose. Turning to my left, I saw a large oak tree. A picnic table sat beneath its grand branches.

There was a man.

My feet, on autopilot, brought me towards him. The scene was so familiar, yet I couldn't place it. Getting closer, I realized he was eating. There was a lovely picnic basket set out on a red and white checkered tablecloth. Real plates, sandwiches, fruit and a bottle of wine chilling in a beautiful wooden bucket.

"Lenora, darling. Welcome." The man stood after patting his mouth with a napkin. Extending his arm, he touched my shoulder and gently guided me to sit across from him at the table.

"Do I know you?" My voice was less raspy this time but still sore for some unknown reason.

The handsome face shied away at my question, looking down as if embarrassed. "Well, not really, but I know you. You've become quite famous around these parts, a bit of a local superstar." Grabbing a sandwich and some grapes, he passed them to my plate. "Please, go on and eat, I'm sure you're famished."

It was as though his words held superior power of suggestion. Immediately my stomach growled, and I found my mouth full of egg salad sandwich. Let me add, *divine* egg salad, some of the best I could ever remember eating.

He returned to his food; another man happy to sit in silence. So, I took a few extra moments to look around. Down the field, I noticed two more large oak trees.

I know this place...

A memory begged to be heard, but only as scratches on a door, desperately clawing at some invisible wall.

...I've been here.

"Now, darling, how are you feeling?" His voice snatched me back. "I will say, you look ravishing, all things considered." With that comment, I now took inventory of what I was wearing; a beautiful yellow sundress that contrasted well against my olive skin. My hair was pulled back into a low bun as I reached to touch the back of my head. Confused, I looked down again at the white sandals that graced my feet. "How..." No. I hadn't been wearing this seconds ago, but to be honest I'm not sure what I had been wearing, thanks to the darkness. I knew for certain my feet had been bare.

"It suits you. I can see now why you've taken his eye; he'd not be a man at all if not wooed by the likes of you. Such a simple, natural beauty you have." His smile twisted while something inside me shifted uneasily. "Yet another shame that we are here to talk business, and not pleasure." His eyes fell to my chest and I moved my arms up around me, worried he could see right through the dress.

"Business?" The fog in my mind was thinning. Not much, but I was getting my wits slowly about me. He didn't feign a response as I looked around again at the table, the trees, the beautiful green hill...

...the scratching became louder as a wall crumbled and the memory came out screaming.

Home! This is your home!

As if on a reel, the last weeks sped by in front of my eyes... Starpathia, Shadow, Cillian, Ivy, The West Tower, magic, the Fallen...the Fallen...Abaddon.

Slowly, I turned my head and made eye contact with the man. That same sly smile was watching intently with his leg bent, ankle across his knee. His hands were rested casually on his leg, one finger gently spinning in a circle, his eyes...his eyes were black.

Abaddon.

I knew it. He knew I knew it. Part of me wondered if he had even told me himself. Those eyes, I hadn't noticed them before, but maybe because I hadn't wanted to.

Trying to hide my fear, I confronted him. "We're not really here, are we? This isn't my home; it's some mirage you have painted."

"Close." He jumped up to walk around the table leisurely, hands behind his back. "True, we haven't actually left these lands you've come to love, but I didn't create this." Stopping, he motioned all around us. "No, if I had a choice we wouldn't be here; this is all you, my dear."

Puzzled, I paused and looked around. "What do you mean?"

"Now, I'm not going to tell you everything at once, it would spoil the fun." Abaddon continued to circle the picnic table, passing behind me.

Of course not, I was his prisoner. But how?

As if on command, the memories flooded in. The tree, the screaming, the woman, the shield, my head...a sharp pain shot through as a reminder.

She was bait. I had taken it, they had taken me.

"By golly, she's got it!" Abaddon skipped and turned before elegantly moving back into the seat across from me. Putting his head in his hands, he placed his elbows on the table to meet my gaze.

That twisted smile dropped my heart to my knees. Disgust stirred, and I thought I might get sick. The weight of what I had done fell heavily on me as I spoke softly. "Who was she?"

Sitting up straight, Abaddon didn't respond.

"Who was she?" I repeated, with a bit more courage than I felt.

Nothing. He was ignoring me, and enjoying it so.

Standing, I slammed both hands on the table as I screamed. "Who did I let in?!" The trees shook as something far off rumbled.

With that he glanced away, a small look of curiosity, surprise even played on his face. "Interesting... now, let's not get our panties in a bundle, shall we? You know who, it's a waste of my breath to tell you."

I had heard stories. I knew Abaddon had a woman who served him. She had attacked Cillian's friends, and anytime her name was spoken, Cillian's face twisted like his blood was raging war beneath his skin. Why, I didn't know. Abaddon was right, I knew. It was smart, I had never seen her so I would have never known her from a stranger. *Cillian, oh Cillian. I am so sorry.*

Biting back tears, I looked down the grassy hill as the wind blew softly.

I failed them. I let Lilith walk straight in the front door, and no one knew.

"They'll know soon enough, my dear. Don't be too hard on yourself. It is her style to just walk right in. There's nothing you could have done to stop her. We were always going to get you, you know."

The thing that was odd finally clicked. He was reading my thoughts.

"How are you..."

Abaddon cut me off with his own matched look of surprise. "They didn't tell you?" His eyes widened and I thought they sparkled. "Oh, you poor thing, they didn't tell you anything at all, did they?"

"W-w-what do you mean?" I stuttered, again trying to swallow my concern.

He let out a chuckle as he sat back, mouth gaping, appearing speechless. "This is a disappointment; I mean, I expected quite the challenge from you. Sure, I knew Cillian wouldn't want to talk about Lilith to his new crush, but to keep you totally in the dark was foolish even for him."

Mind games. Everyone had mentioned it, but no one had elaborated.

"I'm afraid it's much more than that." Shaking his head, he threw his hands up. "Arrogant men. Cillian especially, he has practically handed the entire world over on a silver platter." He mocked a sad face as he spoke. "What will Olam think now? The one weapon they had, now in my hands with no defenses."

Weapon?

"Please tell me they at least gave you a few self-defense lessons?" He questioned.

Yes. I needed to get away, I could summon fire easily enough.

With everything I had I pulled, reaching for the flames but finding nothing. Not even a spark or heat beneath my skin. It was gone.

Abaddon's face fell, another look of pity. "Tsk, tsk, tsk. My sweet Lenora, you are powerless here. But don't fret, you'll have a chance to use them again."

"What did you do to me?" Real fear began slithering up my spine, the kind you can't quietly talk down.

"It's not as if I could take them from you, I just bound you from them is all. You can't summon them in here." He tapped the side of his head.

Mind games. No. That's not possible. The realization hit me like a freight train.

"Oh, but it is," Abaddon replied as he mouthed the word *sorry*.

We were in my mind.

Abaddon stood up and buttoned the top button of his dress coat. "Right again, my sweet. Locked in tight." Smiling, he tapped the side of his head again. "We need to get to know each other better, and in here we can do just that, safely. Well, somewhat safely. Safe for me, not so much for you." He bowed at the waist and winked before walking away. "Now, enjoy your lunch while I go run an errand." With that he vanished, disappearing without a trace.

"Presenting the Master of The Elders, our Lord of Starpathia, Ruler of The Shining City, Olam Shammah." The man projected his aging voice as best he could to fill the room while each Elder rose and stood from around the large circular table. There were six beautifully crafted wood chairs set around, the largest plated with gold and a distinguished white stone set at the back towards the top. Each of the other five held different colored stones with intricate engravings around them.

Olam walked through the double doors, dressed in a long emerald-green robe as he made his way to the oversized gold chair. His face was worn, tired even, as he motioned for everyone to take their seats.

"Thank you all for coming on such short notice. As you all know, Abaddon has begun his tour of assaults. There have already been multiple attacks on our people by the Gangors in the Norwood. Medora was needed, which is why she couldn't attend, but it is time to take our places and provide our aid."

"Sir, with all due respect, we should have done away with this threat a long time ago. Instead, we've left him alone to stew for centuries." Elder Zubair was the first to speak. "If anything, this is our fault. Their blood is on our hands for not doing what we should have when he turned against you." His voice was anything but kind as he aggressively addressed his stance to their Master.

Elder Dondi's face was hardly concealable as she looked to her left, disdain written clearly in her tone. "Would you have had us murder our own, Zubair, just like that? Remember, Abaddon was your friend at one time; the two of you closer than brothers in another life. Are you so quick to forget that world? Master Olam practiced his wisdom in restraint from such things. How dare you insinuate his decision was flawed?"

"Don't you dare speak to me like you know of that, Dondi; I was there. While you played in your forest, some of us have prepared for such days as these." Zubair turned to Olam and stood, a balled fist across his chest as he bowed quickly at the waist. "Send me, sire, let me go into the mountain and end Abaddon before he gets too strong."

Feldrid scoffed, arms across her chest. "What makes you so sure you can defeat Abaddon, brother? He has always bested us all, second only to Olam himself. Surely, you don't think the last few centuries have been enough to change something like that. Did you find some secret magic that none of us know of?" Her eyes narrowed as they fell on him, challenging his pledge.

Zubair didn't flinch as he turned her way, "Now Feldrid, not all of us are dying because of our sins. Some of us can still stand on a battlefield with a chance; a fool's chance, maybe, but better odds than yours." His voice was cold.

Master Olam only barely spoke, as a whisper but one with power and authority. "Zubair, that sin has been forgiven and it is not your place to pass judgment."

Zubair sat with that, head down. "My Lord, forgive me."

"Not me, Zubair..." Olam stated firmly, but with a smile and tilt of his head in Feldrid's direction.

He was annoyed, but wisely he conceded to apologize for his inappropriate remark.

Feldrid spoke again, "Olam, I must ask...although I don't think Zubair could do it, I agree with his gusto and desire to end Abaddon quickly. What more is there to do? He will never stop coming for what you love, and haven't we allowed him times enough to turn back?"

Olam folded his hands on the table as he looked up, intent to make eye contact with each of the three Elders. "We must move The Shining City, hide it. I've left Ivoriene in charge as the sole guardian. She will stay with all those who abide there. There is a darker evil at play here, one that must not threaten the hope for all the humans. Once we have sent the city away, we will make our way to the Tree of Offerings so we may protect those left in our lands who have yet to make it to the city, redeem their ability to arrive one day in paradise. It's time to fulfill my vow."

Feldrid took a deep breath with eyes towards the ceiling, while Zubair stood abruptly, pushing his chair back before walking a few steps to the window on the far side of the room. As the dark blue curtains stilled from the ivory stone balcony, no one dared to breathe. Dondi gently closed her eyes, tears silently being shed.

"Isn't there another way? There must be something else we can do." Dondi's voice cracked as she questioned their Master.

Olam smiled sadly, sympathy pouring out for her anguish at the thought of what they must do. "My daughter, it was always going to be this way; it must be this way. We all knew one day, this would be the road we traveled."

Zubair marched back over, his sword clinking with every heavy step before he slammed his hands down on the table. "Not like this."

"Zubair, there will be a time when justice is served for Abaddon's deceit, but it is not yours to deliver. Right now, as we speak, an evil much greater threatens; shadows no one in our realm of Starpathia, or any of the others, can hope to withstand alone." Olam reminded him. "Now, we must address the needs of the people."

Taking a breath to invite compassion, Feldrid turned to Zubair. "We've watched stars fall and worlds reborn together. So many things have been worthless in these worlds, but him." She pointed a shaking finger at Olam. "Don't you see? It's why we pledged our lives to him. Master Olam has always been the one we would follow anywhere, do anything for because he is the only one in a million worlds worthy of truly serving. The humans won't make it without him, whether in this world or the next. Our creation become their destruction...so let our destruction become their creation."

Olam had been watching keenly, calmly as they worked through the emotions he knew such a day would bring. They had many more yet to battle with.

It had been so easy to slip past each person unnoticed. Every one of them had so falsely settled into the protection that they thought their shields brought, guards down with misplaced faith. With just one choice she could end it for so many, right here, right now...but there was a bigger death, one she didn't want them to miss.

This mission had to be one of restraint, as much as she loathed such things. Her goal was to simply unnerve Cillian after their capture of Lenora; at least that's what she had sold it as.

Moving quickly, she ferried into the castle. Her disguise would work well enough against most of them if she kept her head low. Very few had ever seen her, and she appeared as a wealthy traveler, which wasn't unheard of in this area.

Medora wouldn't be hard to find. All she had to do was knock her out long enough for the shields to fall after she left Cillian his message; it would be more impactful to scare them all. Plus, it was much more fun than simply sneaking back out. They would think they were under attack and act swiftly, so she needed to be fast.

As she turned from the main foyer to duck down yet another hallway in the castle, she was greeted with even more rooms cut into the dark stone walls. There were arched, wooden doors with big iron circle handles on either side of her. For a small castle, it was proving difficult to find the right room. The hall stayed silent as she quietly opened the first door on her left. His room was close, she could smell him. Sometimes, she let her mind drift back to those few weeks, the ones when Cillian had lived among them...

You mean the time he made a fool out of you...

Irritated, she pushed the intrusive thought away.

Cracking open the next door, she inhaled deeply before deciding it still wasn't his. She tried each door, one at a time, until she had reached the one at the end of the hall, gently putting both hands on the cool wood and pushing in. This was his room. Taking one more look down the hall before entering, she closed the door behind her.

There were remnants of a fire, with orange coals still glowing in the corner and smoke slowly drifting up the chimney. A small table with a chair housed nothing; she didn't see any bags or clothes, nothing to show anyone was staying here. She knew, though; it smelled like him. Crossing over to the bed that was perfectly made on the far wall, she sat and rubbed her hand over the coarse, wool blanket. Leaning over to the pillow, she laid her head down, closing her eyes. He had slept here; notes of leather, wood, sweet musk and a tinge of salt filled her nostrils.

Cillian had caught her eye long ago; men had been trying her whole life to do such a thing, but she regarded them as less than. In a matter of days, he had infiltrated the Fallen, bursting in furiously, trying to kill everyone. Lilith had been impressed with the fight he had put up, demanding to see his father, killing quite a few of them before she had disarmed him.

Curiosity...that's what the feeling had been. Curious to know if the rage he exhibited could be useful. His father had died shortly after arriving, realizing his mistake, and wanting to return home. Of course, no one could ever leave once they arrived...well, before Cillian. She decided not to tell him, to keep him clinging to hope until she could learn if he was worth their time. It had taken days to convince Abaddon to let her take over his torture in the Shadow Boxes but, in the end, he allowed her to have him. Later, Abaddon would use her failure with Cillian as an excuse to show off, to go after Anara and successfully bring her in. It had all been to highlight her failure, keep her living with it while he kept the sister in a house.

She had never seen someone fight so hard against themselves, their desires. He never gave in. After weeks of cruelty, she released him to train, impressed with his sheer determination to hold on to the core of who he had tried to convince himself he was, a good man. It didn't take long for her to believe that he may indeed be just that. Sure, he was burdened with guilt over his mother. A guilt that was easy to exploit into pain, but not enough to turn him.

Many times, she poured her influence into his mind, trying to get him to come on to her, but he never did. Lilith reported back to Abaddon differently, all lies because she had never been respected or turned down, both of which intrigued her.

Laughter from the hall grabbed her attention as she shot up off the bed. The steps receded further, revealing that someone had left their room. Walking over to the table, Lilith reached in her robe to pull out a square canvas she had carried with her. She took one final look at the painting before setting it down in plain view. Oh, how she wished she could see the look on his face when he found it.

Chapter 21

The Shining City had been sealed off. Each of the Elders stood around Olam as he bowed his head, hands together, energy flowing from him to encompass the city in a large ball of sparkling light. Speaking an ancient tongue, Olam sent the city away. It simply dissipated, slowly, becoming blurry at first, colors fading and buildings turning transparent. In a few minutes, there was nothing but a massive field of grass as far as the eye could see in its place. "Now they are safe." His bones ached, weary from such power but relief also found its way into the mix to soothe his soul. Olam reached hands to his temples, only one thing remained. The Elder used his connection to all things and ancient words once more to erase any knowledge of such a place existing from the whole of Starpathia. "If the humans find it, we know the time has come when it can be restored once more, so others may enter."

Solemnly, Dondi asked, "Lord, if they do not know of it, how will they have any hopes of finding it?"

Olam smiled, "All those who seek will find, my dear. Always."

It had been what felt like a millennium since the Rosamundi were last summoned; an imperial race of horses that were integral the last time they rode against Abaddon, when he fell from the Elders' grace. Now, they came silently from over the hills at Olam's command. Each distinctively different, approaching their rider.

After mounting his white stallion, Olam commanded him forward with a simple thought. The impressively tall steed had a diamond set in his forehead; his eyes dazzled like lightning. Fubair's red mare followed, mane and tail made of fire. A smokey gray stallion took off ahead of them all, anxious to be joined to his companion. Elder Medora would be waiting. Stepping forward was Elder Dondi, to greet a pale blue gelding, followed by Feldrid on a brown mare that Olam had created from the earth, hoping to reserve what little magic remained in the aging Elder.

Each took turns looking over the large hill that stretched downward towards a glistening lake that was glass, far off in the distance. Beyond the lovely water was the forest that would lead them to the North Tower.

No one spoke as they took off at a gallop, headed for the Tree of Offerings, and although it felt like the end, Olam knew it would truly be a new beginning.

Abaddon still hadn't returned, and I wasn't going to wait around for him either. I had been walking for what felt like miles. Each time I got to the end of my land, it was as if the map reset, duplicating the same green fields and oak trees further away. Taking off the white sandals that were beginning to rub blisters on either side of my foot, I threw them at the air, screaming out my frustrations. With nothing left to do, I sat down in the grass. Pulling my knees in, I rested my forehead on them, desperately wishing for someone's help.

This was madness.

My mind drifted to Shadow again. He had been consuming my thoughts after the fog in my mind had lifted.

My Shadow, where was my Shadow? I needed to know he was safe.

"No, *you* need to get out of here."

Startled, I froze. I slowly looked to my right to follow the sound of a female voice. There, not two feet away from me, stood a woman that I could only describe as a warrior. Half of her long blonde hair was pulled back and braided tightly against the top of her head, while the rest hung loosely around her shoulders. Brown pants and top were wrapped in leather armor, adorned with strange engravings of stars; a cape was attached with a silver broach at the neck. Her wrists held matching brass gauntlets; one hand gripped a slender spear while the other hand extended out to me.

"Let's move, now," she snapped with aggressive urgency as I took her hand to rise, unsure of where she came from, or why I felt she could be trusted.

Then we ran.

Me in my bare feet, her in tall leather boots.

Tearing into the woods, I anxiously awaited the map to reset, but it didn't. Further we weaved through the trees as the air became heavy, light began to vanish all around us. Darkness nipped our heels, the trees fell away, and I felt the familiar forest floor fade from under my feet, replaced instead with cold stone. I kept my eyes attached to the mystery woman, terrified that if I looked away, she might vanish.

Stopping, she assessed her surroundings before turning to address me.

"Well, this is better...I hope. At least he won't find you crying in a sun dress in the same place he left you, that would really doom us all. Now where are we?" Taking a few steps past my bewildered face, the woman searched the dark for something. Where the small light was coming from that illuminated softly around us, I hadn't a clue, but I was beyond thankful for its presence.

"Lenora, where are we?" She questioned again.

Still taking it all in, I stuttered "I don't...I don't know. Wait, why are you asking me?" *Daft*, that's what her eyes conveyed. She looked at me as though I was truly daft.

"We're in *your* mind, you're creating this."

Offended at the thought that I had any control, I raised my voice. "How dare you? I'm not doing this. Up until you arrived, I couldn't get out of that field. If anything, *you* brought us here! Which, I must say, I'm not convinced is any better off than before. Who are you?"

A bit of a smirk pulled at her mouth, but sarcasm came from it. "Look, we don't have time to coddle you today. This is your mind. You control most of what you see; that is until that sick creep shows back up. Once he returns, things could get dicey around here, so let's not make it easy for him to find you. I think until I came your rescue, as usual, you couldn't imagine leaving that field. Seeing me must have broadened your thoughts enough to stretch us somewhere else."

"So, you're telling me I can think us anywhere? That's ridiculous! What if I think about a glass of red wine?" Within seconds my desire materialized. A single glass of red wine appeared on the ground is front of us.

Smirking was no longer the right word. Gloating, yes, the woman was gloating at this point.

"Well...I see. But who are you, and what do you mean you came to rescue me?"

"You called. You kept hoping someone would come help, so I did. As to who I am, it's complicated. Let's just say, for now, I'm a part of you that can step in when you get overwhelmed, an internal motivator."

"Wait. You're supposed to be me? You look nothing like me." Her blonde hair, brown eyes and pale skin in comparison to mine was a testament to that truth.

Annoyed, she continued. "We really don't have time for this. I'm one of the few who roam around freely up here in your head." She tapped the side of her temple. "I can step in when you need me, that's all you need to know. I'm not some stranger; it's why you trust me. I'm a part of you, but you see me how you wish to see me."

"I must be losing my mind. Well, do you have a name, 'me that's not me'?" I said, secretly begging to wake up from this insanity.

Grabbing my hand, she began to drag me further into the darkness, stomping. "I don't care...Woman with a Spear, She Who Must Do Everything...pick something catchy. Now, where are we going?"

The invisible orb of light stayed close as we wandered around the nothingness. I should have been listening or answering, but here I was, trying to name my rescuer who had an innately bad attitude and no patience. "Patience."

"What?"

Smiling, I replied. "Patience. That's what I'll call you, because you have none and I think if you had some you might be a more enjoyable conversationist."

Rolling her eyes, the woman grunted like an ape. "Fine. Now, where are we going? I don't run things in here, you do. Although we would be better off sometimes if you didn't," Patience responded with a hint of resentment.

Honestly, I was lost. That's why we were lost as well. I began thinking about where we should go. Could we hide in here? The invisible orb of light became visible, a bright ball of white that grew to the size of a basketball as it hummed on ahead of us. Jogging off, I motioned for Patience to join. "Follow that, I think it knows where we can hide."

The light soon had us running again, and as we went further, the nothingness faded. Walls began to appear on either side to form a cave-like hall. Patience grumbled something about how we needed to figure out how to leave, not hide, but I was content with hiding until I could learn more about how all this worked.

My hall stretched on, and something about it felt eerily familiar as I slowed to a walk, tiring. The orb sensed my hesitation to go on, so it moved back towards us until I could see a great door. It was square, iron, and bolted into the stone. There was a single latched handle I reached for as Patience came to stand beside me. As soon as I touched the handle, I remembered. This was what happened last time, before I opened the door to reveal the field and meet Abaddon. With that fearful memory, my hand recoiled.

Patience rolled her eyes. "Come on, Lenora, it's just a door."

Before I could protest with why, she squeezed the latch and pushed in, it opened effortlessly.

Inside, there was an office. The lights were blinding as my eyes adjusted to the odd scene. It looked just like a waiting room; there was a frosted half window for check-in, some side tables and a few sitting chairs. Patience didn't seem at all surprised. I blinked a few extra times while she confidently crossed the room to open the far door. I trotted along behind her as her hand pulled down the handle to the next room.

This time Patience did look surprised, even nervous. On the other side of the door was an extremely large circular room, with three doors spaced out equally far apart. Each door had a small window in the middle, towards the top. The doors were white, along with the rest of the room, which matched the fluorescent lights, giving off a hospital feeling. The third door from the left was wide open, which felt odd.

"Lenora, why did you bring us here?" The color had drained from Patience's face, what little there was. Turning, she rushed back into the waiting room, dragging me with her. Once we were there, she shut the door tight and locked it from the outside, before going over to open the frosted window; beyond it held a chair, but no one in it. "No. This isn't right, there is supposed to be a guard here."

Dumbfounded, I watched her pace the room. "Guard?"

"Yes. A manager of sorts, for them in there." Patience nodded her head back towards the door. "It appears someone is missing, and we don't need to hang around to find out which one." Stopping quickly, she shot me a look of pity.

"You really don't need to know, not right now. We need to get away from here, fast. If Abaddon finds this place, you are in a world of trouble. I can't believe you even found this place."

"You're not making any sense. Besides, this place seems safe. It seemed very safe when I thought about where to hide."

Patience laughed. "Ha. It would; you designed it to hide things. I've just never been back here before."

"I did? What things?" Something in that question tickled the back on my mind, as if I were getting close to a memory I didn't need to remember.

Patience sighed. "I'll answer these last questions, but then you hide this place again, as deep as you can, get us far away, agreed?"

I knew. I didn't remember details, but I knew as the whispers started in my mind, the prickling on the back of my neck...I was close to something I wasn't ready to be close to. "Agreed."

"I'm a part of you that has served you well. I have a purpose, a use, but I have an origin too; all your parts do. For us, it was an environment that was overwhelming with big expectations, oftentimes unrealistic. To protect you, I was designed to shut down those feelings, the overwhelm; so you could get done what needed to be done."

Something about her began to feel familiar, like an old friend. Yes, she helped keep me from punishment by taking over when I couldn't manage. She taught me to use my job to cope, she fought back the overwhelm so I could move forward, even if just for a time. A warrior design fit her; she was there to fight for me when I didn't have anyone else to do so.

She continued. "Now, I have always had free rein to wander around in your mind. I'm not dangerous, but I'm not the only thing in here, either. You have other parts, beings that are not as easily controlled. Their origins are more difficult to accept, which is why you've hidden them; you locked them up in there." Patience nodded towards the barred door, the circular room. "This past year, you started asking questions, trying to learn more about yourself. They want to be heard, they want to be found; and right now, would not be a fun time to meet them."

Trying to ignore the lump in my throat, I followed her gaze towards the door.

Why...why did you lock us away?

"The whispers..." Looking towards the door, I felt a pull to go back in.

Patience eyed me intently. "Lenora, what is it?"

Look at us, we need you to listen...why...why...we...we...want...out. Listen!

Screaming filled my ears as I covered them with my hands. Within an instant, I felt strong arms pulling me back out into the dark hall, the orb of light patiently waiting while the door heavily thudded shut, along with the screams.

Desperate pleas filled the eyes of my warrior as she commanded me to get us *away*, asking me to grab on to the happiest memory I could.

Like magic the door vanished, and out of the blackness came a lake with a sandy beach. Looking down, I found myself in some soft shorts with a tank top to replace the sundress. Patience was assessing the area when I heard the soft whinny and joyous laugher of a voice I knew well. Spinning around, I saw Raya, my Raya, as her youthful self. Long black legs, intense eyes, and muscles rippling over her body. Next to her was a girl, someone that had been a both a mother and a sister many times over, in a life when I needed both but had neither. Sara.

"Come on lazy, let's go swimming." Sara gleefully called out as she mounted her big palomino gelding, bareback, and trotted him into the lake.

The smell of horses filled my nose as I watched Sara and her gelding splash into the water. Turning, I looked back to the most beautiful horse; she always had been to me. Standing tied to a tree, she anxiously pawed the ground, wishing to join the others.

Patience smiled. "Good choice."

My face couldn't hide euphoric joy this place had brought my soul. "Oh, any memory with Raya is one of the best. She was always my escape from reality, especially as a teenager. We would create so many different adventures, always running away, always together." Tears ran down my cheeks freely as I stared at the Arabian mare not twenty feet away, my feet cemented to the sand. "Is she really here?" As much as I wanted to run to her, I couldn't imagine not being able to reach out and touch her.

A feisty glint filled Patience's eyes. "She's as real as you want her to be in here."

My heart came out of my throat as I took off in a sprint to throw my arms around the strong neck of the horse who had my heart. The one who loved me for so long, who had always been there for me...but like mist, she faded away, the entire scene vanishing before I could get there.

"I'm sorry, too soon?" His voice sent chills down my spine as he walked forward from where Raya had been. "Ouch, I'm thinking I hit a nerve." Abaddon smiled before looking past me to Patience. "You found a friend! I wondered when we'd start seeing other things in here."

"You filth, how dare you!" Patience threw her spear straight for his head, but he held out a hand and tuned it to sand instead.

With a flip of his wrist, he threw her up against a stone wall and into the shackles that were mounted there. Something gagged her as Abaddon twirled a finger in the air. "Temper. I might not be able to hurt you, but I can contain you."

At some point I had fallen to my knees, crushed by the hope ripped from me; the chance of hugging her just one more time had been *right there*.

"Now, where were we?" Looking over to me he made a sad voice. "Lenora, darling, we are just getting started, and already I have you down. This simply won't do." Abaddon had taken a few steps closer to me as the thoughts beat in my head.

He had taken her from me, he had taken Raya.

Nobody takes Raya.

People had taken things from me for decades. People who should have protected me, people who should have never taken the things they did. Decades of my life had been unrestricted access to whatever anyone wanted from me...not her though, not Raya. No. Nobody touches my horse, nobody stands between us, nobody takes her from me.

Hello lovely, it's been a while.

The heat rose, boiling under my skin as it felt all-consuming. I could hear it in my ears as it muffled out the sounds of whatever this man was going on about.

He took her from me.

What do we do to people who take things that don't belong to them?

Rumbling began, far off as the ground began to shake. My breathing quickened, as did my heart before I lifted my face to meet his. Quietly, I whispered, "Bring her back to me."

Confused, Abaddon replied. "Excuse me?"

Louder, I demanded. "Bring her back."

Standing, I stared him down, fists balled at my sides, shaking.

"Lenora, it's a pony, not a deceased parent." He scoffed.

In one blink, the entire area changed. Patience was gone. We were surrounded by lava, sharp rocks jutted from the ground as I screamed louder than I can remember screaming... "Bring her back, now!" An earthquake began as Abaddon stumbled. A crack split through the stone while pieces fell through, separating the two of us.

"My, my, you are an interesting creature." It wasn't fear in his face. No, I wasn't that impressive. It was complexity, though. For in that moment, I had done something he didn't expect at all. I had become more complex than he had bet on, or he hadn't done his homework very well in my memories.

From behind one of the rocks stepped out a young woman, made completely of fire. She laughed in Abaddon's direction as her face became more human before speaking. "I think it's about time you made your exit, unless you like the idea of burning. Although it would be fitting, you're no stranger to the flames, are you?" Sharp fangs exposed a twisted smile as the fire being glided over, hovering across the ground.

My body was reeling, seething even as the creature came nearer to me. Beads of sweat formed across by skin as the familiar intensity surged in my veins.

"Hello. Who might you be?" Abaddon curiously acknowledged the creature of flames.

"Lenora's not always a fan when I show up. 'Rage' should be a simple enough description for you. You'll find I'm a bit...*more*, than that girl throwing sharp sticks..." She responded confidently.

Abaddon didn't seem amused. "Is that so?"

Bringing her arms up by her sides, the fiery being howled like a primal beast, lava spewing in Abaddon's direction. When she stopped, he had vanished.

"Punk." Her face emerged, a bit more human-like, a deep red as the rest of her body but covered in flames. She smiled at me, no teeth this time.

Slowly, the seething receded as I breathed deeply. "Thank you."

"That was nothing. Thank you for letting me show up; it's been a while. I imagine it won't take him long to figure out how to lock me up too, but let's not make it easy for him." She winked.

Chapter 22

Cillian burst through the door into his room. His eyes registered the lack of movement in the small space, which discouraged him. No sign of her. Not that he thought he would find her here, but he had to exhaust all the options before he left. The alarm had been sounded, the shield had dropped briefly while he had been looking for Lenora in the barn, only to find that Shadow was missing.

As he turned to retreat, a small object caught the corner of his eye.

That hadn't been there before.

Cautiously, he approached the side table. As his vision adjusted to the dim room, bits of color from the object came into view. Shaky hands reached for a canvas that had swirls all over of blues, greens and yellows. Each intricately wound around the other, melting together and a black scribbled signature in the corner, beginning with a large cursive A. He couldn't breathe, as if the air had been emptied from the room. His thumb gently grazed the signed corner. Tears welled in his eyes. He let them stream silently.

The time had finally come, he knew they had Lenora, but he also now knew Anara was alive. Not caring if it was a trap or a hopeless promise fulfilled, he fled from the room, making a silent vow to bring them both back.

Olam had saw the shield fall while they were still far off. Leading in a charge to defend the North Tower from any threat but as soon as they arrived, they learned there was no need.

Relca was shouting orders around like she'd done it her whole life; one was directed at Peeke, as he grabbed Medora's head to heal a gaping wound that would usually require many stitches, had a healer not been present.

Medora shook her head gently, touching the once bloody area that now had closed. "She was fast, ambushed me from behind."

Master Olam didn't need to ask, there was only one smart enough to trick someone into walking her through a shield...Lilith.

Medora sensed the same and looked up as he extended his arm to help her stand, eager to be at attention to the presence of their commanding chief. Once standing, she bowed at her waist, but Olam grabbed the stiff woman, embracing her in a hug.

Medora fumbled for words after the exchange, not wanting to think too deeply about how long any of them would last.

Master Olam spoke. "Next time she arrives, she won't be alone."

"Are we sure teams shouldn't be out looking for her? If we're fast enough, we could track her." Relca agitatedly butted in.

Elder Dondi grimaced at the disrespect that one of her own was showing Olam.

Olam stared at the small woman, her shoulders back and a look of pure disdain on her face. "You are Relca, I presume." The Master smiled.

Relca seemed astonished he called her by name.

"No need. Lilith can ferry. She could be back on her mountain with the blink of an eye," Olam announced, still smiling warmly.

Instead of any surprise, Relca just released an annoyed sigh. "Well, that's helpful."

"Where's Lenora?" Olam looked back with more concern.

"Abaddon has her." Cillian's serious voice added more tension into the conversation. He appeared more determined in his course than Olam had seen in a long time.

Medora hung her head. Feelings of failure no doubt invaded her mind.

"If he has her, I'm not sure anyone can help her. Lenora could have been a game changer." Relca said solemnly.

"Giving up already?" Olam raised a brow at the small woman, less than half his height.

Relca quieted. "I just prefer being honest; false hope never helped anyone."

"She's not a weapon, so stop talking about her like she is one. I will get her," Cillian retorted.

No one spoke as Olam stepped towards Cillian, eying him intently. "You chose not to tell her." It was more a statement than a question, and meant to be factual instead of accusatory.

What was left of Relca's countenance fell as Medora stood, looking stunned. Zubair had just returned from seeing to the Rosamundi, but he had overheard; it was clear from the infuriated look on his face. Dondi and Feldrid both shared a glance of compassion and pity, as a mother does to their child.

Cillian closed the gap between himself and Medora, meeting her head on. "She's a human, not some pawn for our war. Besides, it would have taken years to train her and we didn't have the time."

Medora didn't take her eyes from him, didn't blink. "You've killed her. Whatever happened out there...it's blinded you. The least you could have done was shoot straight with her. That knowledge could have helped us gain ground against him."

"It wouldn't have helped! This girl is trying so hard to hang on, terrifying her would have done nothing. She didn't need more reality checks, she needed to know she was safe, even if only for a moment. Trust me, I know tired when I see it. She's been fighting herself for a long, long time." Cillian defended his choice.

None of them noticed the three strangers walk in, except Olam, as they continued arguing over what would have been a better way to protect Lenora and utilize her at the same time.

A sharp voice rose from behind Cillian. "What in the name of the two suns have you done with our student?"

Everyone shifted their focus to the newcomers, two women and an exceptionally large man, as tall as the Elders. Cillian appeared to recognize them immediately.

Signy's high voice cut through the air. "Let me ask you again, what have you done with our student?"

"You will address our Elders with some more respect." Relca stepped in between the groups. "After all, they are the rulers of this world."

Olam watched the standoff while he wondered where Relca's newfound allegiance had come from, given her disdain for their authority.

Signy moved a hand to her sword, irritated but not the least unnerved by the small woman's posture. "I'm sorry, you don't seem to be in charge nor have enough stature to be speaking to me that way." Jabari had stepped in to place a hand on Signy's shoulder, clearly trying to rein her in before she decided they weren't on the same team.

Elise bowed at the waist to the Elders as she stepped in front of Signy. "What the ill-tempered child is trying to say, is we took a liking to Lenora and want to assist where we can."

Jabari crossed his arms as Medora drilled daggers in Cillian's direction. There was a look of satisfaction across Relca's face as she too moved her gaze his way.

Olam gently interjected to calm the group. "Cillian can lead you to her."

Signy's let her gaze fall before looking back to Olam. "Fine."

"Thank you, Signy. The other two should stay here. I have no doubts Abaddon will focus all he has on this Tower; we'll need their skills." Jabari brought a balled fist to his breast while Elise nodded silently in agreement.

"Pack only what you need; I can give you half an hour." Cillian commanded.

Signy smirked. "I don't need it. We can go now."

Olam watched everyone disperse as they prepared to go their own ways. He hadn't told Cillian what he needed to hear yet, because he wasn't ready to accept it; but he would soon enough.

Lilith had found Abaddon fuming in his dark study, the one adjacent to his Shadow Boxes. It surely meant Lenora was putting up a fight, and that brought her a twisted sense of joy.

"What do you want?" He was being direct and sounded annoyed, which he only ever did when he was facing a problem.

She hadn't changed since arriving from the North Tower, and her boots were leaving small wet marks in the stone floor from the snow outside. Walking across to his desk, she sat on the corner.

He stopped pacing for only a moment to cast a look of his contempt at her presence. "I said, what do you want?"

"You don't want to know how it went?" Lilith snapped. This was the banter that always made her feel like they had been married far too long, even though she would have chosen death over being anyone's wife.

Abaddon continued his pacing while he spoke calmly. "If there had been problems, you would have told me. If there had been grand success, you would have told me. You said nothing, which means you're either here to play games or simply get under my skin, neither of which I am in the mood for."

When he was in a problem-solving space, it was impossible to sweet talk him. They had done this dance too long. "Fine. I want a chance to speak with Lenora."

"No." He continued to pace.

"How did you do it? How did you take her? I thought the Old Law prevented you from such things," Lilith probed.

"I already told you when I sent you out there; on very rare occasions, I can make exceptions," he replied, annoyed.

"Yes, but *how*? You've not done it ever, that I can remember."

"One. I had a spell for *one*. One single time, I would be able to take one of his beloved humans without asking. I've never had a reason to, but we were running out of time. It cost me greatly."

Something was wrong, he was furious and trying hard to conceal it. What had he done? She had to tread lightly with him right now.

He stopped his pacing briefly to offer her a bit of information. "She's weaker than I expected."

"Interesting." Lilith meant it, too.

Returning to pace, he continued. "It's as if they told her nothing, taught her nothing and did nothing. Sure, she has impressive power but no clue how to wield it. She's an emotional mess in there, it makes her very..."

"...unpredictable," she cut in to finish the thought for him.

For the first time he turned and took a long look at her. "Precisely." He held her gaze long enough for her to look away first. There was longing in his eyes as he reminisced on a time long ago, when he had learned her, inside and out, only to use it to rewrite her.

Lilith knew he was remembering how she herself had been when she arrived. He didn't have the time to slowly peel back Lenora's identity piece by piece, though...what did he really want with her? There was obvious logic to obtaining Lenora, but there was something else; a piece missing, one Abaddon was purposely keeping to himself. He would only do that to benefit himself, most likely not a benefit for Lilith. She needed that unknown knowledge and fast.

"Lilith, I need you to keep the Elders distracted. They will come for her here. Get the guard ready to send out the Gangors, prepare to move on the North Tower." He turned his back to continue pacing. He was done with their talk.

"Should we empty the mountain?" Lilith wondered if it truly was time to move.

"Leave the newest here."

"What should we do with those in the Shadow Boxes?"

Abaddon balled up both fists and sneered through clenched teeth. "Those are none of your concern."

Rage stayed close as I made my way down another dark tunnelling hall, the orb of light leading us once more. My fiery companion hadn't said much as she trailed behind me, per my request. It was hard to think when she was close. I could feel the seething heat beneath my skin and my mind would begin to blur.

Do I ask...

You should.

Speaking loudly behind me, I asked the question that had been bothering me. "Did I lock you up somewhere?"

"Ha, no; is that a thing? Granted, you do push me away and really try to pretend I don't exist, but I get it. Anger never was safe for you..."

I didn't need to respond, but I couldn't stop the memories as they flooded in.

He had been an angry man; the smallest thing could set him off. Me. Mostly, my very existence did such a thing...maybe if I had been better.

You were a child...

Taking a deep breath, I willed the memory lane to close and concentrated my steps forward, wishing for another door that would bring me back to Patience. I wasn't sure if her disappearance was my own doing or Abaddon's, but I needed to find her.

Chapter 23

Lilith shoved a small man through the end of the cave corridor, where he tripped over a rock and fell onto the floor below. The man was shaking as he stood up. He had been gagged with an old cloth; his hands tied behind his back with the rope extending into Lilith's slender fingers. One of her least favorite jobs was feeding Abaddon's creature, mostly because she knew it was no more his pet than a starved fire-breathing dragon...one day it might decide to set itself loose. Truly, he didn't hold it here. Why it stayed had always sat very uneasily with her. Apex predators don't hang around for a thousand years just to pass the time. Taking another step over a rock, she pushed the man in deeper and threw a large fire ball into the air to illuminate the eerie cavern, where the darkness threatened to swallow her whole.

Whispers began emerging, slowly surrounding them both. A sharp pain caused her to look down. Her hand burned as she realized the small man had snatched the rope from her to take off running. "It's too late." Lilith knew the Masi was already there.

Black liquid grabbed the rope, wrapping it around his upper arms and carrying him up towards the ceiling. Lilith turned her face as the panicked howling began. She had ungagged him for pleasure. There were unnatural shrieks coming from both the Masi and her dinner, the sound of snapping bones and tearing fabrics as she finished with him, then a thud of what was left hitting the cavern floor.

Lilith resolved herself and turned back to be met face to face with…Lenora. She had chosen to replicate the girl in jeans and a tank top, brunette hair braided to the side. Leaning in, the Masi sniffed Lilith's neck before pulling away to smile. "It's been a while since you came, what a treat."

"We need to know what's so special about the girl, this body you're in." Lilith was snarky enough to cover her fear, she hoped.

Walking around Lilith, the Masi looked her up and down. "What do you truly desire?"

What did she want, truly?

The creature stopped.

Distractions…

Lilith took a step forward. "No. What is the story of Lenora? There's no way you would appear as her for no reason…you knew before I came here."

"Shhhh. We don't need to rush it; why do you think she is so special?" She stepped forward, putting a finger to Lilith's full lips.

Lilith didn't dare to breathe as the icy finger touched her face. In a second, she felt the air get sucked from her lungs, her entire body felt as if it were made of lead pulling her down to the ground. The creature retracted her hand as Lilith collapsed to the floor, her hands bracing the fall onto the damp stone. Her breath returned as she sucked in gulps, begging oxygen to return to her body. Lilith hated this thing. She shakily got to her feet, her face set firmly against it.

The Masi tilted her head ever so slightly, but extremely unnaturally as the ground began to shake and the siren voice filled Lilith's head.

"Buried in shadows of the night,

She will lie till restored is the light.
In death yet life will you find,
And chase away the darkness of the mind."

The words chilled Lilith to her core, but she didn't have the slightest idea what they meant. She risked one more question. "Speak plainly for once. Why did you ask me if she was special? Is she not?"

A twisted smile filled the face of the Masi, and as she opened her mouth to speak, a scream escaped instead. Lilith put her hands over her ears as she shut her eyes tight, daring not a look in its direction. Wind raged through the cavern as the temperature went frigid before the whispers began again. This time Lilith could hear her plainly. "Of course she is, but *he* mustn't discover it. You know, you only need ask. In the end, if you really want to be free of them all, go to the tree where all knowledge lies." With that, she disappeared.

Lilith still didn't know what made Lenora special, but she did know who mustn't find out and what she must do. She also knew exactly where the Tree of Offerings grew quietly.

As I focused all my thoughts on Patience, a door appeared at the end of the hall. This door was small, wooden with an old handle. Pulling it open, a dessert of sand appeared as far as the eye could see, sun burning brightly high in the blue sky. Just ahead there was a small shack, wood with a tin roof, no door but a doorway holding a red curtain. Moving carefully, we headed in its direction, Rage still trailing behind me.

Pulling back the fabric I stepped into the shack, and onto a sand floor. Patience was gagged and tied to a chair in the corner. Her eyes were wide as she grunted a few noises. Crossing over, I bent down to untie her.

Once her hands were free, she removed the gag, screeching in my ear as if the shack were going to blow up. "Now, we go now!"

The three of us were out and running for nowhere in the dusty terrain while Patience shouted orders. "Lenora, get us somewhere else right now. Focus!"

"I'm trying, your yelling isn't helping." I snapped.

Rage was keeping up with our frantic pace, but that had to be easy considering she didn't have legs, her fiery figure floating across the ground. "Let him come, we'll deal with him." Those freaky teeth came out again, clearly she enjoyed the idea of a showdown.

Patience looked genuinely scared when she turned to me. The terrain began to change, sand turning to black smoke as stars above began to form, darkness falling. "Please tell me you're doing this," her eyes begged.

"I don't know. The stars, yes, but..."

The smoke, I didn't do that.

Stars began to drip, melting from the sky like silver paint on a canvas as the black smoke thickened, piling up to my waist all around us. Fear gripped me as goosebumps spread across my skin.

Patience grabbed my hand; dread covered her face. Rage pulled in close. We each had our backs to the others, looking out at the nothingness all around.

Childlike whispers began, as a woman giggled far off in the distance.

"What is this trickery?" Rage questioned.

"Abaddon, right?" I answered, oddly hoping I was correct.

Patience had pulled a dagger from her boot. "He didn't put me in that shack."

"Wait, did I do that?" It had concerned me before, not knowing how she vanished.

Refusing to look at me, Patience answered quietly. "Not exactly. Now remember, Lenora, no matter what happens, you're in control here. We're just parts of you; we can take over, but only if you let us. You don't have to let us."

Rage poured fire into a circle around us, the flames forcing away the smoke at our feet. "Listen to me. You have pushed me away many times, refusing to feel any anger. You can do the same with her; don't listen to that foul tongue."

"Foul tongue. Tst, tst, tst. That's unkind, sister, I'm hurt you think I would want anything more than to help her." The eerie voice was closer than before, but the darkness concealed any form. Only the shifting smoke gave away her presence.

"You don't want to help her; you want to use her for your own vengeance," Patience shouted, bringing the dagger higher in anticipation of attack.

The silence was deafening until the scratching started, like iron on stone. It was the same scratching I had heard time and time again. Chains began to rattle and with the discord, an iron cage appeared in front of us. At the back of that cage were a pair of bright yellow eyes, belonging to the hunched form of a petite woman, cowering naked in the corner.

I knew her.

The voice returned. "Yes, you do...you like to forget her, but you need to be reminded of who I am, and you can't know me without remembering her."

"Lenora don't listen to her, you'll give Abaddon the upper hand if you go there right now," Patience pleaded.

Turning back to the cage, I ignored them both. The girl inside was younger, a teenager, and she had begun to cry as she babbled incoherently. My heart mourned for this pain she was carrying. Without realizing it,

I had put out both hands to separate the ring of fire. Voices were calling to me, but I didn't care. My focus was on the girl in the cage. Crouching down, I grabbed one of the bars to steady myself. "It's ok now, don't cry."

Words whispered out through muttered sobs. "Don't...let...them. I can't take it anymore, please." Her voice cracked. "I don't know how to make them stop. Help me." She lifted her face and I got a good look at her. Bruises littered her thighs, much of her skin was filthy like she had rolled in the dirt. Scars littered her arms, small slashes. Even so, the olive skin, face and long brunette hair belonged to...me.

It was me.

My head began to throb as memories flooded in, so many all at once. Such an angry home, so many attempts at connection, all failed. No one understood, no one cared enough to try.

Fast forward.

Most of the time, I could never remember the partners. I knew I had many, but I never thought about them. I couldn't. It had happened so many times, as if I had purposely sought out men to hurt me.

Faces began flashing, specific places and smells invaded my thoughts. All the awful things they did to me, what I did to please them ...then, all I became to protect myself.

No. I didn't want to go there.

The girl leapt for the door, grabbing my arm as she screamed, sharp nails digging into my skin. Her long hair covered her breasts as she pleaded on her knees, eyes like a wild animal. "Don't leave me here. You abandoned us!"

Pulling away I stood up, backing away slowly as the girl dropped her head, sobbing again. "I'm...I'm sorry...I can't help you. I didn't know how to stop them, I'm sorry."

The girl sat back; head hung low as the cries escaped her throat. Then she fell silent for only a moment.

"I'm so, so sorry."

Manic laughter came from the cage, her chest moving as she titled her head up and back, grabbing her stomach. Lifting her hand, she snapped her fingers, she aged from the teen to a young adult. Standing, she was now fully clothed in skintight black leather with matching black hair set loose around her face, eyes were red. Reaching down, she opened the cage door and stepped out as she tapered off the laughter. "No, you didn't stop them." She took a few steps to the side, the black smoke gathering at her thighs now. "We were so weak back then. I mean, that pathetic thing in the cage? Please. No wonder no one listened to us. Why fight it, right? Embrace it. I mean, if this is all we're worth, just to be forcefully used and abandoned. We were never going to get it back, no matter how many times you scrubbed your body."

I knew her, I hated her.

This is what I had become years after failing to make it on my own, the years I tried to forget. The girl who took before it could be taken, detached and always in control. With her the drugs had arrived. If I was going to be her, I didn't want to remember any of it.

"Hey, I protected you, don't you forget it. That thing in the cage almost killed us all and you were too weak to do anything but lie there, take it quietly while you tortured yourself. We, at least, had some fun on occasion." She grabbed the end of the cage door and swung to the other side.

Swallowing the lump in my throat I pushed back at the memories, the details that tried to force their way in closer, deeper as she spoke. "Where is the girl?" I demanded.

"Oh, don't blame more on me. You locked her up, remember? That was just a presentation by yours truly."

"Lenora locked you up too, but here you are." Rage spoke sternly from behind me after moving the circle of fire back around us.

The woman smiled. "You'll find I'm a bit more powerful than the others, including you, my fiery friend. See, when we ended up in this world, Lenora became unhinged just long enough to let me get out, stretch my legs. I mean, she's been avoiding me, but thanks to Abaddon, we're all locked up together and I'm much harder to put back in the box." She twirled her hair as she drilled those red eyes into me. "You are so ashamed that I am a part of you, and you shouldn't be. I taught you how to survive, when no one else was there to teach you anything. That's it! You can call me Shame; make me feel special like you named these other rejects."

It was too much; I was reeling as I watched the black smoke try to climb above the fire and into our circle. "You don't have to let her in, you are in control." Patience grabbed my shoulders while I continued to fight the memories that clawed at my mind.

Shame laughed. "Her in control, yeah right. That's what she needs me for."

Crumbling, I was crumbling at the thought of becoming the young girl in the cage, again. That line of thinking just increased my panic as one of the memories slithered through a crack...

I had been told my entire life how important my virginity was, to have it taken even if I tried to say no without words...now worthless and unfit for a good man. Sara had been who I ran too, at sixteen, hurting and afraid. Her fury at the marks on my body had been unleashed, but no one else believed me. It was painted as guilt when I didn't say no, instead tightly closing my eyes while I cried in the dark. My honesty had cost me friendships. I decided then I wouldn't tell again.

...taking advantage of the gaping space inside, another memory slammed itself across, demanding to be heard.

Next time I said no, but my voice was too small. When it came out, he didn't hear me. He was so much older than me, he rescued me and I liked this guy, but he could get angry when he drank. Not this time, still too small, mere whispers.

Another rampaged on.

Older this time, wiser. Living with him had been a stupid choice, but if it happened again, we would be noticeably clear, louder this time. Yet again, he pushed us up against the shower wall until we screamed in pain, lashing out angrily. That time it was mistaken for enjoyment. He never forgave the scratches across his face.

Another.

...if we lay still and don't anger him, he'll stay. It's my fault...we can't be alone again...but we don't want to do that...whatever he wants, do it so he doesn't leave.

"Enough. You are torturing her." Patience was at my side as I wept into my hands, my entire body shaking.

Shame got as close as she could to the flames. Her red eyes seemed to dance while Rage met her face to face, furious. "Torture? It's not torture, it's responsibility. This is what she allowed, what happened to us because of her weakness." Her voice raised as she slammed the cage door shut. "You were alone, abandoned, and helpless but I'm not weak. How about giving Abaddon a taste of his own medicine? Let him find me instead, I can manage him better than any of you."

"If you are so helpful, why did she lock you away?" Patience challenged.

Away. I needed to get away, to curl up in a hole somewhere as they continued to argue. There was nowhere to hide here. It was doubtful I could even die in here.

To die. Death meant silence; it meant no more intrusive thoughts to fight.

There were more, much darker things still yet to come. I knew it was only a matter of time. Patience and I had found three rooms; one for Shame, one for the girl who had been abused so often in the cage...Anguish, I'd call her. As I acknowledged her existence, she screamed as an injured animal wails, continuing to sob in the prison I had created out of desperation.

Truly I knew the moment he arrived; Abaddon. Without seeing him, I could feel his sly smile and heavy black eyes pointed my direction from the darkness. He had been watching and learning.

There was nothing more I could do as I laid down on the hard stone ground. Curling into myself on my side, I began to let go. Only one remained, that first door. One that had been trying to take over for a long time, lurking in the shadows of its dungeon. My resolve faltered, as did my strength; I could no longer ignore it or keep it locked away. There had been endless energy poured into keeping the thing in check, countless times it had escaped only to be dragged back, locked in tighter. This part was far older than any of the others; it never screamed but silently slithered. In an instant, I knew the lock failed as I exhaled a breath. The door was open, just a crack was all it needed to escape.

Now it would come for me, and I no longer held the will to fight it. Slowly it would creep, but when it arrived, I knew it would be all consuming.

Chapter 24

Diadred tore through the snowy forest in the mountains and up the sloping terrain at an impressive speed. Signy was riding a small white mare that kept close behind them. Dawn was coming. The late-night rest had been short, right before they entered Fallen territory. Cillian had chosen to go as far north as they could, then cut across to the east and back down behind the mountains in hopes of maintaining some element of surprise. It had taken longer, but even a fool's errand required some strategy. He knew much of the area better than most, and if they were lucky, the Fallen would be making for the North Tower to begin the battle. Abaddon would be making his move now, knowing Olam was close, in hopes to remove him and claim Starpathia as his own. It had never been about a throne, though; there was no actually seated throne in their realm. He wanted the power Olam possessed; the power of creation, what he believed was hidden away in the Shining City. Few who entered ever returned outside, and much of the true beauty of the city was kept hidden, even from Cillian. He had no idea if there was any real power to be found within its walls, but Abaddon seemed certain there was.

Slipping closer the cold deepened, sinking into his bones. Cillian was certain Anara would be kept away from Lenora; it wouldn't be wise to keep them close. He also knew Lenora would be in the dungeons, which is where he would go first. Signy would hunt the surrounding areas for his sister, then they would rendezvous at some outlying cabins south of the territory line. It was a solid plan, they both agreed; but rarely do things ever go as planned.

Lilith had done as Abaddon commanded. Damion was gathering the rest of their forces to move out within the hour, planning to attack the Tower come night fall. Most of them had trained in the dark, they appreciated it and she swore something about the darkness empowered them. There was a reserve of younger recruits that would remain around the mountain, and they had sent extra bodies to Anara's cabin.

Abaddon expected her to go south with Damion and the other commanders, leading them against Olam, but she wouldn't be obeying this time. This wasn't how it was supposed to play out, but nevertheless, she could improvise. Cillian was coming. She had led him here, and Eydis was waiting. Deciding what to do with Lenora, that was still a question. The longer she stayed with Abaddon, the closer he inched to unlocking whatever it was that he needed. If Lilith played this right, she just may be able to get everything she wanted.

"What do you truly desire?"

The words of the Masi taunted her. Her desires had changed so many times as the decades had gone by, even now they were changing. Could *she* change?

Cillian thought so...

She remembered the day she had figured him out.

That day there had been a girl, begging to go home during training. She was so young, barely a teenager, beautiful with long red hair, a face full of freckles and dazzling green eyes. Those were always the ones that triggered memories of Lilith's past, the ones she occasionally pitied, long ago. Lilith held her from leaving, along with Cillian, to help clean up the training area. His face, he masked it, but those eyes yearned to protect the young girl, even though he wouldn't budge against Lilith. Not in a hero way, but in a protective desire that she had never seen here; except recently, when he sometimes looked at her.

Her. He was beginning to believe he might protect her.

As she moved quietly into the mansion, the memory burst through, demanding to be relived once more…

"Damion, take these three back to the Shadow Boxes." The men begged and bargained as they were escorted away. Lilith knew she had to send some so that she could keep the attention off Cillian. It was true Cillian should have returned but she kept him close, pushing him through the ranks to study this man. Once Damion was gone, she turned back to the girl, using a soft voice she hadn't used sincerely in centuries. "What's your name again?"

Confused, the petite redhead lifted her chin, face swollen from crying, but those fierce green eyes were only sharper. "Roisin, my lady."

"Ah, now Roisin, run along and get washed up for dinner." Lilith almost dared a half smile. Roisin didn't question, but simply got up and ran.

Her heart did smile, though, only for a moment before she turned back to head in. With one spin she came face to face with Cillian, only inches away. She stopped short. "Well, that was nice of you."

Quickly she dismissed him, walking off to collect the poles they had used earlier. He followed behind, matching her step while helping her clean up the training area in silence. Once they were finished, he confronted her again.

"You didn't have to do that; I mean, I know why you do it for me, but why her?"

Lilith shot a glare of daggers straight through him, "For you?! Dare I ask what you mean by that?" Her cheeks burned red at the thought.

Cillian laughed; they were alone, so he risked such a thing. "I mean, I know you have been protecting me here, and I'm grateful. I can only imagine it's because of how bad you're hurting." His last words contained no humor, only compassion. "I've watched how Abaddon treats you, how he looks at you. You play his game because you must, not because you want to. Your cruelty doesn't fool me."

Something in Lilith snapped, then tempered. There was no anger she wished to summon, just shock as she looked into those deep green eyes. Heat filled her from her toes. She was speechless, in awe of this new feeling, when one of the commanders yelled across the yard.

Embarrassed at the surprise, she yelled at each of them, annoyed to be caught off guard and muttering about how all men were imbeciles, before retreating into the dungeons. Once she was behind the door she breathed deeply, begging her heart to calm down. She liked Cillian, but she wasn't about to let him ruin what she had here, no matter how good a man he might be. One wrong step and she'd send him off to the pit, just like she had his father.

No. Cillian was wrong.

She had waited too long, had suffered too much to once again be free from Abaddon. Freedom wasn't all she really wanted, though. She also wanted them to suffer, this entire realm, for existing, what it had brought her.

Running short on time and shorter on patience, she moved quicker down the hall. Abaddon would be too obsessed with his new pet to notice much of anything else. Cillian, however, would be extremely focused. Gaining the right leverage to push him where she needed him was imperative now, and she knew exactly where to get it.

This had been what he needed, a perfect storm of information. Although he had missed much of the early pieces, he had caught the end and even taken a quick visit to see the girl in the cage. Life was cruel, abandoned by those who were supposed to protect her. Used by those that should have loved her. In the end, men held power to destroy much of a woman's worth. Some may say it was archaic but, in every world, in every society, it was the easiest way to break someone down. The pleasure of it all was just a bonus. Abaddon readjusted the weight of Lenora as he carried her over his shoulders and up the stairs into the bedroom.

Everyone was gone, so they wouldn't have to worry about intruders, or the noise. He smiled at that fact. She was still trapped deep in her mind, but the parts she had in there were a bit too unpredictable for his liking, turning on each other. He decided to let her fight the war in there while he prepared to ask questions back in the real world.

Placing her on the bed, he took one arm and fastened it with a magic cord to the bedpost. The rope glowed an iridescent green, an enchantment to suppress her magic. He pulled a pair of shackles off a nail that hung in the wall next to various other devices. Grabbing her other arm, he attached her wrist to one of her ankles. Before he had moved her, he had stripped her down and put her into one of Lilith's dresses, a beautiful deep green that made her look ravishing. He wasn't a horrible host, at least.

Placing both hands on either temple, he closed his eyes and released the locks from her mind. From his pants pocket he pulled a small vial. Popping the cork, he placed it under her nose and almost immediately her eyes shot open wide.

He gave her a precious few moments to blink, assess her surroundings and begin to panic as he walked to the front of the bed. Shadows danced on the stone walls from the torches lit on either side of the wood door.

Her attempts at getting free were feeble, but he always loved to watch them try; struggle against the bonds with determination that would later drain into hopeless submission as the fire left their eyes. He stood silent as she asked why she was there; it was an honest question, but he wanted to let uncertainty settle in before he answered. Once more, she snatched her weight against the rope, but they both knew she wasn't going anywhere.

"I thought you might enjoy a break from being inside your head for a while; dangerous place to be if you stay too long. Many times, I've seen men and women go mad when they overstayed their welcome inside themselves, unable to ever leave. We don't want that for you.

Sorry about the dim lighting and the musty smell; this was closer than carrying you up to my house, too many stairs." He smiled. "Now, we're going to play a remarkably simple game. I ask a question, you answer. If you answer honestly, we'll move to the next question; if you don't, I'll pull one of these tools off the wall to persuade you to answer correctly next time. Got it?"

She squinted to look at the far wall, the lack of light making it hard to identify any of the tools he had pointed too.

"First question. How did you get in, did someone let you into our world? That never happens…anymore." He began to pace.

Lenora stuttered. "No…no one. I don't think. My horse and I followed the bells."

"Bells. That's new. But someone had to influence our ward. Was it Olam?"

"Who?" She questioned.

"Master of the realm, my dear...Surely you learned of him in your travels?"

"Well, yes, but I never met him." She raised her voice.

Abaddon paused for a moment before resuming his pacing, his hands now clasped behind his back. "Next question. An old friend told me you controlled the shadows...only Medora's Shadow Sentries can do anything close. How do you do it?"

"I don't know...it seems no one does."

"Oh, come now, you can tell me." He walked over and sat on the bed using his hand to gently stroke her cheek. "No one in our world has ever seen such a thing. This isn't something to fear, but to embrace."

"I don't know. It only happened once; I can't control it."

"You created my creatures, Lenora, to use against them. No one does that without knowing something. Even I couldn't create the Gangors without...help, we'll call it." He narrowed his eyes to show his disapproval.

"Honest, I have no idea. I never asked for any of this." Silent tears slid down one cheek.

"I don't believe you." Abaddon stood and walked to the end of the bed again. "What do you know of the prophecy?"

"What prophecy?" She sounded absolutely stunned. She really didn't know a thing.

"When time is bent by human hands,
His rein will end within mountain lands.
She alone won't be the key,
But Another who longs for them to be free.
Darkness will fall before light will rise,
In hope that one day they will never die."

Abaddon quoted that which had been revealed to him so long ago, after Lilith had arrived. He had thought it was talking about her, but time had proven him wrong.

"When you ferry, you bend time to your will. There is only one other before you that had the power to do such a thing. She did not bring about my ruin but you, you carry the power over shadows. '*With them she will rise, without them you will fall.*' The Masi is never wrong, dear Lenora." He pulled a small knife from the wall; it was dull and chipped iron. "You may be telling the truth, but I was not. I'll have to modify the rules of our game. You see, I'm running out of time and I do hate being rushed. It's nothing personal, but I can't have you bringing about the downfall of everything I have worked for, you understand?"

Making his way back to the bed, he grabbed her one free leg and secured it to another post as she began to fight once more against the restraints. "This rope only dampens your gifts, suppresses them a bit. Now, show me the shadows."

"I don't know how I did it," she screamed as he climbed onto the bed.

He pulled up the dress to reveal her thigh. "I know you don't, but I need to see if I can convince you to bring them out." He smiled as he ran the small dagger down the side of her face. "Don't worry, I won't kill you; but you may wish I had when we finish."

Olam looked at the Tree of Offerings with sadness as he reached out a hand to break a branch from the tree. Once separated, the white barked grew and wrapped into a bulb at the top, creating a single staff. In his hand he held the star-shaped stone from his amulet, which he placed inside the staff bulb, triggering a response, more small branches to encase it. This tree held so many stories. It was a history of so many worlds that were before and would be after. A dance of light and darkness bound in its bark. Tomorrow it would be bound in blood.

Stepping outside the shield he chanted in the old tongue as he raised the staff before shoving it forward. With his hands went the shield, the front of the dome pushing to extend north with unmatched speed. He was going to encase the Fallen's territory, Abaddon's Mountain and the North Tower all in together. They would know, they would see it pass, but it no longer mattered. He would fortify this barrier much more than Medora's, one that would contain the darkness, for as long as possible. It was to protect those left in this realm of Starpathia, to contain the battle and strike what would happen here from the record, for now.

Once he was satisfied the shield was in place, he wrapped a separate dome of protection around the Tree of Offerings. As he finished his spell, loud thuds approached from behind, enough to make the ground shake. Olam turned to see the Mandros on either side of Elder Dondi as she commanded them to stay with the tree, another line of defense to protect the single most important life in their realm.

Olam took the long walk back to the North Tower, whispering blessings on the trees before exiting the forest. Elder Dondi watched with him as everyone continued to bustle about, preparing for battle. You could feel it, the anxiety that arose from many of the humans. Medora met them at the edge of the tree line, and as they passed by, she created a fortified wall of magic. It would be their last line, fully encompassing the Tower and the small town that resided around its base. Into it she poured her heart, everything she had. Satisfied, she too turned back towards the Tower.

At the bottom of the narrow staircase sat Balfour, his grand forest guardian. The gold sigil on his chest glowed bright as Olam approached him. Balfour bowed to his Master. He inclined his head as they passed by, proceeding to the tedious conversations that would follow his arrival inside. There were mere hours left before the nightfall which would bring the Shadow Sentries with it; as well as immense sorrow for many.

Chapter 25

Cillian had been hesitant to let Signy take the lead, but the trail of bodies he was following told him it had been a wise decision after all. He hadn't heard much of anything, other than the occasional thud or slice of her sword as they made their way through the dark, wet passage between compounds within the mountain. The back entrance had been easy enough to find, but too small for Diadred to pass through. He had gone off sulking, commanded to wait for them out front. If memory served him correctly, this current tunnel would dump them near the living quarters of those awaiting their initiations. To his surprise, there were more of the Fallen left than he had expected; all inexperienced, it would seem, since Signy had not even slowed enough for Cillian to assist. Stepping over another body, he lowered his bow while pausing long enough to study the young man's exposed face. His tan skin and brightly colored tunic were a dead giveaway that he was from the West Tower. Who knew what pain and lies had driven him here. It was such a shame, all those whose lives were to be extinguished this way. But he knew, as did Signy, that they were beyond saving...or that's what he chose to tell himself.

The loud metal clank from a heavy door brought his attention back forward. Pushing into a quick jog, he caught up to the small assassin as she moved silently into the next room. It was dark, like most areas in this dreadful place. Cillian threw a ball of fire up above them to illuminate the dining area they seemed to have found themselves in. He knew where they were. "Signy, this is where we part ways. Take that door on the left and follow the stairs up until they lead you out to a training courtyard." He motioned to the door across the room.

"High up, right?"

"High as you can get without going up to Abaddon's mansion." He shrugged.

"Good. I'll see you soon."

Off she went, as silent as the air around them.

Apparently, not only could Signy move impressively fast with a blade, but she had superior vision from far away. The idea was to try to locate where any outlying buildings were, and any guards that would indicate something special resided close by.

Cillian went through the door on the right, which opened into another dark stone tunnel. Moving quickly, he drew his bow, preparing to loose an arrow if needed. It was eerily quiet being so close to the Shadow Boxes. He wondered if Abaddon had emptied them, but that didn't seem right.

The next door opened into a small room with three more doors. It was a maze in these halls, easy to get lost if you didn't know the way, and this mountain was the last place you wanted to open unknown doors. Choosing the middle one would take him to the Shadow Boxes at the end of the hall, so he moved through center door with haste. His father used to take him hunting about this time of year, he had taught Cillian to move swiftly and silently.

At the bottom of the stairs, he reached for the last door. On the other side was a place of nightmares. As he breathed in deep, the wet dark air filled his lungs. It was so heavy down here and dark, incredibly dark, but he wouldn't dare any light. He moved his hands across the door to find the latch and as stealthily as possible, entered the hall.

Utter silence had never graced these rooms, Cillian was sure, and it made him even more uneasy. A few long strides had him bump into a door. Pushing, he tried to move it back, but something caused it to resist. Moving around the protruding door, his foot contacted something soft and the faintest dripping noise could be heard only a few feet away, as a metallic tang hit his nostrils.

The hair on his neck rose as his gut twisted uneasily, responding to that smell that filled his nose. He decided to risk the faintest light as he ignited a small flame from his finger. Orange light flickered, and Cillian moved his hand down to be met with the face of a woman, her eyes missing from her head. It was her body that kept the door from swinging back in.

Something was very wrong here.

In one hand Cillian produced a short black blade, easier to wield than his bow. In the other hand he took a chance and made a ball of fire to throw above.

As the light illuminated the narrow hall of the Shadow Boxes, he once more faced a scene of nightmares. This time, however, it was real; not some manipulated memory in his mind. Even for Cillian, the macabre display in front was enough to make his battle-hardened face look away, until he found his ground again.

One thing he knew for sure; he was alone here, at least for now.

Stepping over the body, he passed by another human strewn in the walkway. This man's eyes were also gone. The dripping noise belonged to another poor soul who had found himself thrown over one the Shadow Box doors, blood slowly dripping into a small puddle that gathered below his head.

Only one of the doors remained closed, one he hesitantly opened. Inside there was the form of a small woman, hunched over in the corner. At the center of the room sat a wooden bucket full of blood, and symbols like nothing Cillian had ever seen were painted all over the stone floor. At certain points within the symbols, the eyes had been placed. This was dark magic, something not of the Elders or this world.

Abaddon was dabbling in something unknown.

The only good news here was the lack of any signs Lenora had been present for the massacre. Now the question remained, was it better she was not here, or worse?

Lilith had been swiftly navigating through the deep snow on her way to the cabin when she first spotted the small woman. It was a streak of pure luck that she had just stepped from behind a large pine, which gave her the ability to crouch back down out of sight. This woman was a foreigner to Lilith, only her drawn sword and silent movement spoke to her mission.

Cillian was here, and it would appear he had chosen to go after Lenora yet trust his sister to this warrior. *Cute.*

She was obviously just that; a skilled warrior. Dangerous beings could always size up other dangers with acute accuracy. Lilith knew the extra guards would be nothing for this woman to overpower; she would have Anara easily. This was a bit annoying. Without his sister, she would have less leverage over Cillian.

Maybe she didn't need him.

Abaddon wouldn't even leave the mountain over this girl, and neither would Cillian.

"You know what makes her special, but he must never know."

She had learned to be adaptable, rethink plans and produce more solutions. Lilith may not know exactly what Lenora possessed, but she did know it was something. With that it was decided, and in the blink of an eye she ferried into the mansion.

Cillian was after Lenora, too. Maybe they had become more than friends, maybe she would be even more useful than his sister. *Men in love were always dumb, easily manipulated,* Lilith thought as she ran down the hall into her room. Upon entering, she crossed the floor to the wardrobe and threw open the door, digging at the back for a small item. Her hands met the cool, rough form of rock. Pulling it out, she clutched the black, misshapen item. It was an odd thing, black rock with symbols that only ice would reveal; at least, that was what she had been told. Summoning the cold, she wrapped the lumpy figure in ice, before throwing it to the ground. As chunks shattered across the floor, a small medallion with an odd symbol on the front appeared.

There was a hole in the center that led to the hollow space inside. It was said to summon the shadows under the mountain, the Masi. Whispers nipped her ears as she recounted the day she received this gift...or curse.

In her early days, over half a century ago, she had found herself caught in a trap of the creature's; Lilith had entered the lair alone, wandering farther than she should have. In a panic, she told the shapeshifter a story, one of tragedy and longing, her deepest anguish. Instead of attacking, the Masi listened, then granted Lilith this gift. She had appeared to Lilith that day as an old lady. As she handed the rock over, she promised great power if Lilith ever desired to open it; but she warned Lilith not to stick around and watch it unravel. One drop of blood would release an agent of justice from the Masi. Who truly knew if it would work, or if it was another trap; but today, it would be worth the risk to find out.

Abaddon wouldn't be in the mansion; Lilith knew something was off, and he was unraveling.

She always knew deep down when the time came, he would fail to deliver on his word. As twisted as the darkness had made him, as powerful as he was, in the end he wanted others to fight for him. He had promised her power, tortured her, kept them hidden away, but at his core he was a coward. Whether by design or choice, she knew he couldn't engage this old Master of his.

It didn't matter. She no longer needed him, she just needed Lenora.

Climbing off the bed, he stood and grabbed the small, star-shaped metal medallions to return them to the wall. Lenora's stifled sobs had tapered down but not stopped completely. He had resorted to a more direct approach after she had spit at him, choosing to brand her thighs with the stars. Abaddon had to give it to her, she was tougher than expected. No amount of anger or pain coaxed anything from her.

Grabbing a small piece of linen from the dresser, he walked to her left arm. In his excitement he had cut deeper than intended, and she was bleeding a fair amount. "Don't need you passing out, my dear." He kissed her forehead after binding up the wound.

They had been in here for hours and she hadn't been able to do the first bit of magic. It was infuriating.

This girl would end his mountain reign.

No. There must be something he was missing.

He was running low on patience and time; Lilith and the Fallen would be closing in on the North Tower at any moment now. It wasn't enough, all of them, in the end. He needed more power, he needed more from Lenora; or he just needed to kill her now.

That thought angered him more, thinking of what he sacrificed to get her here. It had cost him, more than he had known, or intended. His powers had begun to fail him, it's why he had to leave Lenora's mind. If he weren't so sure it would kill him, he'd go back to the Masi, demand a restorative spell. That creature had been the one to give him the incantation, the words and practice to be able to bind Lenora here against her will, defying the Old Laws. What he had done to those left in the Shadow Boxes...he had secured Lenora, but as payment his own powers were waning. A small payment the Masi failed to mention.

There was one more thing he hadn't tried. It was risky, but he was becoming desperate. "Why don't we go visit your friends again?" Abaddon put his fingers to her temples, locking her inside her mind once again. Within moments her head slumped to the side, so he decided to gently remove each restraint and put the torn dress back across her shoulders. Walking over to the single door in the room, he locked it with a metal bar. It infuriated him, the need to lock the door for his own protection. Putting her back in her mind had drained him, though. With every passing minute more of his power left, as if something were slowly leeching it from him. Maybe Lenora thought couldn't do anything while she was pinned down, there was no hope, so he would give her a chance to escape to see if that would motivate her instead.

He had one more spell. If she could produce the shadows, he could take them from her.

Slowly I opened my eyes, repulsed by the light coming from outside.

Outside.

My hands grasped soft green grass as I pushed to sit up. The scene was blurry, but as it came into focus, I could see mountains in the distance and feel brisk autumn air on my face. I was in a valley, a beautiful one. There was a creek nearby, and I heard the small falls made by the rocks. Birds were singing in the trees. It was perfect; maybe it had all been a dream. As I went to stand, I winced in pain from the weight I put on my arm. There was a blood-soaked rag tied around it.

Each sense was slowly coming back, but when the burning began on my thighs I simply cried out. Pulling up the sundress I once again found myself wearing, my eyes found the raw skin that had been burned. Six-point stars had melted the flesh aside.

Anger rose from my chest, but grief washed it down when I realized nothing had been dreamt. He had locked me back inside my head, but every memory followed. There was no way to escape this hell that had become my life.

Not that I would be missed back home, but my animals…who knew where Shadow was. Abaddon refused to tell me.

Cillian. Ivy. Signy. I would miss them; they had started to become my friends.

"Well then, why don't we go get them back?" The sassy voice cut through my thoughts from behind. It sent chills up my spine. I could already see the leather before she came into my view. "Shame. Isn't that what we named me?" She laughed.

My voice came out smaller than I intended, but I guess all the screaming earlier had left me a bit hoarse. "What do you want from me?"

"Control. Let me take the wheel when he wakes you back up; I'm more useful than you give me credit for." She crouched down to meet me eye to eye.

"When you are in control, we aren't *in* control and people get hurt."

Shame shook her head gently. "When you don't let me help, *we* get hurt."

"Where are the others?" I looked away, trying to find relief from her heavy stare.

"Preoccupied at the moment."

"What did you do with them?" I didn't try to hide my concern.

Shame rolled her eyes. "Goodness, Lenora, what do you think I am? I can't hurt them; I just made them take the long way to reach you is all." Shame looked at me, her face softened, and pity flashed in her eyes. "He's going to do it again, you know, and if you don't give him what he wants, I don't think he's going to let you walk away."

"Fine, just let him kill me!"

Shame looked offended at such blatant resolve. "You don't mean that. Even though you dream of death, I know you want to live."

"I can't give him what he wants!" I screamed as new, hot tears came down.

Shame let her face fall, she came and sat down next to me, grabbing my hand. "I know, but I think I can. Let me try." She grabbed my chin and lifted my face. With a thumb she brushed one of the tears away.

It broke me. I leaned into her as I sobbed. I loved and hated her all at once in that moment. "I can't, I can't trust you."

Shame just smiled. "I know you can't, so I brought a friend." Her arm went past my face, pointing off to my left. There, past the tree line of the forest heading up to the mountain moved a dark, hunched shadowy figure. Slowly, from one tree to another, it walked. Whispers had begun snaking into my mind as the temperature dropped around me.

"No."

"Oh, come on Lenora, it hasn't been let out in so long. It's lonely, I think."

"Why did you bring it to me? Do you know what you've done?!" I stood up, wishing for Patience or Rage to come intercede, trying to imagine anything else other than the twisted creature that wished to be seen.

"You did this, Lenora. You let it out, not me. The two of you can chat while I get us out of this pickle you placed us in, once again. Give me control!"

The fear was undeniable, I felt it everywhere. My breathing shallowed as each wound Abaddon inflicted screamed in pain. Thoughts of having to endure another minute with that evil man consumed me. I couldn't, I couldn't go back. Never again, I wouldn't make it again. No matter what it took, I wouldn't let anyone touch me that way again.

He would have to pay for his crimes.

Chapter 26

Night had fallen. The Shadow Sentries appeared one by one, seen through the shield that shimmered clear as glass. Shadow Sentries were the first line of defense between the Fallen and the gifted humans that remained at the Tower. Elder Feldrid had been ordered to stay in the Tower as her health continued to decline. Elder Dondi was sent out to the Tree of Offerings and instructed to hold her position there with the Mandros. Elder Zubair, his lions and small force were on the ground with the rest of those willing to stand against the Fallen. Olam commanded them only to engage when the shield fell.

One by one trees caught fire over the hill, ablaze high in the sky until a line of them were engulfed. Elder Medora and Master Olam rode out to give the opportunity of surrender. Medora had been appalled that Olam was willing to give them the option, but he was unswayable.

The Rosamundi ate up the ground with their long strides, throwing old snow behind them. Three of the Shadow Sentries accompanied Medora and Olam as they approached the line of forest that was burning. There were two or three hundred Fallen, it seemed, and countless Gangors clinging to the trees, snarling like attack dogs awaiting their master's command.

Three men had come to the front, each dressed in fine black clothes with silver accents. One man stood in front of them all. Olam had been told about him; Abaddon's right hand.

"Damion, is it?" Olam asked from atop his horse, which stood high enough for a human to walk underneath its belly. Damion didn't respond, he just stared, his slick black hair reflecting the flames around them.

Olam calmly stated his proposition. "You can all turn around, leave, and we will not pursue you, but I ask that you come no further."

"Abaddon told us to tell you, if you concede The Shining City, he will spare the humans who are loyal to you. They will live a wonderous life as slaves to the rest of us." Damion twisted a smile and the other commanders laughed, while cackling spread further behind them.

"Why don't you send these people home? They don't all have to die for your insolence." Medora was irritated, her mount just as much since he could barely seem to stand still, teeth bared in the direction of a Gangor who was slinking closer than it should have been. One of the Sentries had moved in, sword drawn in between the creature and its commander. Another Shadow Sentry flanked Olam while the third remained motionless at the back; it stretched open its wings, doubling in size, while shadows oozed out like smoke all around them. It was enough of a move to stop the laughter.

"Leave this place," Olam commanded again as he turned to leave. Most of them would fall immediately, as do ants under a shoe; no match for him and used only as dispensable pawns by Abaddon.

Medora paused before turning to do the same, but she didn't succeed. Not all dogs can be commanded. That Gangor decided to spring up, tackling Medora to the ground. Her loyal Rosamundi reared, coming down on top of the creature before he could attack again, but it was too late, a chain reaction had already begun.

Gangors took flight, heading for the Tower as fire came from the Fallen's army. The largest Shadow Sentry screamed an unholy echoing sound as it grew once more, shadows reaching from the ground and smothering any who came close. Master Olam shot his staff up as a shield of light protected him and Medora, who quickly retrieved her mount before they took off, galloping back to ensure the safety of the others. Two of the Sentries followed, but one stayed behind to pick off any that dared come close.

Fire was going to rain. They needed to draw it away from the Tree of Offerings.

Both tore past the trees with a speed only the Rosamundi could offer. Olam pulled up just shy of the fortifying shield that surrounded the North Tower, with Medora at his right. There were ten more Shadow Sentries who proceeded ahead of Olam. Swords drawn, the ancient creatures began to hum a song of old while the shadows moved out in front of them, a fog spreading over the snow through the trees. Medora dismounted and drew the heavy blade that hung at her side, her enchanted horse ready to face battle with his master. Olam stayed atop his stallion, staff at the ready, watching the flames move closer; shouts of the Fallen and screeches from the Gangors attempting to get through the shield, rang in his ears.

Here they would make their stand. Here, so many would choose death as their own hatred for that which they couldn't understand consumed them, for they had bought so deeply into the lies that they could no longer see truth. Olam spoke a few words in the old tongue and gave a moment of mourning for those that would fall this hour. He could hear the screaming, as they moved into the shadows. One by one, they were pulled into the ground to be returned from whence they were created. Those that made it close enough to the Sentries themselves would learn swiftly that fire would not protect them.

Gangors however, were another foe entirely. Diving out of the sky like bombs, they attacked the Sentries, shredding whatever they could get their teeth into. Two had already fallen to the creatures. Just their robes lay in shreds as the shadows abandoned them to their fate, absorbing into another close by. Medora found herself in close combat again, and it didn't take long for the black blade she wielded to be covered in blood, pulling it from the side of a Gangor.

Olam continued to use his staff, beaming out a light shield that pushed the creatures back when too many came too close. The Shadow Sentries that remained began absorbing what remained of their comrades, growing larger each second. A few of the Fallen had slipped past, battering the shield with streams of fire from their hands.

A flash of red caught the attention of the Elders as a wall of flames pushed out of the forest into the shield. Medora took a knee and threw her arms over her head. She was too far from Olam as he tried to protect her from the heat, unable to reach her quickly enough. Instead, her horse had; the large steed abandoned his fight to rear up in front of his Master. Flames engulfed the Rosamundi, incinerating the animal to dark ash that littered the snow. Medora cried out in suffering, her view of the animal replaced instead with a far-off Damion and another commander, walking confidently from between burning trees.

Medora stood wielding the sword as the fire around them burned away. Olam had climbed down beside her. "That took a lot from them; they will be weakened for a time."

One of the Sentries moved to put itself in front of the Elders once more. This one had grown more than fifteen feet high. Most of the first wave of Abaddon's soldiers had fallen. It was the Gangors that posed more of a challenge. Olam hadn't seen Abaddon or Lilith, each of whom could stand against entire armies on their own.

This massacre was far from over.

Abaddon rarely extended olive branches, but for this to work he would need to seem sincere. Pulling Lenora's brown hair from under the shirt he had placed back on her, he watched her closed eyes flutter back and forth. He didn't know what was going on in there, but it was of little concern to him. Stepping back, he frowned at the sight of her in the baggy long sleeve and pants that now graced her body. She had looked much better in the dress.

He woke her up once more, and as she groggily came too, he placed her own boots next to her on the bed. "I've decided to let you go."

Blinking repeatedly, her faced twisted into confusion. "You what?"

"You heard me. Get your boots on and get out." He expected her to jump up at the command, but she didn't. Instead, she sat up slowly, taking a moment to study her surroundings again. "I've concluded you are worthless to me, not even worth the energy to dispose of you. The prophecy must be wrong; you are no weapon of power," he stated while leaning against one of the bed posts.

She took a long look at him, her face blank while she moved to touch her cheek, wiggling her feet and fingers slowly. "I'm back."

"Yes, yes. Now get out of my sight before I decide you looked better tied to this bed." Abaddon smiled and motioned to the door.

Lenora grabbed the boots, placing her feet in each, and stood slowly. "You locked the door." She pointed to the bar.

"Ah, that. One moment." He strode across the room and removed the barricade, swinging the door open with a hand motioning to the hall. "You are free to go."

He expected her to be uncertain, afraid, maybe run. He expected her to be petrified, frozen solid or cry. What he did not expect was the widespread grin that found its way to her face as she leaned against the post of the bed instead of moving towards the door.

The confidence she spoke with bordered arrogance in her next words. "You aren't going to let me go. No one like you just gives up. You want me to run, to hide, to play into your sick game. Well, I don't like to run in boots."

Surprise was not something he managed well, mockery even less.

Had she just toyed with him the entire time, with an act?

Lenora walked over to the wall, selecting a small knife that was caked with dried blood. Using it, she cut a strip of fabric from the shirt she wore and used it to tie her long brunette hair into a bun on top of her head. "That's better. I always did want to chop this hair off. Control is a funny thing; how little you really have, even when you do get it."

Abaddon's face wouldn't budge. He held it as stone, calculating his response. This was intriguing, unexpected, but there was an air of familiarity. Her tone, this arrogance. He knew it. Now who did this remind him of?

"Personally, I like the long hair." Abaddon finally spoke.

"One more reason to hate it." Lenora snapped back.

"Well, as fun as this is, I do have places to be." Abaddon's patience was wearing thin and killing her was still on the table if she couldn't offer him anything. One last thing he could manage before his powers left completely.

She didn't try to conceal it as she slipped the knife she was still holding into the waist of her pants. "You haven't exactly been hospitable. The things you did to us, well, I found them quite vile."

"Really? Well, I must say I rather enjoyed them." Abaddon had begun to play with a small ring of fire he created.

Lenora walked over, flames dancing in her eyes and a soft smile on her lips. "Is it because we couldn't fight back? My guess is you can't do much unless the object of your obsession is restrained; safer for you. Now, that sounds like a coward to me. Or someone who didn't have power to begin with. What do you think?"

He didn't respond.

Stopping mere inches from his face, she pushed him into the wall. "I don't think you could handle me without your magic ropes."

Gritting his teeth against each other, he refused to peel his gaze away. He raised a hand to touch her cheek before back handing her across the face. Blood dripped from her busted lip as she looked back, boldly smiling. Lenora slowly took a few steps back as he followed, fire seething up both of his arms.

The door to his left suddenly exploded, shattering and sending pieces across the room. A sharp burning surged up his right arm as he moved away from the blast. Looking down, he snatched a dagger-like piece of wood from his flesh. Blood oozed through the torn fabric of his shirt.

He quickly summoned more fire to his side, pushing streams of flames in the direction of the explosion. It had come from the other side of the door, not Lenora. A dark figure appeared from the doorway, moving through the blaze. There was a cold chill that invaded the room as the faceless being moved about, attached to the ground. Abaddon lowered his arms, silencing the flames as the new guest came to a stop in the middle of the room. "What sort of new devilry is this?"

Lenora had emerged from crouching beside the bed.

"A new gift from our friend. Well done, Lenora."

"It's not me." Lenora's tone was an honest one.

He dared not pull his eyes away from the strange creature who had entered. Its appearance was that of a cloaked being, faceless, but there were no arms or legs that were visible. Black, solid, nothing of smoke or shadows loomed. It didn't seem to breathe or move at all, but stood between them and the only way out of the room.

Abaddon chanced a small movement, one towards the bed, shortening the gap between him and Lenora.

Nothing changed.

"What's the likelihood it's friendly or indifferent to either of us?" Lenora lowered her voice.

Abaddon huffed a small chuckle at the idea that this thing might just let them leave. "Ladies first." He said, mocking the idiocy of the question.

Yet it didn't bother Lenora as she followed the wall to the left, one leg over another. Three steps in, still no response.

Abaddon decided to follow, but as he took his first step the toe of his boot met a small chain he had forgotten to put back on the wall. The faceless head turned to lock dead on Abaddon. The sound of the links hitting together on the stone floor seemed much louder than it should have, because it was no longer the only chain. Lenora had frozen solid with hands against the wall, while the creature produced chains of black liquid from its now fully visible, cloaked arms. Two chains went into the floor and came back up, grabbing Abaddon's ankles. Taking the fire from within, he turned his body red, burning away his clothes and attempting to melt the chains while flames exploded out towards the dark being.

It didn't work.

He might have incredible power, no matter how brief, but something told him none of that would help him with this foe.

Lenora had taken advantage of the distraction and ran, successfully making it out of the room, leaving him alone. Chains continued to wrap around his legs, body and arms. They were heavy and cold as ice as each began to pull Abaddon forward. It didn't take long before his body was covered in the links; there was nothing else he could do. As his body drew closer to the cloaked demon, something caught the corner of his eye, movement in the door.

There she stood, watching.

Of course, it was you.

Something so surprising, yet not, for he would have done the same.

He smiled, trying his best to ignore the burning cold as the being consumed his body into itself. There, in the doorway was the owner of this beast; or better yet, the borrower. For as the darkness crept closer to his face, he knew this thing had a much older master than the beautiful woman who stood with her eyes locked on his.

Tears welled in her eyes as she watched Abaddon be consumed by the creature her medallion had released. She shouldn't shed a tear, this is what she wanted; but as he smiled at her, there was a sorrowful rage that burned.

He had still won; this is what she had become, thanks to him.

She should leave now. She had been warned not to stick around after sharing her blood, but she needed to watch, needed to know he was gone for good. It sat nicely in her head, the idea that this thing would bring him to the Masi for torment...but who knew what was happening to him. He could be dying, changing, or being sent elsewhere. Honestly, it didn't matter as she saw the last bit of his head disappear.

Swiftly, she turned to leave in pursuit of her next task at hand.

Lenora hadn't seen her in the darkness. In her effort to escape, she had run right past her, then vanished. No doubt she had ferried, hopefully not far because Lilith needed her. Not that she wanted to hurt her. Truth was, the Masi knew and Abaddon *thought* he knew...now Lilith needed to know. There was still a war waging outside, and although Abaddon wouldn't get to see it happen, she was going to take all that he had promised her, using Lenora to her advantage.

As she prepared to ferry back outside, a shadow down the hall caught her attention just in time to see a flaming arrow fly past her head. She knew instantly who it was; *Cillian*. It wasn't the first time he had shot flaming arrows at her head. No matter, she would leave him...then guilt hit. There were no promises the thing behind them wouldn't take him too.

Instead, she sprinted to the left, down the hall and up the stairs, leading him back towards the training courtyard outside.

The frigid air felt wonderful as she threw open the door, quickly jogging into the snow. Cillian kept right behind her, bow at the ready.

"Lilith." His voice was angry but calm. "Where is she?"

Slowly she stopped, turning his way but continuing to take small steps backwards to maintain distance between them. "Well, since we seem to have more of your women as of late, you'll have to be more specific of whom you are asking for." Lilith gave him a half smirk, curious who he would name first.

"I'm not here to play games. Give me the one you took." He drew his arm back a bit more on the bow.

"You know we can't take anyone. Your sister came willingly, remember?" She jabbed the memory at him.

Cillian smiled. "She'll be home soon enough. Thank you, for the gift of letting me know she was alive. I'm still not sure why you did it. The great Lilith couldn't be doing something kind now, could she?"

"Oh please, don't accuse me of such wicked treachery. I am a lady, after all. I saw your assassin, the one you sent after her. Cute thing. You do have an eye for women, Cillian, I'll give you that. Shame though." Lilith clapped while they continued their dance towards the edge of the yard. She watched his face closely and saw a gentle drop in his mouth as he pondered her words, searching them for truth.

"Lenora didn't come willingly, I know it. How did you do it?" He spoke through clenched teeth.

"That, I truly can't answer. I may have played my part, but I didn't take your precious lover."

"She's not my lover." Cillian bit back.

Lilith had backed into the stone fence; a quick look below confirmed her suspicions. It was time to go. "Well then, I guess you won't mind if I borrow her for a bit. See, Cillian, Lenora and I have a date of sorts; girl-talk only I'm afraid. I'm sure we'll all see each other soon. I hear there's a battle underway, eventually I'll need to show up. Scout's honor, I will return your 'not lover' in the condition I found her. Well, I'll try." She blew him a kiss before calling wind to her side, shooting herself up into the air and off the mountain ledge.

Chapter 27

Ferrying had been easier, more controlled that time even though we hadn't gone far. Never would I let Shame think she had a hand in that though, it was much easier than expected to kick her out of the driver's seat once my feet contacted the ground. Taking in a huge gulp of fresh air, I marveled at the lights dancing in the night sky. Streaks of blues, greens and reds stretched high above the trees. Snow had begun to fall around me; it melted and soaked through my pants, numbing my thighs while I scrambled to my feet. Turning, I could see the mountain; a ledge-like courtyard sat high above while a bird flew into the sky. It was surreal to be free of that suffocating place.

"Lenora?" The female voice came from behind me.

Startled, I spun around. I hadn't heard anyone approaching, but I was relieved to find a familiar face staring back at me, even if it did have blood on it. "Signy, what in the blazes are you doing here? And who is that?" There was another woman anxiously pulling at the ends of her fur coat. There were no signs of battle on the stranger, like those that Signy wore. She was also dressed much more appropriately than any of us to be in the snow. It was beginning to fall heavier, and my thin blouse wasn't providing any real warmth.

"Rescuing you, but it would seem you're doing a mighty fine job of that yourself. This is Anara, Cillian's sister." Signy tilted her head in the direction of the young woman.

"Cillian's here?" My heart fluttered a bit at his name.

"Of course. He's looking for you. Best we try to find him. I doubt he'll leave that place until he knows you're safe." Signy shook her head.

Heat filled my face while my cheeks burned red, and it wasn't just the cold that brought it on. The welcomed reunion was short lived, though. The dark bird flying near the mountain, the one I had seen moments ago, wasn't a bird at all.

We saw her, just briefly, in all black and flying straight for me. Faster than any animal, arms out she slammed the full force of her body into mine. Air felt nonexistent, as if an elephant had sat on my chest. My head was dizzy and I believed I might pass out, but I fought against her as best I could. Frantically I kicked, screamed and thrashed about, but she had wrapped arms of steel around me. Blood could be tasted as my mouth filled, lip swollen even more than before. Looking up, I recognized the injured woman from the woods. It was Lilith. Her black hair had come loose and whipped behind her; we were moving so fast all I could do was watch scenery blur behind us.

I don't know how long we flew together, likely mere minutes. Suddenly, those arms released me and I fell straight down into the snow. She dropped me from high up, and when my shoulder found the ground I heard it pop as I screamed out in pain. Never had I dislocated anything, but immediately I knew that's what happened to my shoulder. Rolling over, I tried to take a few deep breaths, hungry for air I couldn't seem to find. The sky was coming into focus as the world stopped spinning. I heard water rushing nearby and began to feel the cold seeping through my clothes and into my skin once more. I needed to get up, now.

Struggling to stand, I leaned into my good side, hoping to protect my shoulder from any more trauma. There were two women now walking towards me. One was Lilith, the other was frail and blonde. I noted two cabins near where I stood, and snow was falling moderately, so I began to dig for fire. It was here. I knew it was, Rage had shown me, as I coaxed her forward in my mind. How dare that woman show her face. I didn't care who she was; because of her I had endured things even nightmares couldn't produce at the hands of a madman. It was her fault. She was responsible for my pain, for my torture and how Shadow was nowhere to be found.

She knows where he is...

Something inside begged me to entertain the small hope that my horse was alive.

Flames had arrived. My hands felt the heat, yet no pain, as the fire danced and nipped from my fingers to my wrists.

"Well, well. Easy now, dear, we wouldn't want you to hurt yourself." Lilith stopped a few feet away, clearly unimpressed with my display. The other woman just seemed downright angry; her face couldn't hide any of it. Her eyes burned bright blue as streaks of the same color danced under her skin. "This is Eydis. She's going to help me today, and so are you."

Lifting my head and stretching my neck, I huffed in her direction. "I'm not going to help you, at least not for nothing."

"Smart girl, I'm listening." Lilith smiled.

"You have something of mine. A black horse. I doubt Abaddon needed him, so I assume he left him with you. Hand him over, and I'll let you speak long enough to entertain your proposal."

Lilith took longer than I liked to answer. That meant she either didn't know and needed to think, or she didn't wish to share the truth.

"I don't have him, but I would be willing to help you find him if you agree to come with me." She tried to sound sincere.

It was an easy answer; she didn't know. "No. No deal."

"That's a shame. I had really hoped to return you to Cillian without any more injuries. I'm sure Abaddon marked you up nicely already."

There was a change in her tone. I should have caught it, but Rage showed up instead.

Flames flew from my left hand while I used my posture to continue guarding my right shoulder. Eydis moved to respond but Lilith stopped her, instead pushing a forceful wind that knocked me back down to the ground. Instinctively I tried to fall to my left, but I failed as my right side hit the ground. Pain ripped down my arm as I howled, tears freely falling and nausea filling my stomach.

Lilith was by my side, and before I could respond Eydis was holding me down. Pain once again shot through my arm when Lilith pulled, hard, until a clunk let me know my shoulder had returned to its rightful position. Upon releasing me, they slapped around my face, calling my name. The pain was enough to knock someone out, but I stayed conscious. Lilith's eyes finally cleared into view while she helped me sit up. No part of me wanted to thank them. I wanted to leave, I wanted my horse and I wanted to find Cillian.

"I'm still not helping you." I stared directly into Lilith's eyes.

The corner of her mouth turned inward as she crouched down to my level. "No, I didn't expect you to, but you'll be much easier to move if you're not screaming in agony."

With that, Eydis bound my arms and legs with a blue cord of lightning that burned.

"Well, that's a nice touch." Lilith seemed surprised.

Eydis didn't smile but looked less angry as she responded. "I've been practicing some new things while you were away."

"Good. I'm sure we'll need them." As she finished her statement, an elbow met my temple, and once again my world went black.

Cillian swiftly found his way down to the ground after watching Lilith carry someone off. It had sounded like Lenora, but it hadn't been confirmed until he met up with Signy. Upon their reunion, he embraced his sister in the tightest hug he could remember giving. They had both shed a few tears before Signy cleared her throat, reminding him there were more pressing matters at hand. Cillian glanced at his sister. It was dangerous for her to come along, but even more dangerous for them to leave her. He wasn't letting her out of his sight.

Diadred, loyal creature that he was, had responded to the cries of Lenora but had arrived too late. They needed to get back to the North Tower as soon as possible. He was certain Lilith would bring Lenora there. Her reason was still up in the air; to use as a weapon, or a bargaining chip with Olam?

Diadred was quite large but carrying three people would be taxing. They wouldn't be able to go as fast as usual. Still, it was the most effective way to get back.

They'd covered over half the distance to the Tower when they stopped to give the poor boy a break. He was stoic more than anything else, but Cillian could feel the shallow breathing against his legs. It had been hours since their last rest, and everyone was feeling it. Snow was falling harder, and Signy was trying to hide the discomfort of the bitter cold as evening set in. There wasn't much to offer besides a small flame from Cillian's hand, so he decided to go into the woods in search of wood to start a proper fire.

Being a forest, it was teeming with branches. Finding them under the fresh snow was the more difficult part. Half an hour passed and he had only found a few measly pieces. The trees held theirs high, so pulling some down wasn't an option. Pushing further in, he spotted a dark mass off in the distance. Setting the wood to the side, he fashioned his bow and knocked an arrow, just in case. A Gangor maybe...as he moved closer, it began to come into focus through the snow. It was large, walking slowly towards him. Cillian took a deep breath, pulling the string back a bit more to fire, and then the mass lifted its head. The shape of a horse emerged through the screen of white, a black horse. It had seen him but wasn't moving off. Lowering his bow, he slowly stepped forward with a hand outreached. "Shadow?"

The horse moved its ears forward at the sound of his name, something familiar. A few more paces and Cillian was directly in front of him, now able to see why he hadn't tried to move away. Reins that came down from his nose had become tangled around his front left leg. Small steps were all the boy could manage. After cutting him free, Cillian gave the rest of his body a good once over for injuries. He found a few cuts and scrapes, along with some large gashes on his rump; all things that would heal in time. Thankfully there had been some spare rope tied onto the back of his saddle, something Lenora had said she always takes on trail rides. Using it, he bundled up some more wood and added length to Shadow's lead. Dragging him along would slow them down, but leaving him wasn't an option. Lenora would never forgive him for that.

Olam and Medora had dropped back behind her shield. The Gangors were overpowering the two of them as the Shadow Sentries continued to battle the Fallen. One of the Sentries emerged through the shield to report their enemy's retreat. But Olam knew it wasn't retreat, it was reorganization; they were going to bring down the shield.

The respite provided valuable time to fortify the defenses around the Tower that housed the most vulnerable, and Olam decided to address those that had chosen to fight for his people. There were only about one hundred, maybe less that stood alongside the Elders to stand in defense of this threat. A threat many didn't truly understand.

"Today, you stand against those that would see you enslaved. You stand against former countrymen that you may know, those who have been wrapped in the chains of lies. Today, you stand as brave men and women who fight for truth, for the future of your world. In standing here, you do not stand alone. I stand with you; I will not forsake you, this day or any other. Today, your very presence makes a vow, that you stand against darkness. A vow I will honor. Today, no matter what comes, know that you will be among those held in honor. For many, you stand to lose much, gain little, but I tell you as you stand here today; you may lose your life, but in death find freedom. There will be a place for you, one day, because of this choice to stand with me. This day will not only shape the future of Starpathia but all the realms within it, and I will not forget." Pausing for a breath, tears filled his eyes as he looked out on all their faces. He knew each of them by name. Before turning away, he saw the heavy eyes of Relca at the front. "Yes, even you, friend."

Relca wanted to turn away from Olam's words, to be angry, but she couldn't. In that moment, she didn't know why, but she knew she would die for Olam. He was worth fighting alongside, to the death; him and his city.

Lilith had ferried all three of them away; it was faster than walking, but it had taken a lot from her. Keeping to the outskirts, she allowed them all a long rest. When morning came, she walked calmly into the encampment, amassed on a hill outside of the shield around the North Tower. Eydis trailed behind, pushing Lenora forward, wrists still bound behind her. Many of the men and women quickly stepped back out of their way. Some even gave small bows in Lilith's direction. One might say it was her army, and it was now, if no one challenged her. They didn't know Abaddon was gone, and with Eydis at her side, no one could best them.

There were many fires spread out, trees still burning, and Gangors moved amongst the people. She found Damion at the center, along with the other two Abaddon had put in charge of more trivial things. Not that they could do much. They might be more powerful than most, but nothing compared to her or Eydis.

"Look who finally decided to show up." Trenor spoke up from his seat against one of the few trees not burning.

"Eventually, someone was going to have to help you guys get in the front door. Unable to do it on your own, I see." Lilith stopped in front of him.

Reddel, the other commander, sat next to Damion with a smug look on his face. "Who's this?"

Before she could respond, Damion cut over them. "Where is Abaddon?"

She shrugged. "Am I meant to be his keeper? Abaddon arrives when he wants. You should know that by now," she replied, brushing him off.

"Something the two of you have in common." Damion commented. "Who are these two?"

"You two don't remember me?" Eydis whispered angrily.

Lilith walked around the fire, a hand raised to keep Eydis standing down as she saw the pain in her face. "They aren't important, and you don't need to know. Touch either of them and I'll remove your hand. Now, let's bring this shield down."

Damion mumbled something before walking off. Reddel followed. Trenor took a step towards Lilith, leaning over as he whispered in her ear. "Remember honey, you're not Abaddon; we take orders from him, not you. You're just kept around as a bedroom plaything, nothing more."

He didn't get a full two steps away before she used the wind to pull him back, throwing him to the ground and removing all the air from his lungs. Unable to breathe, he choked, frantically clawing at his throat. It had taken little effort from Lilith. Damion turned back to reprimand her, but it was too late. Trenor's body had gone limp, brown eyes and mouth wide open.

Stepping in, he snatched her upper arm. "We need everyone we can get, so it would be best if you didn't kill everyone who pissed you off."

"You don't need everyone; you just need me. Get them ready, we're going to bring down the shield." Lilith snatched herself away, grabbing Lenora and walking them down towards the Tower.

Eydis stood off on her own. It was clear being around all those people was difficult, near the commanders who, at Abaddon's order, had hurt her as well. Briefly, a pang of guilt for what she was going to do sliced through Lilith's mind. Eydis was just to be used as muscle and Lenora as bait, yet Lilith wished to have Lenora as a weapon instead. Shoving the thought aside, she turned back to Lenora. "You know, it would be easier if you fought alongside me."

"Why would I help you destroy the people who keep trying to protect me from you?" Lenora replied, annoyed.

"Don't just think they are trying to save you. You're as much a pawn to them as you are to me. At least see it for what it is, Lenora. I'll grant you freedom from this world if you help me. No one here is trying to save you; they're just using you."

"Cillian is." She snapped.

Lilith stared, momentarily surprised at her boldness. "I see." She turned to hide her face. "You aren't the first, he's tried it before. Don't think you're special."

Lenora was quietly seething. "You're right, I'm nothing special, but I know jealously when I hear it. Sounds like you're just angry he didn't try to save you."

Lilith froze. Wind began to blow furiously about her while flames danced in her eyes before she spun around to face Lenora. "What makes you think I need saving?"

"Lilith." Eydis interceded.

Cooling the flames, she stepped back. They had a purpose here.

Eydis had begun to hit the shield with lightning that came from both her arms, as those blue streaks returned and flames danced from her fingers. Damion had arrived on the other side, throwing as much fire as possible at his section. The Gangors descended, using their claws to slice at the barrier. Lilith mustered as much wind as she could, funneling it down to the middle of the shield and pushing with everything she had. She heard a shout from behind as fireballs launched into the air, coming down on top of the shield.

It was only a small area the Fallen were attacking, but that was the plan, to cause enough chaos for it to fall. Once it fell, it was doubtful Medora would be able to focus enough energy to raise it again.

Chapter 28

It was hard to believe this is where I had found myself. Immersed in a magic world, I had entered so afraid but had fallen in love with its entirety, unsure if I ever wished to return home. Now I stood on a battlefield, in a war I didn't understand. There was little to do other than gawk at the sheer power being thrown into the shield; how could anything still be standing? It was hard to imagine the strength they must be pouring into keeping the shield up.

A pawn...this wasn't even my world.

Crackling rang out, high pitched as spidering cracks spread from the lightening Eydis was firing into the shield. The Fallen rushed down the hill, charging with battle cries. In a blink, the entire thing fell like glass. There was screaming on either side as I watched Elder Zubair lead a charge with his lions, followed by many familiar faces from the Tower. Medora ran in, sword drawn, multiple Shadow Sentries coming in behind her.

Lilith was pulling me away, my legs like wet noodles beneath my weight. The two most powerful women here were keeping me at their sides as I continued to watch the horror unfold. Gangors dove in, grabbing people with claws, throwing them to one another in the air as they screamed, torn open alive. Flames went everywhere, burning those without the gift of fire. Water was streaming from Relca, extinguishing what flames she could before wrapping others in a bubble that could drown them. Olam emerged from behind the flames, far away from us, riding atop a white horse. He was stretching out his staff, pushing a tornado of bright white fog onto the field. It disoriented many of the Fallen and provided some much-needed cover to let the injured retreat if they could.

People continued to scream, some in agony, others is celebration. The smell of fire, smoke and blood filled my nose. One of Zubair's lions was overpowered by too many Gangors. Death was everywhere, and all I could do was watch while Lilith suffocated or Eydis electrocuted the life from anyone who came close to us.

Time is a funny thing during a battle; I'm not sure how long it all went on before I saw him. We had moved further north, around the path to the tree Shadow and I visited, set back now from the main attacks. Diadred's legs tore at the ground, carefully jumping over the bodies strewn all around. Cillian was atop him slinging arrows at the handful of Gangors that were close. Signy had also entered, swords drawn, heading straight for the Tower. Balfour was outnumbered near the stairs, under attack from fire on all sides. My heart leapt for the creature who had terrified me upon my entrance to these lands.

Screams were at the forefront of my mind as I fell to my knees, but no sound left my throat. There was no way I could call for them. It would be selfish and unfair. For I knew if they came for me, they would perish.

"Lenora!" came a call from the right. My heart sank as I locked eyes with Elise. Her arms were up with her force field as she screamed my name again, louder. This caught the attention of many others. Jabari came running, his chains snaking the ground in front, headed straight for Lilith.

"No!" The cries left my mouth before turning to beg both women for mercy. "Please, don't harm them." Lilith ignored me.

Lurching backward, I tried to distract them, heat boiling beneath my skin. Lilith grabbed my shoulders, holding me back from advancing while Eydis stepped forward.

Eydis had her blue flames by her side, waiting for my friends to make the first move. She was beginning to revel in her powers, daring people to try her. It was hard not to notice others now heading our way. Elders were easy to identify far away with how tall they were, and Dairdred, he was running.

They had heard her; they knew I was here.

Jabari shot his chains around Eydis as Elise protected him with her force field. Eydis sent currents of lightning through the chains back to Jabari, knocking him to the ground. Lilith lifted her arms up and the snow began falling again, heavily. The white flurries caused a screen of confusion for everyone, a perfect distraction for Lilith to pull me further away. This time I fought against her. She mumbled something while a woman screamed, and the snow broke enough for me to see Elise engulfed in blue flames. Jabari's chains were now attacking him, wrapping around his chest and neck until it snapped, rolling forward as he fell.

Throwing all my weight, I lunged, kicking away; Elise was still screaming, and I had to get to her. The others were too far. Free of Lilith for a moment, I tried to summon fire to burn away the bindings on my wrists, but the flames did nothing.

Screeching came from above; a Gangor was close.

People were dying again, because of me, but this time I knew them. I fell to my knees as Elise fell to the ground. Blue flashes could be seen through the snow, Eydis taking the life away from another.

No. Not another.

As Lilith grabbed me again, the snow began to lighten. I dug deep, begging for the power of the shadows once more, if only briefly, to punish them. To drag the Gangors from the sky and bury them, to destroy Eydis for her crimes.

It was granted.

Sitting back, I felt the familiar rattle in my mind, the other sounds drowned out as I summoned the shadows to my side. Closing my eyes, I heard faraway unnatural screaming cut through the cold snow. Lilith had moved from behind me, yelling something as she unleashed power to push away those who were coming closer. Time began to slow all around me.

Elise and Jabari's faces flashed before my eyes, dead. They were here for me. Eydis didn't have to kill them. The seething heat rose, Rage begged to appear, but I quieted her. This had gone on long enough. Scents of burning flesh hit my nose as the flames ignited behind my eyes. Shame laughed while Patience called out before I silenced them all.

They deserved to pay, they all deserved to perish.

You know you can, you have the power to pass this judgment...

A new voice spoke seductively.

Standing up, I looked around to see the snow cease, fresh powder half-burying lumpy bodies across the field. Shadows drifted like smoke around my feet. I heard muffled yelling, but I didn't heed it. The usual burn in my wrists began to diminish as my bonds snapped away. Shadow Sentries came to my side, three of them. I thought I had summoned them, but instead I watched as my hands took their own power away from them. Each Sentry became smaller until they simply ceased to be, replaced by only a robe that lay in the snow.

The shadows were gathering deeper around me, up to my waist now, pulling more and more before I looked down to see them moving around my arms like black, translucent snakes.

It was time.

Twisting them around once more, I commanded them out. Some took the shape of wolves, going after any of the Fallen they encountered. Others left my side as Gangors, taking to the skies to pull them out of it. Fashioning a snake, I sent it after Eydis. It went straight for her neck, but she saw it too soon, dodging the advance.

"She told me you had something going on in there." Eydis smiled, shoving a hand in her direction. "Isn't it amazing, the power we can wield? At first, I was so focused on revenge, but now...beings like us should rule. Master Olam has allowed this to go on for too long, not doing anything. They are no longer fit to be the deciders of fate in this realm. Join us. Between the three of us, there's nothing we couldn't do."

Her blue eyes were ablaze, locked into mine, and for a moment...*this is wrong...but...she burned Elise alive with that power...*

"You didn't use it how you should have. Elise did nothing to you, you could have let her go." I didn't have time for talking or sympathy as she laughed in response, mocking the snake I had sent her way, not realizing it was only to get her attention.

"Lilith said no one was to lay a finger on you, but I can do wonders from right here." Eydis smiled and lit her flames as her entire body coursed with those familiar blue streaks beneath her skin.

Large wings appeared from behind me as the shadows twisted up and around my body. A long neck emerged above, shaping into the head of a dragon with two horns. The body emerged as its tail wrapped around, spikes protruding from the end. Stretching its wings and stepping to my side, the massive creature roared before leaping into the sky. "She gave me no such warning."

Eydis threw flames from one arm and lightning from the other, but it had no effects on a dragon made of shadow. Roaring, it bellowed black smoke in her direction. The smoke itself took on a life of its own, binding her as with rope. It was no epic battle, for the shadows could not be destroyed; not really.

Walking forward, I didn't speak.

Ropes of shadow clenched tighter until the blue faded from her eyes; the electric color turned to gray. She began to plead for her life, but I cut her off.

"If you would have only spared her, I would show you mercy; but you don't deserve any such thing."

With that, I allowed myself to be engulfed in a rage that put my entire body to flames before commanding more shadows to consume her. They dragged her across the muddy snow towards the forest. Where they were taking her, I cared not. I only followed long enough to hear a final scream cut short before she disappeared into the darkness.

My dragon had stayed close, attacking anyone who neared me, no matter what side they were on. Not taking the time to stop the beast. Turning around, I felt the power surge through my blood. In mere moments I had gone from helpless, to one of the most powerful beings on the battlefield. Raw stenches of death hit me in the face, filling my nostrils, burning my lungs. Red and black blood streaks ran across the snow. Fires still burned as smoke rose from mounds on the ground. Very few were left standing. Not far away, Lilith was single-handedly holding off Diadred, Medora and Cillian. A shadow wolf was chasing a young man into the woods, refusing to accept retreat. My creatures had slain many, and as the shadows returned slinking across the ground to my side,

I heard them. With the return of each shadow, the cries of their victims returned with them. I had killed, relentlessly and without conscience or hesitation.

You're no better than they are.

Looking down at my arms, I flinched in pain as strange symbols appeared carved on each wrist. Something had changed. The heaviness of it all nearly brought me to the ground.

"My child. We finally meet." A soft voice caused me to look up. He was an Elder, very tall with long white hair. I had never met him, but he held a staff of light that warded away my shadow dragon. I knew it was Master Olam. As guilt cascaded down on me, I cast the shadows away, no longer wishing to hold them. In a moment of shame, I threw myself at Olam's feet and began to weep.

There weren't words, I had none.

Someone grabbed my shoulder as a familiar voice filled my ear. "Lenora, you're going to be alright."

"Cillian?" Raising my head, I met the green eyes of the man I had thought I wouldn't see again. His freckles were smeared with black blood, hair all out of place, but he was here. Throwing my arms around his neck, my weeping continued.

We had survived.

He would never let either of them out of his sight again. At least, that's what he kept telling himself. Standing guard in the hall between the two doors in the North Tower, he anxiously awaited their exit. One room housed Anara, his beloved sister, who was getting dressed. Behind the other door was where Lenora could be found, who had asked for three consecutive baths so far. He didn't want to begin to think about the horrors she had endured.

That would be for another day.

She had barely spoken at all, and wouldn't look anyone in the eye. Her shadows had taken countless lives on both sides.

Cillian thought longingly on the others he would never see again. Elder Feldrid had died on her own, peacefully during the night, after seeing her sons one last time. She died proud that her boys kept harm from all those in the Tower, even after the forest guardian Balfour fell. There had been a few of the Fallen who had surrendered. Their fate was undecided.

It wasn't all over, not yet.

Olam had called a meeting of the Elders, also requiring the presence of Cillian and Lenora. They were to meet at the Tree of Offerings, and to bring Anara. They should be feeling relief, but Cillian wasn't. No one knew where Abaddon or Lilith were, and the marks on Lenora's wrists certainly weren't of this world.

"Is she done yet?" Signy had walked up.

"I'm not sure...do I ask?" Cillian wanted to give her space.

"We're already late. I'll get your sister; you check on your girl." Signy smiled.

Cillian shot her a warning look. "Lilith is still alive. We don't let them out of our sight."

Putting her hands up, Signy retreated. "I won't."

Knocking lightly on Lenora's door, he waited for a response; a weak 'come in' came from the other side. Entering slowly, he saw her sitting on the bed, wrapped in a blanket. She had wet hair, dressed in fresh clothes. There was a pile near the wall that was smoldering. She had lit something on fire.

"Cold in here?" Cillian pointed towards the pile.

She didn't move as the monotone response was released. "My clothes. They smelled like death, so I burned them."

His heart sunk as he sat beside her. "It's going to all be ok."

"When?" She shot her head up to meet his eyes for the first time. They were swollen from tears and aged from the days she had lived; there was no fire to be found.

Cillian took her hands in his and noticed the marks on her wrists. She had scrubbed them raw in a desperate attempt to remove...whatever had happened out there. Olam had reassured her provisions would be made to remove them when they met at the Tree of Offerings, but the marks unnerved her. Honestly, they did everyone; it was old magic they did not know. "One day, Lenora...maybe not today, or tomorrow, but one day it will be ok."

She didn't believe him. She couldn't right now. That was fine. He would keep saying it until she did, no matter how long it took.

"It's time to go, isn't it?" Standing up, she let the blanket fall and pulled her hands from his.

He followed her out the door. She wasn't looking for a response, she was looking for a way out. Not just out of this room, but a way to leave all that had happened here.

Yesterday, seeing Shadow the first time on the battlefield had lifted my spirits just enough. It had been the salve I needed to walk off that field when Cillian had trotted him up to me. He had hidden my horse deep in the woods, hoping it would keep him safe from harm, and it had.

Today, seeing him brought pain. It was no salve, but a burning reminder of something I didn't deserve, just like Cillian's kindness.

They made their way through the woods silently. Cillian had to leave Diadred behind when they left for the tree. Olam asked him to part ways for good with the noble creature; it was Diadred's turn to rest. It had been a heartbreaking goodbye to watch, one neither understood but didn't question, both trusting Olam's decision.

Cillian didn't try to make small talk during our short travel; it was the one relief. In the past, we had been comfortable in silence together, but not today. Signy and Anara trailed behind on their own mounts, both able to feel the tension that lived settled permanently around me.

As we neared the Tree of Offerings, I found myself scratching at the symbols on my wrists once more, blatant reminders of what I had done; what I had become in the blink of an eye amidst my suffering. Coming into the clearing, it was still beautiful. The tree was stunning. This entire area had been sealed off from the destruction only a day ago. The snow was soft and white, not tainted with blood or ash. The trees in the immediate area were all healthy, not a scorch to be found. The serene place should bring peace, but it just amplified my discomfort.

Something like me shouldn't be allowed in a place like this.

The Elders were gathered near the tree, but not under it. Only Olam was found there. The three of my companions dismounted and walked over to him. Each Elder stood dressed well, amulets around their necks with star-shaped stones that were glowing softly. The tree itself was humming with power this today, along with Olam's staff, a low audible noise.

Dondi smiled as she greeted Cillian. Signy and Anara walked over to Olam as I sat frozen on Shadow, not wishing to get off. My desire to run away from all these people was so deep, so primal I didn't think I could avoid it. Picking up the reins, I clenched my hands until the whites of my knuckles were showing. Biting the inside of my lip, I prepared to use my heels to urge my mount forward, to run far away before a touch gently settled on my leg. Looking down reluctantly, my gaze fell upon the concerned face of Signy. She knew I was ready to bolt, so she offered me a hand down.

As I walked over to the group, the voices ceased. All eyes turned to me. They felt heavy, their stares.

You don't belong here.

This was true enough, I didn't; but I didn't belong in my own world either.

Before anything could be said, applause emerged from behind a tree. The clapping was slow, deliberate, and the hands that produced it were pale. Lifting his head, the same sinister smile that haunted my sleepless nights spread across his face, eyes that sparkled dark as coal. "What a touching reunion. Please...everyone didn't get dressed up for me, now did they, *Master Olam*?" Abaddon dragged out his title.

Cillian and Signy had already drawn swords, along with Medora, but Olam commanded them to stand down. Hesitantly, they obeyed.

"We wondered when you might be joining us." Olam stated plainly. Many turned in confusion towards the gentle Master.

Cillian was the first to speak. "You invited Abaddon?"

Olam moved forward to put himself a bit more in front of the group. "No. Abaddon has moved on from here. Of course, he was always a puppet, even if he didn't know it. This creature is far more ancient, and until yesterday, had been unable to move from its prison." He used his staff to motion towards Abaddon.

Hands up, his smile broadened. "I always told him he would show me his world one day. He believes me now." A giggle left his mouth as Abaddon tapped his wrist gently. "It's been ages; this world looks so different from the last. How long has it been since you locked me away?" Olam just stared him down with no response.

"No matter. You know why I'm here. You have something of mine."

Both of my wrists began to burn from the inside. The symbols on them started to bleed. As I looked down in surprise, a small cry escaped me from the pain. Cillian knew the moment our eyes came together; it wasn't hard to draw the same conclusion. He moved in between me and Abaddon, Signy joining him, weapons drawn again.

"Come and claim her then, you snake." Signy spat at him.

Abaddon walked closer. "I don't need to; I already have. Your girl made her choice when she borrowed my power for her judgements. She killed in my name, whether she knew it or not. Olam knows the law; she belongs to me."

It hadn't gone to plan, at all.

Lilith had known all along Lenora had power- even if she could barely wield it- but she didn't expect the explosive display that happened. Everything was ruined, all her plans; but at least she was free.

She had decided to run, to take advantage of such a luck where she was able to walk away.

Until she saw him.

Lilith had followed, unable to believe her eyes when she glimpsed Abaddon walking through the snow, headed south. Her stomach had turned; if he was alive, she would never feel free. Him confronting Olam was even more confusing; he wasn't powerful enough to take them on alone, so why was he here?

Something about him was different...he carried himself in a way she had never seen.

She was close enough now to overhear the conversation, things she didn't fully understand. Her jaw tightened as the words left Olam's mouth...it wasn't Abaddon.

It can't be.

In that moment Lilith knew what she had done, the price paid, whom she had released to make her claim. That thing had used them all, it was a trick. Neither Abaddon nor Lilith ever spoke of it, but they both wondered why it never left the mountain. It had been caged, even before the creation of this realm. For centuries, no one had known, no one had desired to set it loose...until her.

Lilith had unleashed unspeakable evil.

Olam commanded his people to stay their weapons. "Your powers are useless here, my friends."

No one really listened this time. They didn't trust whatever was happening. Cillian wouldn't hand over Lenora or Anara without a fight so soon after getting them back. This thing was evil, all evil. Lilith could feel it in her bones as a chill ran down her spine. It wanted everything, to cover this realm, all realms in inescapable darkness.

What had she done?

Her instinct was to leave, to run while she still could but when she saw Cillian throw caution to the wind, putting himself in between others. She paused.

There was no more time to contemplate, when something began pulling her forward.

"Welcome, my child." The chilling voice acknowledged Lilith's presence.

There was no running. She knew as the symbols on her wrists carved themselves, shooting a burning pain through her hand. She had become bound to this new tyrant as well.

Stepping out from behind the tree, Lilith caught everyone's attention- except the thing that wore Abaddon's skin- as she strode confidently up to his side. Turning, he locked eyes with her for a moment. "You did well. I knew I could count on you, eventually."

It didn't need her now; she knew it.

There were few choices left in this game, but she'd rather die than stay in servitude any longer, especially to this monster.

Chapter 29

No one spoke as the silence deafened the forest around us. The leaves of the Tree of Offerings began to rustle gently in a light westward wind.

What have I done?

Olam came to me with a hand on my shoulder, his bright eyes dazzling with both longing and joy. "Lenora. You're a daughter of my world; don't let anyone tell you different. I brought you here, you have never been alone. In the end, you must remember...remember this day, remember whose you are, and you will find your way."

It was a goodbye; I knew how those felt. They were familiar, but this was something more; a king I didn't know was claiming me as his. My heart swelled with a love, a sorrow I didn't understand as tears filled my eyes.

With his staff, he pushed us all behind him, to the side behind a gentle but secure force field. Each of the Elders had stepped around the tree, commanded not to interfere. Dondi was crying.

Abaddon called out again. "Olam! Blood for blood. She belongs to me, even you cannot keep her from this fate."

Olam spoke as he stood beneath the white oak. "Take me instead."

"You?" Abaddon vanished and appeared directly in front, nose to nose with the Elder.

Lilith stood frozen in surprise.

"You would sacrifice yourself for a lesser creation, such as these?" he responded in disbelief.

Olam smiled. "Yes."

"Master of All, the only Creator of Life, handing himself over to me." The creature was contemplating the offer. "This is *mur-goth*, unexpected, as you say in your tongue. How do I know this is not a trick?"

"Who made man? Who made the suns, the moons? Was it not I? Do you dare question my word?" The skies darkened as the voice boomed from Olam, causing each of us to look away.

Abaddon shrunk back in astonishment before collecting himself again. "Name your price. Without you, there is no one to keep me here, think of the chaos across all Starpathia. It would be like the days of old. Surely there are terms for such an exchange?"

"You will be unable to touch the Elders. You will release Lenora; she will no longer be bound in your name." Olam replied.

"Done." Abaddon didn't hesitate.

The symbols on my wrists disappeared, as did the burning.

Olam pulled a single clear blade from his sleeve. It shined like glass. With one hand, he made a cut in the other; bright red blood dripped down his arm before he placed a handprint on the base of the tree's white trunk. My heartbeat quickened; Cillian was shouting, but we were contained by Olam's shield, unable to do anything. Lilith locked eyes with me, hers full of guilt and shame, a weight I understood.

In that moment, we were looking into a mirror. Each one, the same.

"Do not interfere." It was a command, not just a warning from Olam as he cast his staff aside.

Abaddon began to change. He melted into black smoke, shadow and liquid, transforming himself into something of nightmares. The shield came down as Olam closed his eyes, arms stretched out. It was then I realized, he wasn't being taken somewhere, he was not being bound to this creature like I had been.

Olam was going to die in my place.

"Say my name." The female voice screeched at Olam.

He hesitated before speaking. "You are known by many. The Masi, Darkness Maker, Queen of Vengeance, and Angel of Death."

The foul smell hit me in the face, as Cillian commanded us to look away.

I didn't.

It was finishing its transformation and made the Gangors look like kittens. Six arms and legs, it crawled unnaturally with two heads. Each head had a set of six eyes, with four black fangs. Shadows pulled at its legs while black liquid struck out like snakes from its body.

Signy pushed Anara and I further back. Trembling in fear I watched the thing grow, moving closer to the tree. Before I knew what was happening, Olam began to moan as he suffered at the hand of the Masi. It was devouring him, and it was over as quickly as it began; his torn body fell to the ground at the base of the tree.

Out of nowhere, Lilith was sprinting towards Cillian.

She was going to kill him.

Crying out, I lurched forward, but Signy tackled me to the ground while Anara screamed. He was too close, the creature shot out black liquid from its body, straight for him; but it never made its target.

Lilith had thrown herself in between the two.

It was cold but burned like fire as the black tentacle-like liquid bound her. Cillian tried to reach out for her. She yelled at him, "Get back, you fool! You must stay away from it!"

Slowly the liquid pulled Lilith in as the creature morphed again, focusing on its prize.

"Let me try," Cillian begged as Lenora reached his side, grabbing ahold of his arm to pull him back.

"And let you die, too? It's tempting, but I've made my choice. Besides, it's not that bad..." She began to bite her bottom lip to keep from crying, the pain was excruciating as it snaked into her mind. "...you deserve a much longer death; this is too easy." Lilith tried to laugh.

Cillian let his concern show as he shook his head. "You always had it in you, I always knew it was there. That heart of yours wasn't turned completely to stone."

Lilith frowned. "Don't you dare disgrace me in death; people might think I've gone soft." She coughed, struggling to breathe as her voice flinched. The creature was morphing again and she was up to her chest, being absorbed into it. "You and I never would have worked, you know."

Her resolve fell while she held Lenora's stare, no longer could she lock out parts of who she was, and the compassion stirred for her. Lilith knew the path she walked; it was one she too began centuries ago. The beginning of suffering, the weight of the guilt, the shame that she was clothed in, the rage and sorrow. "Lenora. You survived, don't forget that; but don't let what you've done turn you into something you're not. This thing taking me, I can hear it. It wants you to fail, like I did. This isn't over. It's free to move now, and it wants you still. Don't give...it...the...satisfaction." Lilith gulped in one last breath as the rest of her disappeared.

Her last thoughts were of the past.

What if she had friends like Lenora, whom might she have become in her suffering?

She smiled one last time, for in that moment she realized...she did.

Long ago, there was a man, who saw glimpses of who she had been before. That man believed she could be herself once again, not simply the cold cruelty that defined her.

As darkness descended, the terrifying screams overtook her mind for only a second before silence fell. Olam's voice found its way through the vast black space she drifted into. "Your sacrifice will not ever be forgotten. You were once called by a different name, yet you've forgotten it. This time, you will forsake the name he gave you and I will give you a new name...today, you will receive life anew, *Galine*."

The Masi had morphed into a hooded being as it took Lilith before disappearing entirely. Signy, Anara and I ran to Olam as soon as it was gone. Only a white robe lay on the ground, streaked with red blood. Cillian scanned the tree line carefully to ensure the threat was gone before rushing up behind me.

The leaves began to fall from the tree. The tree twisted from the center of its trunk, pulling apart and growing as a sheer portal appeared in its center. The quiet chanting that had begun after Olam fell, ceased, the Elders opened their eyes and lifted their heads.

"Oh, dear children; all is not over yet. Each of you shall make a choice. You can stay here, or leave." Dondi spoke softly.

Confused, I replied. "Leave to where?"

"Dear Lenora, you can return home..."

I stepped forward. "I can?"

"...or you can move on, into another realm of Starpathia; another world of Olam's."

Home. I could go home.

It had never felt that way, though; I had been a foreigner there and a foreigner here, but maybe I could find a true home now. Looking back at the faces I had come to know in these lands, the thought of leaving them tore my heart in two. Turning my head forward, I studied the sacrifice made for me to live, a powerful being that I barely knew, who gave all.

"What is this other world like?" I cautiously asked.

Dondi smiled. "I don't know; it is not by my power you are sent on."

"Can they come with me?" I locked eyes with Cillian, and smiled.

"If they want to."

Signy stepped up. "But what is to happen to this realm, our home? That thing wants to destroy...everything."

"Do not fret, Signy, we will protect the people here. The Masi's power is more limited than she yet knows, but I do worry for you three. It does not give up easily and will try to move over all Olam's lands. This place will be safe, though; we will stay. Finally, the Closure here has been completed. This realm of Starpathia will be cut off forever, I'm afraid; this is the last door." Dondi explained, as she motioned towards the portal in the tree.

"This realm?" I questioned.

"Oh yes. Truly, you didn't think this was it? Starpathia is vast, beyond your understanding. It encompasses all the realms of our Creator, Master Olam, and there are many." Dondi beamed with pride.

Anara stepped closer as she spoke up. "I wish to stay." Her auburn curls bounced around her determined face.

"Anara?" Cillian questioned with astonishment.

"Don't 'Anara' me." She grabbed her brother's face in her hands. "You have brought me home; let me enjoy it. We've always needed different things. Let me be at peace here, but do not feel guilt at leaving. She needs you; I don't anymore." Leaning in, she hugged him deeply as a few tears fell.

"You don't have to come, Cillian; I can go alone." I forced the words out, even if I didn't mean them.

Signy laughed. "Not alone. I've always wanted to leave, and you're bound to get into trouble along the way, but not without me."

Waves of gratitude washed over me as she stepped up by my side.

"What about my Shadow?" I hadn't forgotten the friend who brought me here. He was faithfully waiting along the tree line.

"I wouldn't think of parting you two. Signy, would you get him for her? Now, pick up the staff, Lenora; you will need it. Keep it close, keep it safe." Dondi commanded.

Gently, my hands grasped the smooth white bark. The light in the top was dull, the stone cracked. It was taller than me.

Cillian hadn't spoken, and I refused to look at him. I wanted this to be his choice; I couldn't fathom the thought of saying goodbye. So, I took a step forward, tears in my eyes, before someone grabbed my hand.

"You're not shaking me that easily." His voice soothed my soul as I turned to face him. His eyes were glistening. This was hard, but most choices here had been.

"Once you pass through, you cannot return; not here at least. We've never sent humans through the Tree of Offerings, I'm afraid, so I don't know what to expect," Dondi cautioned. "Now go."

Squeezing Cillian's hand, I let him lead the way as we passed through, into the unknown, with Signy one step behind. I felt weightless as we moved further in, walking on nothing. The staff in my hand transformed into an amulet tinier than my palm. Small branches from the white oak still encased the broken six-point stone, graying the farther we moved from the tree.

Dondi called after us as the tunnel began to close, while a light illuminated ahead with dazzling colors.

"Remember today, for it has changed everything."

THE END

The story continues in book two of the Tree of Offerings Trilogy: **Veiled in Glass and Silence.**

Read on for a sneak peak of the first chapter.

CHAPTER ONE

Veiled in Glass and Silence

"Perfect is relative, and anything perfect isn't perfect at all."

Pushing the whispers away, I ignored its implied insanity. Today was a perfect day. The palace floors were shimmering brighter than usual, as the ocean breeze drifted in through the balcony, tousling my hair. Rhythmic clicking from my heels on the marble floor gently sang in my ear, while sweet whiffs of lavender filled my nose. Passing by each of the grounds staff, they gently bowed with a smile, then resumed preparations for the Violet Gala. Flowers from all over the isle were brought in and displayed, from aster to purslanes, lilacs and sea thrift. Waves of white fabrics and all shades of purple invaded the kingdom for a solid week, before a grand ball that was hosted every year in Spring. Quickening my pace, I lifted the front of my dress to descend the spiral staircase. If I hurried, I still had time to visit the gardens before meeting Queen Mirria for afternoon tea.

Not surprisingly, the gardens were busier than the palace. With only seven days left before the violet sunrise, marking the start of the year and the day of the dance, preparations were keeping everyone busy. I had come down here for a bit of quiet, but instead found myself immersed in more decision-making clamor.

"Lady Lenora. What do you think of this arrangement?" One of the flower masters stopped me, motioning to a beautiful vase filled with cuts of purple and white flowers with greenery accents. The man was dressed in a tuxedo, as are all men who worked in the garden; he waited anxiously for my reply.

"Wonderful." I smiled shyly. "Good day to you, sir."

Dodging more questions, I tried to appear mission-bound to avoid any more interruptions from the staff. Moving along the marble walkway, I passed into the greenhouse where people bustled around, watering new plants, tending to and praising the new growths. Pausing briefly to admire a water lily beginning to bloom, I stood in awe of its simple beauty. Reaching out, I touched the delicate white petals ever so gently, just a brush of my finger...my temple burned as pain shot through my face. The white petals became streaked with blood, dripping from the center.

You must get us out!

Screams filled my ears and pain invaded my skull. The servant woman tending the blossoms next to me transformed suddenly; from a well-dressed greenhouse attendant of plump proportions to a frail maid in rags who clawed at my dress. "Free us!" Jumping back, I knocked one of the pots from the shelf as my shoulder made contact, shattering as it hit the floor.

Confused, the greenhouse attendant ran to my aid. Her plump and proper form had returned. "Lady Lenora, are you alright?"

Annoyed and embarrassed, I straightened my dress, fussing about the poor plant whose roots lay exposed on the ground. "I'm fine, just tripped is all. Carry on."

Moving out of the greenhouse, hoping to avoid more stares, I entered one of my favorite parts of the garden. In the far corner, hidden away was a fountain that moved its small cascading streams over large stones and into a small pool. The ground was only dark dirt, per my request, surrounded by many archway trellises housing multitudes of dark green vines that hung down, providing seclusion. In the center was a small bed where three Violet Isle Stars made their home; a local plant that produced beautiful six-point, star-like blossoms in deep violet. The Isle of Kenosopia was known for the rare flower. My part of the garden here was a secret, horribly kept from the place staff but successfully kept from the Queen. Quickly I shed my heels, digging my toes into the cool earth, and moving to run my hands in the water running over the wet rocks.

"I thought I'd find you here." The sharp female voice came out from behind me, following the rustling of vines.

I ignored it.

"She'll have my head if you're late."

Matching her tone, I replied. "That day can't come soon enough. In that case, I choose being late."

Turning, I looked at the petite woman standing at the edge of the sidewalk. Her sapphire dress matched the fierce blue eyes and paled her blonde hair that was carefully tied up in a bun with a matching ribbon. The two of us couldn't be more different with my curvier figure, emerald dress, olive skin and hazel eyes. My hair was deep brown, long and straight, falling far past my chest, down my back.

No more could we continue the stare off as we both broke into ravenous laughter.

"Lady Vera, why don't you come join me?" I taunted.

She rolled her eyes, took a few looks to ensure we were alone and slipped off her own heels before plunging her toes into the cool dirt. Vera was my absolute best friend, one of the only friends I had in the palace. The two of us were known to stress the Queen on occasion.

Vera was rambling on about something, but I barely noticed while I gently splashed the cool water repeatedly. The whispering had returned, louder than usual after my small mishap in the greenhouse. Try as I may to forget the face of the frail woman, it kept pushing itself forward in my mind.

"You aren't even listening, are you?" Vera stood, annoyed.

Leaning my head against the back of the stone wall near the water, I sighed heavily, avoiding her stare.

"Oh boy, I know that look." She replied crossing over to sit next to me on the simple bench. "More visions, huh?"

Gently I lifted my head to meet her gaze. "Am I going mad, Vera?"

"No. Well…you have always been a bit; you know, mad, on your own." She rocked her shoulder into mine playfully.

Turning my face back to the water, I gently stroked the smooth stone. I wasn't in the mood for her jokes. It amazed me, the power that water had, even such gentle streams, to smooth the roughest of rocks over time.

"It's just bad thoughts. Nothing bad happens here, you know. Your mind is playing tricks on you like Queen said, that's all." Vera stood and retrieved her shoes. "Are you going to tell her again?" Concern filled her deep blue eyes.

Resigning I followed, brushing the dirt from my feet and using my fingers to remove any from my toes. "No. You're right, I just wish they would stop. The tea does nothing for the headaches anymore, I've just given up on it."

"Don't tell her that." She warned.

Using my right hand to wave her off, I simply stated my resolve of not speaking about it further. Vera was right; I didn't need to concern the Queen with such silly troubles, she had enough on her plate. The two of us hurried through the rest of the gardens and across the courtyard in the direction of the awaiting tea we were both late for.

Queen Mirria had a grand palace; the bottom two stories were made of shimmering silver marble. The top floors, along with the single largest tower were made solely of mirrored glass. You could not see through them from the outside, but one could look out from the inside. It was a stunning work of art, these grounds we had come to reside in.

Tea was to be taken overlooking the Queen's private gardens. A glass sitting room sat at the base of her private quarters, on a balcony overlooking an impressive display of flowers. Upon my first visit, I found it downright unnerving to walk on the mirrored glass, but now I strode across the apparent floating floor with ease. Vera fussed once more over my hair that I hadn't taken the time to contain, something the Queen preferred, as we stepped onto the balcony under the entryway.

"You're late." Her voice stated the obvious, calmly disappointed. Delicate, long hands that held three gem rings set down her glass teacup, which clinked ever so tenderly against the matching plate beneath it.

Letting Vera go before me, she entered with a curtsey and an apology from both of us. "Sorry, your Grace. We were awestruck by some of the flowers in the garden, helping the caretakers make a few arrangement decisions." I followed behind with a matching curtsy, before we each shuffled into the plush blue chairs set around the table.

"The masters of the garden are just that, masters; they do not need your opinions on such simple tasks. Let them be to do their work during such an important week."

"Yes, your Grace." Vera and I replied in unison before servants stepped in to prepare each of us tea. The aromas from the loose leaves that had been held under the steamy water were pleasant, floral and fruity, with a hint of spiced earth.

The Queen had chosen a simpler gown this day; white, with light blue trim to match the pale blue stones that dangled from her ears. Her light brown hair was piled into a tight bun as usual to help support the crystal glass crown that sat upon her head. She was going on about preparations with Vera. Letters had gone out for the Violet Gala, with fewer responses than last year. It was frustrating, the Queen didn't understand the drop in attendance. She was going to send them out again. Clearly, there must have been a logistical problem because everyone *should* want to come.

Vera was given the honor of assisting in planning the gala this year, so she updated the Queen about the food, the gowns, and the music while I gently swirled the light amber liquid around my cup. Looking down, I watched as many of the gardeners bustled about beneath us, cutting flowers, watering and caring for the Queen's prized plants.

"...what do you make of that, Lenora?" Raising my chin in response to my name, I met the Queen's pale blue eyes.

"Why yes, that sounds lovely, I should think." I quickly replied, taking a hurried sip of tea.

The two women turned to me in surprise before the Queen spoke again. "You think the lack of responses to my Violet Gala is lovely?"

Almost slamming my glass down, I corrected myself. "Not at all, your Grace. I must have misheard, I thought we were speaking of the music for the dance."

Vera shot me one of her looks while the Queen eyed me suspiciously.

Wait. There was an opportunity here, one that I almost missed. "Why don't you send Vera and I into Sandmere? We can personally deliver your invitations; that way there are no more accidents along the roads."

"Lenora, I think that would be less than ideal." The Queen shut down the idea.

Vera gave me another look that begged me not to press the issue, but I didn't heed her warning. "Queen Mirria, we would consider it a high honor to advocate for a festival as grand as this. Vera and I have been in your service close to a year now, with no visits permitted off the grounds. This could be a wonderful opportunity for all of us.

The Queen softened her face, lifting a small smile in my direction. "I know. You two missed most of the celebration last year. It's lucky we found you when we did. You girls looked dreadful when the guards brought you in, but now look at you two...like daughters I never could have. You are safer here. Look around; don't you want for nothing?"

Reaching across the table she grabbed each of our hands, but after a moment I withdrew my own, still devoted to my cause. "Your Grace, I cannot...we cannot ever repay you for your kindness. You saved our lives and we are forever in your debt. We could go with escorts, multiple guards. Please, your Grace?"

"No. This is the end of the discussion. Do not ask me again."

Vera piped up. "My Queen, we are forever grateful for your hospitality, we do not wish to upset you further."

"Thank you, my dear." The Queen stood and approached me, back of her hand to my forehead. "Lenora darling, how are those headaches? Are you still drinking your evening tea from Manidhar?"

Meeting her gaze, I lied. "They're much better, your Grace, I haven't had one in weeks. And yes, the tea has been helpful." I smiled the sincerest smile, as she bid us good day and retreated to her quarters, handmaids following close behind.

Vera pinched my arm with a sour look across her face. "What are you doing?"

Pausing, I turned to ensure we were alone. "Leaving."

Acknowledgments

It takes a village to raise a book, is an understatement. To think that it took over a year, to get here, typing one of the last sections before we go to print. Without the following people, 'Bound by Blood and Shadow' would have never made it to your hands.

Cory, my husband, my biggest cheerleader and my love. You are one heck of a man, placing so much on hold to encourage me into pursuing what has been one of my largest accomplishments, other than marrying you…and birthing the children, of course. Thank you for the extra support from putting kids to bed, feeding the farm or cooking dinner while I agonized over deadlines and had a few less-than-ideal meltdowns.

To Wesley and Daniella, who are far too young to read this but one day might…mommy loves you dearly and didn't mean to yell from her hammock after she couldn't log onto her laptop that one day, I'm sorry.

Leslie, one of the most amazing women I know whose friendship, without, this book would have never begun. Thank you for believing in me before I did, loving me in my darkest moments and providing hours of advice while you juggled your own life.

Dedra, my mother-in-law, the woman who fiercely loves her children and treats me as her own. Thank you for your support and amazing balcony deck where some of my best scenes were written…oh and the wine.

Bronwyn, my unofficial proofreader and fellow book nerd. Thank you for the time you sacrificed to fix my grammar, which really needed your extra eyes and your insistent celebrations to lift my spirit.

Clara Carlson-Kirigin / Prometheus Editorial, my amazing developmental editor, who not only worked with me extensively but went far above what she had to. Thank you for reaching out to direct me and not backing out of our contract after you saw my true anxieties surface with obsessive blurb rewrites.

Steve Leacock / Leacock Design Company, my graphic designer, you are a rock star. Thank you for being willing to take on this project, listen to my banter and not fire me after hand drawing thousands of leaves I later asked you to delete.

Sean, the father who rallies behind any of my visions with financial support and encouragement. You never think my goals are too big or too crazy. Thank you for all you've done these past few years, I'm beyond grateful.

Ben, the one male who was willing to read my 'not romance' manuscript and critique it from a point of view I don't have. Thank you for taking the time to organize your thoughts, unbeknownst to you, encouraging me during one of the darkest nights in this publishing process.

Jenny, one of the first to put eyes on my manuscript, spurring me to believe that being an author wasn't so far-fetched of a dream.

AK, for helping me search BAM to study books and judge them harshly. Also, I promise to base a character after you in book two, then kill them off, per your request. It's in writing now, it must happen.

There are so many of you, who put in something to bring this story to the page. Thank you to each of the one's who donated their time, money, expertise or words of wisdom. To my launch team, you were awesome; we couldn't have done it without you. To all the authors who spent hours on the phone with me, commented direction in groups or simply shared their stories, thank you.

To the professor I cannot name because it was so long ago, the woman with red hair who took an interest in my writing before anyone else; you made an impact. To Edgar Allen Poe, the first author to turn my head in school; you brilliant man. To C.S. Lewis who showed me fantasy and the Bible could coexist, regardless of what others had told me.

Finally, Father, my Creator and Savior, the ultimate fantasy author and to whom I owe my life; thank you for such an opportunity as this.

About Author

Born in South Florida but growing up on the Florida/Georgia line, L.R Bryant was raised in the woods before she began writing. Red clay, tall pines, horses and bringing home every stray was the usual rhythm of life for this wild farm child. From a young age she dreamed of far-off places, multiple realms, incredible creatures and magic that could fiercely protect or destroy. As she grew so did her world, expanding well beyond what most people could see or feel.

Known for writing any paper the night before, over complicating book reports and sharing colorful versions of recent events, Bryant has always been a natural storyteller. After high school she took only one college course at a community college, a creative writing class where an eccentric red-haired professor took an interest. Yet, the real world would keep her from realizing the extent of such writing talents for another decade.

Those years were filled with many lives lived and endless lessons to file away. Marriage, divorce, motherhood, dead end jobs, incredible opportunities, wealth and poverty would be just a few paths this life would bring. But through all the ups and downs, one thing never left...the ability to spin magical realms, alternate realities and wonder like no other from the back of her horse.

Then one day, grief pushed this weaver of tales to write again.

It was now time to pour those worlds out, the stories that needed to be told, characters voices who needed to be heard. With the best support and publishing team around, echoing the same encouraging words from a stranger so long ago, Bryant took a chance. One story would change her future, transforming into a debut novel. With it her title morphed from 'good with words' to 'published fantasy author' and she intends to continue that for many years to come.

Printed in the USA
CPSIA information can be obtained
at www.ICGtesting.com
LVHW020546111123
763658LV00011B/20